SHINOBI

COLE GIBSEN

flux
Woodbury, Minnesota

First Edition
First Printing, 2014

Book design by Bob Gaul
Cover design by Ellen Lawson
Cover images © iStockphoto.com/20694625/Igor Zhuravlov,
iStockphoto.com/14458776/Iya Terentyev,
Shutterstock Inc./112652780/takayuki,
Shutterstock Inc./42996295/DigitalHand Studio
Photo composition by John Blumen

Flux, an imprint of Llewellyn Worldwide Ltd.

Library of Congress Cataloging-in-Publication Data
Gibsen, Cole.
  Shinobi/Cole Gibsen.—First edition.
      pages cm
  Summary: With graduation nearing and Kim regaining his memory, Rileigh is ready to celebrate but Sumi not only regains her memory, too, she performs a ritual to switch bodies with Rileigh, draining her ki and placing her in grave danger.
  ISBN 978-0-7387-3911-3
  [1. Samurai—Fiction. 2. Martial arts—Fiction. 3. Supernatural—Fiction.
4. Reincarnation—Fiction. 5. Love—Fiction. 6. High schools—Fiction. 7.
Schools—Fiction.] I. Title.
  PZ7.G339266Shi 2014
  [Fic]—dc23

                                                              2013038149

Flux
Llewellyn Worldwide Ltd.
2143 Wooddale Drive
Woodbury, MN 55125-2989
www.fluxnow.com

Printed in the United States of America

Acknowledgements

A huge thank you to my tireless champion, the woman who dons a cape when no one is looking, my amazing agent Nicole Resciniti.

Thanks for the continued support from Brian Farrey-Latz, Rhiannon Nelson, Kathy Schneider, Mallory Hayes, and the rest of the amazing people at Flux.

To my crit partners Brad Cook, T. W. Fendley, Sarah Bromley, and Michelle McLean, thank you for your invaluable wisdom. Without you, my books simply wouldn't be.

To my Southern Illinois Bookends, your support is invaluable. If it weren't for my Wednesday night lattes with you guys, I'd probably be fitted for a straitjacket already.

A special thanks to the beautiful and gracious Hasume-San, Umeka-San, and Tsutsujime-San. Thank you for always making my release parties memorable.

Thank you to all my amazing readers and fans. You're the reason I do what I do. Thank you for your love and letters. There's no feeling like knowing people love your characters as much as you do. Thanks for allowing them to spend time with you.

To Grandma and Grandpa. I'd hate to think what my imagination would be like without all the time I spent nurturing it in your backyard.

1

When I was a samurai, rites of passage were performed in ceremonies of steel and blood. But here, in the twenty-first century, everything was done with paper—kind of anticlimactic if you thought about it. High school was officially over. From this day forward, I was an *adult*. If they weren't going to cut our hands with ceremonial blades and make us sign our names in blood, the least they could have done was rig our diplomas to shoot confetti when we opened them. Something other than the standard, "Your childhood is over. Here's a piece of paper."

"Rileigh! Can you believe it?" a voice shouted through the sea of green caps and gowns. I closed the folder that held my diploma and looked up to find my best friend Quentin weaving through the various families and graduates milling about the lawn outside the gymnasium. His unzipped robe billowed around his suit like a cape as he pulled me into a hug. "It's over!" He tore his graduation cap from his head and threw it in the air. "It's finally over! Doesn't it feel so ... amazing?" He grinned widely.

"Sure does." I forced a smile. But the truth was, as happy as I was to finally graduate high school, I couldn't help but feel Gimhae Kim's absence like a dull ache in my side. When I fantasized about this moment at the beginning of the year, Kim was waiting for me at the end of the ceremony, his arms open wide.

Q pulled away and held me at arm's length. "You could have called him, you know."

I dropped the forced smile. Leave it to Dr. Q to always know what was wrong. It was one of his more annoying traits. "Yeah, well, you could have called ... " I racked my mind for the perfect comeback but came up blank. When in doubt, there was always my old standby. "Your face."

"Ouch. Get me to the hospital, I've just been burned." He smirked and let go of my shoulders. "I know this is a touchy subject for you, I just don't understand why you won't return his calls. You love him, Rileigh. And even though he doesn't remember you right now, you know he loves you too. Didn't you two have fun at prom?"

"We did but ... I don't know." I sighed and waved a hand in the air. "It's not the same now that he doesn't remember who I am—who *we* were. I miss Kim so much, but spending that night with him at prom, and seeing the way he looked at me—like he didn't know me ... I felt more alone with him than without. I know that probably sounds crazy."

The humor left his face and he turned away. "And it's all my fault."

I immediately wished I could take back my words. I knew how guilty Quentin felt about accidentally erasing Kim's memory. And on our graduation day, I didn't want him to be anything but happy. I reached for him, but he sidestepped my hands. "Q, don't blame yourself. If you hadn't altered Sumi's memory, we'd all be dead. You saved us."

"At the cost of Kim's identity."

I opened my mouth to argue, but before I could a deafening squeal threatened to burst my left ear drum.

"We did it!" Michelle, my friend and fellow past-life samurai, bounded in front of me. Her mess of red curls, unwilling to be restrained by her French braid, stuck out at odd angles beneath her graduation cap. Before I could stop her, she grabbed my hands and spun us in a circle. "We graduated! It's so exciting!"

After several seconds of spinning, she abruptly released me. I stumbled a couple of steps and sucked in several large breaths in an attempt to pull my stomach out of my knees.

"You're not happy." She looked to Q. "Why isn't she happy?"

"Who's not happy?" Braden asked. He and Drew, the remaining members of our samurai team, walked over to us. Braden stopped next to Michelle and gave her a kiss on the cheek. His bare legs and flip-flops stood out among the heels and polished loafers around us.

Drew, who'd graduated several years ago, had watched the ceremony from the bleachers—the seat beside him noticeably empty. Like me, the smile on his face couldn't quite mask the sorrow in his eyes.

"Rileigh's not happy." Michelle pointed to me.

Drew shot me an understanding look, and I responded

with an appreciative smile. With Kim's past-life memories gone, I'd lost a boyfriend, but Drew lost a brother. To make matters worse, Drew lived in the same apartment complex as Kim. I couldn't imagine what it'd be like to see your past-life brother every day only to have him look at you like a stranger.

"What's not to be happy about?" Braden cocked his head. "We just graduated and I'm naked. Could life get any better?"

"Wait, what?" I jerked back as Q burst into laughter.

Michelle rolled her eyes.

"What do you mean you're *naked*?" I asked.

Braden's lips quirked into a grin. "It means that the only thing separating me from this delightful spring breeze is thin silk." He pulled at the robe and let it fall back against his chest.

"Um, ew." I wrinkled my nose and took several steps backward, wanting to place as much distance between him and me. "Why?"

He shrugged. "Drew bet me. He said he'd pay me twenty bucks if I went through the entire graduation ceremony with nothing under the robe." He held his arms up in triumph. "Easiest money I ever made."

Drew folded his arms. "Okay. But before I pay, how do I know you're really naked? You could be sporting boxer shorts under there for all I know."

"Don't believe me? I'll show you." He grabbed the zipper at his neck and pulled it down several inches.

"No!" Quentin, Michelle, and I screamed in unison. I quickly spun on my feet to avoid seeing anything that might require an eye-bleaching. "Let me know when the coast is clear." Facing the opposite way, I let my eyes wander through the throng of happy graduates with their families. A bizarre sense of nostalgia overcame me as I took in the people surrounding me. It was weird to think this would be the last time I saw some of them, maybe even the last time I set foot on school grounds.

An invisible ribbon laced around my chest and pulled tight. How strange to stand before a door, close it, and know it could never be reopened. I hoped with everything inside of me my relationship with Kim wasn't a closed door—that despite the odds stacked against us, we'd find a way to get his memories back.

"Rileigh." Michelle giggled. "It's okay. You can turn around. I promise I'll make Braden behave."

He snorted. "You can try."

"*Braden*." I made sure the threat was evident in my voice even if a smile pulled at my lips. "I swear if you unzip your robe, I'll axe-kick you right in the ... " But something caught my attention and my words trailed off. At the edge of my vision, behind a woman wearing a large purple hat, I thought I caught a glimpse of a face half-hidden behind shoulder-length blond hair, ducking behind a family posing for pictures.

No. It couldn't be.

I stepped to the side and craned my neck for a better look. Unfortunately, the constantly moving crowd pressed closer to me, making it impossible to find him—if he'd been there at all.

"Rileigh?" Q asked. "What is it?"

"Probably nothing." I didn't turn around, too afraid I'd miss him. "I'll be right back, I ... want to say goodbye to my math teacher."

"But you hate Mrs. Adkins."

Without responding, I weaved through the crowd, dodging the flailing arms of excited parents and graduates. As I made my way farther, I caught a glimpse of a crisply ironed shirt collar, followed by the heel of a brightly polished shoe. These could have belonged to anyone, but the pounding of my pulse told me otherwise.

When I reached the edge of the crowd, I spotted him retreating at a brisk pace halfway through the parking lot. I'd never catch up to him in time. And from this distance, it was impossible to make out his face. I'd have no way of knowing for sure who he was. Unless . . .

I glanced around to make sure no one was watching. Lucky for me everyone was too busy laughing and taking photos to notice the girl standing at the edge of the parking lot, picking up a stone just large enough to fit inside her palm.

I muttered a quick prayer that karma would be forgiving if I nailed a perfect stranger in the noggin. If, however, the guy was who I thought he was, then he deserved what was coming his way. I lifted the rock over my head and chucked it.

"Son of a—!" the guy cried out after the rock bounced off his head. He whirled around and, even though he was several yards away, confirmed my worst fear. I could feel the heat from his glare through the dark sunglasses shielding his face. The same glare he'd given me a lifetime ago right before he killed my soul mate—my Yoshido—and forced me to drive a dagger into my gut to avoid being taken captive.

There was no mistaking it.

Whitley was back.

2

Whitley's lips twisted into a smirk as he approached. "A little primitive, don't you think? One of the world's most fearsome samurai has been reduced to throwing rocks?"

"I make do with what I have." I glanced behind me to make sure the other samurai hadn't followed. Recently, Whitley and I had been forced to work together to take down a common enemy. But after we'd defeated Sumi, he'd disappeared and I'd thought that was the last I'd see of him. Clearly, I'd been mistaken because here he was, walking toward me. Each step closer made my stomach roll with dread.

The last thing I needed was for my friends to find Whitley here, considering he'd killed them all in a past life. A bloody parking lot murder was not the way I wanted to conclude my graduation. I couldn't spot them through the throngs of people, but I had to get rid of Whitley before they came looking for me.

He smiled. "That's what I like about you, you're resourceful."

"Want to know what I like about you?"

"Hmm?" He tilted his head to the side, shifting the hair draped over half his face so I could see the shiny, pink scars underneath.

"Your absence. The only reason I haven't killed you is because you helped me get rid of Sumi. So you should probably leave before I change my mind."

"So cocky." He folded his arms across his chest. "How do you know I'm not letting you live for the very same reason?" He took a step closer.

My muscles reflexively tightened, readying for a fight. I shifted my weight to the balls of my feet.

Whitley must have caught the movement because he rolled his eyes. "Please. You think I'm here to kill you in front of all these people?"

"*Try* to kill me," I corrected.

He made a face. "Whatever. Look, I didn't come here to start a fight. Besides, as much as I hate to admit it, you and I make a pretty good team. I thought you might be interested in backing me up on my latest mission."

Yeah. This from a guy who'd tried to ritually sacrifice me before burning my house down a year ago. "What mission are you talking about?"

He grinned, obviously pleased by my interest. "Sumi. Or as I knew her in the past, Chiyo Sasaki."

I clenched my jaw at her name. Sumi, as it turned out, had been the money and brains behind the attack on our village a lifetime ago—the attack that led to my death as well as the deaths of the rest of the samurai. In this life, she'd used her mind-control powers to manipulate the minds of Kim, Q, and the rest of the samurai. She'd also tried to block my ki powers. When Q tried to erase her memory so she'd no longer be a threat, she pushed Kim in front of her so his memory would be erased as well. Needless to say, I wasn't her biggest fan. "Sumi doesn't remember who she was. She's harmless."

"Is she?" Whitley raised an eyebrow. "Think about it, Rileigh. How much does anyone really know about the effects of Quentin's mind-altering abilities?"

"Well..." But my words trailed off. The truth was nobody truly knew for sure how Q's abilities worked—including Q himself. I shrugged.

"Exactly." The smile melted from his face. "Which is why I'm here. I don't know about you, but I'd sleep a lot better knowing the one girl who wants us both dead, and actually has the power to do it, is out of the picture."

"Out of the picture?" I folded my arms across my chest. "How much more out of the picture can she get?"

He leaned in. "How does six feet under the ground sound?"

I dropped my arms to my side. "You want to kill her."

"I guess you really did earn that diploma." The grin returned to his face. "I don't care what everyone else says about you, I think there's a brain inside that little blond head of yours. But right now, I'm more interested in the warrior than the brain."

I regretted not throwing a bigger rock. "Are you out of your mind?"

"We worked so well together last time, and you have those nifty ki powers that make everything so much easier."

I frowned. As a samurai, killing came second nature. But when we killed, it was justified. Going after a girl who could barely remember her name wasn't honorable. It was like hunting an animal with broken legs. Not to mention the fact that she claimed to be Kim's soul mate. The world ran on balance. For every light, there was a dark. Sumi was Kim's inyodo. In other words, his opposite. And if she died, the world would correct for the tip in balance. If we killed her, then Kim would die as well. And that was a risk I would never take. "I can't help you."

Whitley jerked back like I'd slapped him. "Are you kidding me? You're pulling the samurai high-and-mighty card? Please. You know if she had her memories, she wouldn't hesitate to kill you in your sleep."

"I know." I glanced behind my shoulder for any sign of my friends. It wouldn't be long before they came looking for me, and I had to make sure Whitley was gone before they did. "But I'm not her." And thank God for that. "I'm not going after someone who isn't a threat—especially if it puts Kim's life in danger."

He stepped so close to me the spiciness of his cologne stung my nostrils. "You don't know for sure she's really Kim's soul mate. Besides, if you believe that Sumi, even without her memories, isn't a threat, you're a bigger idiot than I thought."

"Now hold on—"

He cut me off. "In case you've forgotten, she's transcended. If she regains her memory, she's going to have full use of her powers. Not only will she be able to manipulate minds again, but she'll be able to do so much worse. Remember your Kentucky fried boyfriend?"

Bile burned the back of my throat as the memory of Yoshido resurfaced, his sightless eyes staring at me from where he lay sprawled on the ground. The smell of his burnt flesh was so vivid my stomach lurched. "I'd rather not. Thinking about that makes me regret not killing you when I had the chance." I reflexively cracked my knuckles.

Whitley held his hands up. "Hey, I was only following orders, not to mention operating with *borrowed* power. And that's Sumi's thing. She likes to get other people to do her dirty work. If she gets her memories back, you won't know who she'll send after you or what kind of power they'll be packing. I don't know about you, but I kind of like to sleep at night."

I relaxed my fingers. He had a point. But still, I couldn't justify going after someone who was no longer a threat. "I sleep just fine at night. The Network has her under surveillance. If she awakens, trust me, I'll be the first to know."

He snorted. "Forgive me if I'm less than confident in the Network's abilities. After all, they were all but useless in helping you when Sumi had her ninjas ambushing you at every turn."

Another good point. Man, it was annoying how much sense he made today. A tingling sensation crawled along the back of my neck, alerting me that someone was headed our way. I glanced behind me and saw the bleached-blond tips of Q's head as he wove through the crowd. *Son of hibachi.*

I grabbed Whitley's arm and yanked him behind a nearby SUV. "You've got to go. If the other samurai see me talking to you, well, they're going to be a lot less forgiving."

"Rileigh?" Q yelled from the edge of the parking lot.

I motioned for Whitley to stand still and moved from behind the SUV. "Oh, hey, Q," I called. "I just ran out here to grab my lip gloss."

He frowned. "But you're parked over there." He pointed in the opposite direction.

"Huh. No wonder it's taking me so long to find my car."

He stared at me a long moment without saying anything. Finally, he nodded. "Okay. But hurry up. Your mom's looking for you. She wants more pictures before we leave."

Sure she did. Because the nine hundred she took during the ceremony weren't enough. "All right. You go on ahead and tell her I'm coming. I'll just be a minute."

He hesitated, frowning, before finally turning around and making his way back into the crowd. Once he was out of sight, I released a long breath and ducked back behind the SUV. Whitley leaned against the hatch with an obnoxious smirk on his lips. I shoved him, more out of fun than necessity. "Okay. You have to go. *Now.*"

He stumbled and jerked out of reach before I could shove him again. "Fine. But I want you to consider something. For all we know, Sumi could be faking the amnesia—biding her time until she catches us off guard. Do you really want to give her the opportunity? I just thought if we worked together we'd have the upper hand."

Faking her amnesia? A shudder rippled through me. It was a thought I hadn't even considered. But even so, how would we know for sure? "Whitley, I—"

"No," he interrupted. "Don't answer me right now. Just… think about it."

I bit my lip. What if Whitley was right and Sumi was biding her time, waiting for the perfect moment to attack? It was certainly a theory worth investigating.

Finally, I nodded. "Okay. I'll think about it. But if it turns out she has her memories, we can't kill her. I won't risk Kim's life. But maybe we could get the Network involved. Maybe we could lock her up for good."

He grinned. "It's a start." He spun on his heels and walked away.

"Wait!"

He glanced at me over his shoulder.

"How will I get in contact with you?"

His grin widened. "Don't you worry. I'll be close by." Without waiting for me to respond, he disappeared behind a row of cars. Even though he was out of sight, the sound of his chuckling lingered, giving me the impression I might have agreed to more than I'd bargained for.

3

Japan, 1491

Chiyo sat silently as her friend Miku worked the bronze kanzashi into her hair.

"Tell me again, Chiyo," Miku said excitedly as she arranged Chiyo's hair. "How handsome is he?"

Chiyo grinned broadly and swiveled on her knees so she could face her friend. "Oh, Miku." She grabbed Miku's hands to stop her own from trembling. "He is surely the most handsome of all samurai." She giggled. "I was so scared when I heard my father arranged my marriage to a warrior. I was certain I would be the wife of war-ravaged old man. But when I spied on him as he spoke to my father . . ." She sighed happily. "I am sure he is descended from the Sun God himself."

Miku quirked an eyebrow. "My, that is handsome! I cannot wait to see him."

"You will not have to wait long." Chiyo let go of Miku's

hands and tucked a wisp of hair behind her ear. "I overheard Father talking, and the wedding will be soon." A rush of excitement rolled over her as she considered all the details to be planned. First, her wedding robe, then—

Miku's squeal of delight interrupted her thoughts. "What is his name?"

"Yoshido," Chiyo answered, relishing the taste of it on her tongue.

"What a strong name." Miku sighed.

"It suits him well," Chiyo agreed. "You should have seen his muscles." Chiyo flexed her own small arms in imitation. "I bet he has the strength of six men—no! Ten!"

Miku laughed, and Chiyo grabbed her hands, pulling her forward until both girls collapsed onto the floor in a giggling heap. When their fit ceased, Miku rolled her head against the floor and looked at Chiyo. "How did you manage to spy on him?"

Chiyo idly flicked the dangling coral beads of the kanzashi. "I waited until the servant brought them their tea, and I snuck a glance."

Miku gasped. "Did your father see?"

Chiyo made a face. "Of course not! He would be furious. But I think Yoshido saw me. I mean, he looked *directly* at me."

"He saw you!" Miku squeaked. "What was his expression? Did he look madly in love?"

Chiyo swatted her friend. "Miku, honestly! How does one *look* in love? He looked like a warrior is supposed to look, I guess—very serious."

"Maybe he did not want to alert your father you were there," Miku offered, "so he could not stare at you longer."

Chiyo laughed. "Yes, I suppose that must be it." But she knew that wasn't exactly true. Yoshido's reaction at seeing her had been more than disappointing. Chiyo had smiled at him—but he'd only given her a polite nod in return before turning his attention back to her father. The memory burned through her and killed her laughter. No matter. Even if he hadn't fallen in love with her at first sight, once they were married, Chiyo was sure she could make him love her. She'd stop at nothing until he did.

Miku shook her head. "I think you are the luckiest girl alive, Chiyo." She sighed wistfully.

Chiyo nodded in agreement. She was to be the wife of a samurai. She'd never want for anything. And she'd have the respect of all. But there was one tiny downside. "Father said I must learn to defend myself."

Miku rolled over and blinked at her. "What? Why?"

Chiyo shrugged. "Father said it is the duty of a samurai wife to defend their household. I'll also be expected to kill myself should I be taken captive." She shuddered at the thought of plunging a dagger into her own stomach. "Can you imagine anything so vile?"

"No," Miku answered, her eyes wide. "Let us pray that never happens."

"It will not. I am sure the training is more ceremonial than reality. I cannot imagine anything so horrible happening with such a strong warrior to protect me."

The girls erupted into another fit of laughter.

From outside Chiyo's window, a horse cried out, followed by the sound of shouting. The girls stopped giggling and quickly sat up. From the garden, more voices cried out.

"What do you suppose is going on?" Miku asked.

Before Chiyo could answer, her door slid open and one of her father's servants rushed in the room. He closed the door, pressed a hand against his chest, and gulped for breath. "Bandits have breached our walls," he said between gasps. "We must get you hidden. Immediately."

Terror gripped Chiyo's heart with icy fingers. "What do they want?"

"You. They must have heard of your arranged marriage and assumed they can get a ransom from your future husband." The servant ran to the window and surveyed the gardens. He glanced at the girls a moment later. "We are going to have to leave through the window."

Miku grabbed Chiyo and tried to pull her forward, but Chiyo dug her heels against the floor. "What about my father?"

The servant's face crumpled, and Chiyo had her answer.

"No." Chiyo placed her hands over her mouth. He had to have been mistaken. She'd find her father, and he'd be okay— everything was going to be okay.

Outside the clashing sounds of metal mingled with battle cries.

"Chiyo, hurry!" Miku's voice was tight with panic. She waved Chiyo over to the window. "We need to hide!"

Chiyo glanced at the door. Could she really leave her father? What if he wasn't dead—only hurt? What if he needed her to take care of him? How could she abandon him?

"Quickly!" the servant hissed.

Before Chiyo could move, the door to her room was thrown open and two men entered. The men wore tattered clothing, their skin speckled with blood Chiyo was quite sure was not their own.

The shorter of the two men stepped forward with a katana drawn. He smiled, revealing a mouth of crooked, yellow teeth. "Which one of you is Chiyo?" he asked.

A scream bubbled up Chiyo's throat. But before it could escape, Miku's hand tightened around Chiyo's wrist in a vise-like grip, a warning to remain silent.

"No!" The servant ran in front of the girls and drew a small blade from his obi. "You cannot have her. I will die first."

The bandit shrugged. "I am happy to fulfill your request." Before the servant could move, the bandit lunged forward and drove his blade through the man's chest.

Chiyo and Miku both screamed as the servant fell to the floor. He blinked lazily at the ceiling and drew in one long, ragged gasp before growing still. Blood pooled beneath him like a rising tide.

The bandit shook his blood-stained sword, spotting the floor in dots of crimson. He raised an eyebrow at the girls. "Let us try this again. Which one of you is Chiyo Sasaki?"

The second bandit pulled an arrow from his quiver and drew it in his bow. He aimed the gleaming tip at the girls. "Answer carefully."

Chiyo's heart thundered inside her head. Beside her, Miku whimpered. This couldn't be happening. She was only weeks away from having the life she'd always dreamed about. But now, all around her the pieces of her perfect life shattered like porcelain.

Chiyo glanced at her best friend. Miku stood beside her, pale and trembling in terror. Chiyo knew there was no escape for herself. And since she was sure to lose everything anyway, maybe she could at least save her friend. She gently pried Miku's clamped fingers off her wrist, took a deep breath, and stepped forward. "I am Chiyo Sasaki."

The archer released his arrow. Chiyo gasped and clenched her eyes shut as it flew toward her.

A second later, instead of feeling the bite of a metal tip into her chest, she heard the thump of something hitting the floor.

She opened her eyes and found Miku on the ground, staring up at her with sightless eyes. An arrow protruded from her chest.

"No!" Chiyo shrieked. She fell to the floor and reached for her friend. But before her fingers could graze Miku's robe, two rough hands grabbed her arms and jerked her to her feet. The world spun around Chiyo as she was dragged through the door and pulled from her house.

In the span of a couple heartbeats, she'd lost almost everything: her father, her home, and her best friend. Still, she held on to hope as best she could. She still had one thing.

Yoshido. He was a samurai. *Her* samurai.

Chiyo swallowed the sobs clawing up her throat as she was thrown on top of a horse.

Yoshido would come for her. He would avenge her father's death and make these men pay. Chiyo was sure of it. Samurai, after all, were men of honor. There was no way he'd let her down.

4

"Aren't you so excited about college?" The girl standing in front of me pulled a strand of long brown hair over her shoulder and twisted it around her finger. I'd spent the last five minutes trying to remember her name and kept coming up blank. I thought it started with an L—Linda? Laura?

"I'm going to Michigan State," she continued. "I cannot *wait*! I think I want to major in political science, or maybe marketing." She smiled expectantly, as if waiting for my approval on her life choices.

Okay then. I'd play along if it made her go away.

I forced a smile to my lips. "That's great. There's, uh, a lot of good career opportunities in those fields." I had no idea if that was true. My eyes darted to the clock on the wall. How much longer could I keep this conversation up without revealing I had no idea what her name was? We took history together last year, but that was the extent of our relationship. For the life of me, I couldn't understand why she'd shown up at my graduation party. But after glancing around the room, I realized there were quite a few people here I didn't know.

Huh. Maybe I wasn't the social leper Carly, Quentin's twin sister, always insisted I was. But the more likely answer was they'd come because Debbie, my mom, had sprung for catering, giving me the only party with a taco bar.

"Rileigh?"

When I looked back at my former classmate, her eyebrows were raised, like she was waiting for the answer to a question. *Crap.* I tried pulling my smile wider. "I'm sorry. Today's been so exciting I just can't seem to stop my head from spinning. What was your question?"

She waved a hand in the air. "Trust me, I understand. I only asked where you're going to go to school."

My cheeks twitched, an ache building along my jaw from the strain of keeping the smile in place. "Oh, I'm staying local."

Her smile melted. "You're staying in St. Louis? *Why?*"

God, I was so tired of that question—the same one Debbie asked me nearly every day. Before my mom became a talent agent, she'd spent her teen years as a model traveling the globe. She loved to lecture me about how important she thought it was for people to travel before they settled down. It wasn't that I didn't have the option to go away. I'd received acceptance letters from schools on both coasts. A year ago, I would have jumped at the chance to embark on a new adventure across the country. Exploring the globe was something Yoshido and I once talked about doing a lifetime ago—but we'd never had the chance. Now it didn't look like we'd have one in this life either.

A lump formed in my throat, and I struggled to swallow it down. Maybe it was stupid to stay for a guy who might never remember me—remember *us*. But I couldn't give up on him ... not yet. I didn't expect anyone to understand, so I'd found the best explanation was the shortest. "The college I'm going to has a really great criminal justice program—"

She made a startled sound. "You want to be a cop?"

I didn't know what I wanted. But since I was actively involved in the secret government agency known as the Network, it was the only thing that made sense. "Um, something like that ... "

Her mouth dropped in horror. "But you're a *girl*."

"Last time I checked." I looked over my shoulder and, as luck would have it, Q glanced up from the taco bar across the room. *Help me*, I mouthed before turning around, the fake smile firmly in place.

"That's crazy, Rileigh. You're so small. Do you really think you'd stand a chance if some guy attacked you? You'd die!"

This time I didn't bother to stop the smile from sliding off my face. "Gender and size have nothing to do with a person's ability to fight. A warrior's strength lies within the heart," I added, quoting my past-life mentor, Lord Toyotomi. "Don't you remember what happened to me last summer when I was attacked by those muggers in the mall parking lot?" I would have been surprised if she didn't. The incident made the news, and the entire school talked about nothing else for several weeks afterward. "I handled them just fine."

"*Ohhhh.* I get it. This is one of those post-traumatic stress things, right? You have something to prove?" She patted my shoulder sympathetically. "Don't worry, Rileigh. I'm sure you'll get it all figured out. You have two years before you really have to decide on a major."

I nearly choked. Why was it people assumed if a girl wanted to take on the job of a warrior or a fighter she must have some sort of brain injury? My fingers tightened into fists, and a familiar tingling sensation pulled across my chest as my ki flared to life.

"I see I've arrived just in time!" Q looped an arm around my neck. "I'm sorry to interrupt your conversation, but Rileigh is urgently needed in the kitchen. Some sort of chips-and-dip crisis."

The girl stuck out her lip in a pout. "That's too bad. It was really great catching up with you. We'll have to exchange emails so we can stay in touch."

Before I could answer, Q yanked me toward the hallway. "Don't you worry. Rileigh's excellent about keeping in touch." He turned his head and whispered in my ear, "With her fists."

I giggled, and the knot of tension inside me dissolved. Once we'd made it down the hall, he pulled me inside my bedroom, shut the door, and leaned against it with folded arms. "Want to tell me what that was about?"

"Meh." I flopped onto my bed. "Any chance we can skip Dr. Q's psychoanalysis and move onto the cupcake-eating portion of the night?"

"Are there any red velvet?"

I snorted. "How long have we been friends? Do you think there was any chance there wouldn't be red velvet?"

"You don't like red velvet."

"True. But I like you."

His arms fell to his side. "Rileigh, I'm so sor—"

"Don't!" I sat up. "If you apologize to me one more time, I swear I'll punch you. What happened to Kim was not your fault." I patted the bed beside me.

Q sighed and shoved his hands in his pockets. He shuffled over to my bed and plunked down beside me. "If it's not my fault, why do I feel so terrible? Sometimes, I think maybe you should punch me—because I deserve it. I took away the love of your life."

"No." I rested my head on his shoulder. "You saved him. And me. The only thing you deserve is a mountain of cupcakes served on a platter by one of my mom's underwear models."

He laughed. "Well, you get on that."

I smirked. "That's what she said."

"Not in my world." He grinned mischievously and threw an arm around my shoulder. "Now, want to tell me why you were making the 'Rileigh Martin Fists of Fury' at poor Lisa Pope?"

"Lisa! I knew it started with an L!"

Q shook his head, his chin bristling the hairs on the crown of my head. "You're avoiding the question."

"I'm not avoiding anything."

Q snorted.

I scowled up at him. "It's just that Lisa was talking about college and when I told her where I was going ... " The words died on my tongue and I shrugged. "Am I making a mistake?"

"What do you mean?"

"I could go away, you know. I received acceptance letters from colleges across the country but ... I ... " I shook my head.

Q nodding knowingly. "You can't leave him."

"I can't. But at the same time, I know I can't put my life on hold for something that might never be." A dull ache throbbed inside me. "He might never remember me, Q. I know that. But I can't let go. At least, not yet."

"Oh, honey." Q gave me a tight squeeze. "Nobody expects you to let go."

A girl's high-pitched laugh breached the door, and I went rigid beside him. "I know Debbie meant well, and it is graduation and all, but I'm just not in the mood for a party."

He glanced down at me as a smile slowly uncurled on his lips. "Your wish is my command." He stood suddenly, leaving me scrambling to gather my balance before I face-planted on the bed.

"What are you going to do?"

He walked to my closet and threw the doors open. He pulled two blankets from the top shelf and rushed over to me where he dumped them in my lap.

I raised an eyebrow. "Q?"

"Take the blankets to the roof. You, me, and the rest of the samurai will have our own party. We can just chill outside, watch the stars, talk, whatever! It will be great."

It really did sound great. But there was a problem. "What about all the people here? Debbie will freak if I leave my own party."

He waved a hand through the air. "That's the easy part. I'll tell them that Kara Littner's party has Jell-O shots. This place will be cleared out in ten minutes flat."

I blinked at him. "Q, you're a genius."

"I know." He pulled me to my feet. "Now take the blankets to the roof. I'll tell Drew, Braden, and Michelle the plan and get them spreading the rumor. When everyone's gone, we'll come up." He opened my bedroom door and pushed me into the hallway, right in front of my mom.

Debbie arched a perfectly manicured eyebrow and folded her arms across her chest. "Rileigh, what are you doing with those blankets?" Beside her stood her boyfriend—and Network official—Dr. Jason Wendell. The look on his face was far more suspicious than Debbie's accusatory glare.

"Um." I cleared my throat. *Think, Rileigh!* What plausible reason could I have for carrying blankets out into a party? *I smelled smoke and thought I'd tear these blankets into strips and tie them into a rope so we could escape.* No. Two blankets would never make enough rope to reach the road from our twelfth-floor condo. Maybe, *Me and my classmates were feeling nostalgic and thought we'd reenact the team-building parachute fun we had in elementary school gym class.*

I bit my lip. Of the two, the latter had more credibility. But before I could speak, Q swept to my side. "Get back, Deb." He shoved me between the shoulder blades, making me stumble forward. "We found Terrance McGill sitting on Rileigh's bed and rumor has it"—he lowered his voice conspiratorially—"he has bedbugs."

"Dear God!" Debbie jerked back. "Rileigh, take those to the trash chute immediately. We'll buy you a new bed set tomorrow."

"Will do." Q and I exchanged sly grins.

Dr. Wendell's frown deepened, but I ignored him as I brushed past. He controlled my Network assignments, but he certainly didn't have any say in how I spent time at my own party.

Q and I emerged from the hall. Michelle caught sight of

us and wandered over. "What are you guys doing with the blankets?"

Q wrapped an arm around her shoulder. "We're starting our own private party on the roof. But first, I need you, Braden, and Drew to help me clear the room. Get the guys and meet me by the kitchen bar. I'll give you the details there."

She smiled. "Sounds like fun!" She spun on her heels and disappeared into the throng of students.

Q turned to me. "Okay. You go to the roof and we'll meet you there in ten."

I leaned my head against his shoulder. "You are the best friend a girl could have."

"I know. Now get out of here." He gave me a gentle shove toward the door.

"Okay, I'm going." I took a step forward and stopped. "Bring me up a nacho plate? With extra—"

"Jalapeños," he finished. "Fine. Now *go!*"

Giggling, I turned back to the door. Only a true friend would kick you out of your own party with the promise of extra jalapeños.

The night was most definitely looking up.

———

I spread the blankets out on the roof and sat, leaning on my hands so I could tip back my head and look at the sky. The city lights masked the glow of stars. Even so, the sky was remarkably clear, a velvet blanket of black just waiting to envelop me.

I crossed my ankles and sighed happily. The night's

chill would soon be gone, replaced by the sticky summer humidity that always made me long for cooler climates.

If you hate the weather so much, you could have picked a college up north. You could have picked a college anywhere.

I flopped back on the blanket and threw my arm over my face in an attempt to drown out the nagging voice of doubt that had plagued me ever since I decided to stay in St. Louis. It wasn't like I'd based my decision solely on Kim. The other samurai were here, as well as Dr. Wendell and my work with the Network. Staying was the right decision.

So why did it feel so wrong?

The rooftop door behind me squealed open and shut with a soft click. I didn't bother to move my arm from my face as rubber-soled shoes padded across the concrete. "Did you remember to bring my nachos?" I asked.

"Extra jalapeños?" A distinctively not-Quentin voice responded—a voice I hadn't heard since prom. I sat up with a gasp and spun around on the blanket. I blinked several times to ensure my eyes weren't playing tricks on me. "Kim?"

He stood silently, wearing jeans and a tight black T-shirt. His hands were shoved into his pockets.

I cautiously climbed to my feet. A fluttering sensation like thousands of flying cherry blossom petals blew through my stomach. As much as I wanted to hope and believe it to be true, I knew the guy standing before me wasn't *my* Kim—the samurai who shared a lifetime of memories with me, the samurai who held my heart.

This Kim—well, I loved him just as much, but because I knew my love was one-sided—his presence filled me with a hollow ache. "W-what are you doing here?"

The muscles along his jaw tightened before he spoke. "You never returned my calls after prom."

"*Yeah...*" I dropped my eyes to the toes of the ballet flats I wore because Debbie didn't think sneakers were appropriate party attire. "I'm sorry I didn't call you back. It's not that I didn't have a great time and all, but—"

"But what?" He moved closer. The smell of his sandalwood cologne enveloped me, threatening to pull me into a pit of memories I wasn't sure I'd be able to dig out of.

I stepped back. "But... I lost someone really important to me recently and... I guess I'm just not ready for a relationship. I'm not over him."

"That's good." He pulled his hands from his pockets and grabbed my arms, his touch electrifying my skin. "Because I'm not over you."

My pulse thrummed inside my head. This couldn't be real. Maybe I'd fallen asleep on the blanket and was dreaming. "What are you talking about?"

He placed his hands on either side of my face and drew me forward so that only a breath separated his lips from mine. "I remember, Rileigh. I remember everything."

Before I could respond, his lips were on mine, kissing me in such a way that I knew—without a doubt—my Kim was back.

5

I pulled away from his kiss with a gasp and brought my hands to his face, wanting to feel with my fingers what my eyes refused to believe. "Is it really *you*?"

"Yes." He placed his hand over mine and drew them toward his lips, kissing the inside of my wrists.

Delicious shivers ran down my arms and along my spine. I blinked rapidly, trying to sort through the mess of emotions tumbling inside me. "How? Your memories—Q erased them and—"

His lips met mine again and swallowed my words. He could have them. When he'd lost his memory of the past—of me—I thought I'd lost a piece of my heart. But now I realized it hadn't been lost, only missing. And now that it was back, words no longer mattered.

"When I went to bed last night, my dreams were filled with past-life memories," he said. "And when I woke up, it all clicked into place. I remembered everything."

"That's incredible." I slid my hands to his neck and pressed myself against him, wanting to feel the thrum of his pulse as proof that I wasn't dreaming. He responded by snaking his arms around my waist and pulling tight, as if by sheer force we could fuse ourselves together to prevent ever being torn apart again. His head was low so his breath tickled along my neck. "I warned you I would never let go."

A strange sort of hiccup escaped my lips, a cross between a laugh and sob as I remembered when he spoke those words to me nearly a year ago when I was the one who didn't remember him. So many things had transpired since that meeting—so many attempts by others to keep us apart and yet, finally, here we were.

Behind us, the metal door leading into the building screeched open, and Kim and I jerked apart. Still, he slipped his fingers through mine as if unable to fully let go.

"What the—?" Q stood in the doorway with his mouth open, balancing a plate of nachos in one hand and holding the door open with his other. Braden and Michelle peered over his shoulders, their lips parting in unison.

"What's the hold-up?" Drew called from behind them. He appeared a second later but jerked to a halt the moment he stepped around Q. His eyes traveled from me to Kim to our interlacing fingers. "I don't understand ... "

Kim smiled. "Brother. It's so good to see you again."

Drew staggered back a step, nearly colliding with the nachos teetering in Q's grip. Michelle darted forward and placed her hands under the nachos, preparing to catch them.

"Please tell me this is you—*really* you." Drew spoke

slowly, as if choosing his words carefully. "This last month, thinking that I'd lost you forever—"

"You've lost nothing," Kim said. "I remember everything—from this life and the last."

Without warning, Drew launched himself at Kim. I released his hand and darted out of the way before I became the mustard in one very beefy sandwich. Michelle squealed, and Braden laughed out loud as they rushed to join the group hug. Someone snagged me by the arm and pulled me into the mass of laughter and tangled limbs.

Warmth radiated throughout my body as I clung to my friends. It was crazy to think that only moments ago I wasn't sure if this day would ever come. And now, everything was perfect, or at least thought so until I noticed a distinct absence from our group.

"Q?" Carefully, I untangled myself from the knot of arms and backed away from the samurai. Q hadn't moved from his spot at the door, only now the nachos were scattered at his feet. Lines of worry etched across his brow.

"What's wrong?" I took a step toward him. "Isn't it great that Kim's back?"

Q blinked several times before answering. "Of course it's great." He gave a weak smile.

"Really?" I crossed my arms. "Because you're wearing the same expression that I have right before I get a cavity filled."

"I know. It's just—" He looked to the sky, as if searching for the words. "It's just—if Kim remembers ... " He sighed and ran his hands through his hair.

"If Kim remembers ... " I prompted.

"There's something wrong with my memories?" Kim asked.

Startled, I looked to my right to find Kim beside me. I'd forgotten how supernaturally quick he could be. Michelle, Braden, and Drew stood behind him, the smiles gone from their faces.

"No!" Quentin shook his head rapidly. "There's nothing *wrong* with your memories. I wasn't sure you'd ever get them back. Rileigh's missed you so much—everyone has."

I hugged arms across my chest to ward off the chill creeping down my spine. Something wasn't right. Kim glanced at me and, given his tightly pressed lips, I knew he felt it too. "I sense there's a big *but* coming, Q."

"You're right." He nodded. "And I'm not saying that something *is* wrong, but I was thinking—and this is just a theory because I'm pretty new to this healer stuff." He licked his lips. "You guys know I don't fully understand the extent of my powers. And the night I'd erased Kim's memory by mistake, I'd only known about my powers a couple of days. I had no idea if my attempt to wipe Sumi's memory would even work, and if it did, how long it would last. Now that Kim has his memories back..." He shrugged helplessly.

The meaning of his words hit me like an axe-kick to the gut and I grabbed onto Kim's arm to steady myself. "Son of hibachi."

Kim's head jerked back as if he'd also been struck. "You mean—"

Q nodded. "Exactly."

Michelle brought a hand to her mouth, and Drew went rigid beside her.

Braden looked at everyone and frowned. "I'm sorry, am I missing something? Kim's memory is back. I fail to see the problem."

Michelle dropped her hand, her skin visibly paler. "Quentin is worried because he erased two sets of memories that night. If one person got their memory back, it's only logical that the other person would have too."

Braden's eyes widened. "No. Oh, God. You mean ... her?"

"Sumi." Kim spit her name through clenched teeth. Afterward he grimaced, as if the word alone left a foul taste on his tongue.

My fingers reflexively curled into fists. "If she has her memories back, she's going to be pretty pissed we took them away in the first place."

"Agreed." Kim nodded. "She'll want revenge. And the first ones she'll come after will be you two." He motioned to Q and me.

Q and I exchanged uneasy glances.

Drew folded his arms across his chest. "This is serious."

Angry heat flushed beneath my skin. It wasn't fair. I'd only just gotten Kim back and five seconds later we had to deal with Sumi. For the millionth time, I wished I could have a normal relationship—one where I didn't have to worry about my boyfriend's psycho ex-fiancée trying to kill me. "It *is* serious," I agreed. "Sumi's tough, conniving, and let's not forget how annoying it was that she kept sending ninja to kill me. But Q and I handled her once. We can handle her again."

Q shot me a skeptical look.

"Rileigh." Kim shook his head. "I'm afraid you got lucky last time. She was able to alter our minds, to make us all think we hated you, with only a fraction of her powers. Now she'll be coming at you with her full powers—"

"Which means she'll be close to unstoppable," Q added.

Kim nodded, his lips forming a grim line.

I gave a frustrated laugh. "So what are you saying? We're dead no matter what, so we shouldn't even bother to fight back?"

"No." He raised his hands. "That's not what I'm saying at all—the opposite, in fact. If we have any hope of taking down Sumi once and for all, we're going to need backup."

My stomach dropped. "Oh no. Isn't there another option? Some other solution we haven't explored? I hear honey badgers are pretty good fighters. Maybe we can have one shipped to us and—"

"I'm sorry, Rileigh." He shook his head. "But desperate times call for desperate measures. Your safety is something I won't risk."

"Son of hibachi," I grumbled.

"Do you want me to get him?" Michelle pointed to the door.

Before Kim could answer, I raised my hand to stop him. "Don't bother. I'll do it." With a sigh, I began a slow march to the stairs. The man was like a wart, annoyingly embedded into my life. When I alerted him to the new situation, it certainly wasn't going to help get him out of my business. But there was no denying we needed his help.

It was time to get Dr. Wendell.

6

There you are!" Debbie stopped tossing paper cups into a garbage bag long enough to wag a finger at me as I trudged through the door with the rest of the samurai in tow.

Dr. Wendell glanced up from the vegetable platter he was covering in plastic wrap. His eyes widened in silent alarm when he caught sight of Kim standing beside me.

"Don't you know how rude it is to abandon your party?" Debbie continued. "Everyone left shortly after you disappeared. They must have been so insulted."

Maybe not insulted—but they sure were going to be angry when they found out there were no Jell-O shots.

Debbie picked up a stack of abandoned plates and shoved them in the bag. "Where did you run off to anyway?"

I exchanged a glance with Kim. How was I going to get rid of her long enough to get Dr. Wendell alone?

Lucky for me, Q whispered "I got this" in my ear as he brushed past me. "I have good news and bad news, Deb."

"Oh, Lord." Debbie pinched the bridge of her nose. "What is it *now*?"

"Remember when I told you about the bedbugs?"

She narrowed her eyes. "Yes."

"The good news is I was wrong. Terrance McGill doesn't have them."

Her body relaxed. "Thank goodness for that."

"The bad news is he has fleas."

"What?" Debbie screeched. The trash bag fell from her hand.

Before I could question what he was up to, Q grabbed my arm and lifted it in the air. "Rileigh already has several bites."

When I didn't immediately move, Quentin nudged me with his hip.

"Oh ... *right*." I rubbed my arm. "I do."

"Me too," Michelle added, scratching at her own invisible bites.

"Yup," Drew said, itching his leg.

"All over!" Braden scratched wildly at his stomach and back.

Kim only nodded and swept his fingers through his hair.

"Oh, God!" Debbie spun a circle, her eyes darting wildly around the room as if anticipating a sudden bug ambush. "What do we do?"

Kim shot Dr. Wendell a pointed look. He, in turn, gave a subtle nod before slamming the roll of plastic wrap against the counter. "This is a very serious situation," Dr. Wendell said. Debbie covered her mouth with her hand and nodded. "Then this is what we're going to do. Debbie, I need you to run to the store and buy the biggest bug bomb they have."

Leaving the garbage bag at her feet, she raced to the counter and snatched her car keys from a bowl. "What are you going to do, Jason?"

"I'm going to finish cleaning, and then I'm going to get us a hotel room. We won't be able to stay here tonight if we're fumigating the apartment."

To my relief, she nodded. If Sumi was coming after me, the safest thing for my mom was to get her out of the house.

"Rileigh," Dr. Wendell continued, "do you think you can stay at one of your friends' houses tonight?"

Q raised his hand. "She can stay at mine."

"Good." Dr. Wendell clapped his hands together. "Let's do this." When Debbie didn't immediately move, he slapped his palm against the counter. "Hurry, Deb! Before they breed!"

The color drained from Debbie's face. With a quick nod, she dashed to the door, her high heels wobbling dangerously in her haste as she exited the condo, slamming the door behind her.

After several heartbeats, Dr. Wendell walked around the counter and climbed onto a bar stool. "I don't know what's going on, but from the looks on your faces, something tells me I'm going to need to sit to hear it."

"Kim has his memory back," I said.

"That's wonderful news!" A smile flitted across Dr. Wendell's face before it quickly dissolved into a frown. "But I think I see the problem. If Kim has his memories, then logic would dictate that so does—"

"Sumi," Kim finished, folding his arms across his chest.

"Right." Dr. Wendell took off his glasses and rubbed his eyes. "Let me start by saying, Kim, that I'm thrilled to have you back and on the team."

Kim nodded.

"It's too bad," Dr. Wendell continued, "that your return coincides with such a serious situation. Luckily, the Network has a plan ready for this very outcome."

This was news to me. I exchanged a sideways glance with Q. "You're not going to kill her, right? Sumi and Kim—"

"No, of course not!" He waved a hand in the air. "The Network is well aware of Kim's connection with Sumi, as well as your connection to Whitley. We know that killing either one of them may inadvertently put either of you in great harm."

"If by great harm, you mean our *death*, then yeah. That would be pretty harmful."

Dr. Wendell frowned at me before continuing. "No. The Network prepared for Sumi's possible awakening by preparing a cell specifically designed to contain her and her powers. We have a transport truck with the same perimeters so we can safely transport her to the headquarters in New York."

Braden clapped his hand together. "That sounds great!"

I wasn't so sure. "You say this cell can hold her, but for how long?"

Dr. Wendell slipped his glasses back on. "As long as it takes."

"What does that mean?" Kim asked.

"It means the Network will do all they can to rehabilitate Sumi. But if that proves to be futile, we'll hold her ... " Dr. Wendell shrugged. "Indefinitely."

I narrowed my eyes. "That's your plan? Hold her in a cage forever? This is Sumi we're talking about—the most powerful kunoichi to ever live. Fat chance you're going to be able to rehabilitate her. You might as well put a shark in a swimming pool and ask it not to bite anyone."

He laced his fingers together and rested them on his lap. "I understand your concern. But I assure you this cell will be able to hold her. We can't kill her—not without risking Kim's life. So if you have a better idea, I'd be open to hearing it."

"I—" But the words died on my tongue. Truth was I had nothing. I locked eyes with Kim but he only frowned. I then looked to each samurai, hoping to find a solution among them, but as I met each pair of eyes, they only turned away with sad shrugs.

I sighed. "All right. Cage it is. Do you at least have a plan for getting her *into* the cage?"

"It's like I said," Dr. Wendell continued. "We've had a truck engineered specifically to transport her. I'll call and have it sent here. In the meantime, I need all of you to go to Sumi's house and address the situation. There's a chance we might be reacting over nothing. None of us fully understands the extent of Q's powers, correct? So there's still a chance Sumi could be without her memories and, therefore, quite harmless."

A knot loosened inside my chest. Maybe we *were* getting worked up over nothing. "So what do we do if she doesn't have her memory back?"

Dr. Wendell sighed and raked his fingers through his hair. "I'm afraid we're going to have to contain her regardless. We can't take any chances."

"Agreed," Kim said. He turned around so that he faced us. "All right. We have our mission."

I bit the inside of my cheek to keep from groaning. I'd had Kim to myself a whole fifteen minutes before the Network managed to assign us a mission.

"Remember," Dr. Wendell added, "your objective tonight

is strictly surveillance. On the off chance Sumi has regained her memories, I don't want anyone confronting her until the truck arrives. Is that clear?" His eyes targeted mine.

I met his gaze with my own unwavering stare. "But if she attacks—"

"You retreat," he finished.

I jerked back. "You want us to run away like cowards? Are you forgetting what we are?"

"No one is accusing you of being a coward, Rileigh. I simply know that Sumi's powers killed all of you in your past lives."

"We were caught off guard," I argued. "Besides, now we have Q, who might be every bit as powerful as Sumi." And I'd be lying if I didn't admit there was the teensiest part of me that wanted her to pay for all the hurt she put me and my friends through.

Quentin cleared his throat. "Let's not make any assumptions about what I can or cannot do. I'm not sure *what* I'm capable of, let alone the extent of my power."

"Exactly." Dr. Wendell nodded. "We need to go into this situation with extreme caution. I will not put anybody at risk."

"But—" I began.

"No *buts*, Rileigh!"

I snapped my mouth shut, stunned. After all the crap I'd given him over the last year, Dr. Wendell had never raised his voice to me before.

He slid off the stool looking more exhausted than he had a minute ago. "Look, I'm sorry. I didn't mean to snap like that. I just refuse to take any chances when it comes to Sumi. She bested you once before."

"That's ancient history," I reminded him.

"Yes, it is." He crossed his arms and locked eyes with me. "But that's the thing about history; if you don't learn from it, it has a funny way of repeating itself."

7

We crept through a cow pasture, having abandoned our cars several miles away on one of the many country roads in Waterloo, Illinois. It was better we stayed off the roads and away from curious eyes who might wonder what the six of us were doing in the middle of the night with swords strapped to our backs.

The long grass in the field pulled at our legs, making shushing sounds as if warning us to remain hidden. As we approached, several cows glanced up at us, only to drop their heads disinterestedly back to the ground in search of clover after we'd passed.

Kim led our group, with me following closely behind. Q and Drew walked on either side of me while Braden and Michelle brought up the rear. Her frequent glances over her shoulder let me know she was doing her job, checking to see if anyone was sneaking up behind us. Even if they were, it was a long shot their attack would go undetected by my danger premonitions—a tingling that buzzed beneath my skin whenever an enemy lurked nearby.

Kim stopped just before the crest of a hill, dropped to the ground, and pointed to the dimly lit farmhouse just ahead— the home of Sumi's adoptive parents. We fell to a crouch beside him. He glanced at each of us, his eyes asking if we knew the seriousness of the mission ahead. We nodded, one after another.

If I hadn't known better, as I found myself kneeling in a field under an open sky with a sword strapped to my back, I might have assumed I'd traveled back in time to my days as a samurai in Japan.

History has a way of repeating itself.

I shook my head, trying to dislodge Dr. Wendell's words from my head. But I was too late—a shiver danced along my spine as the memories of our last battle, and ultimately our deaths, replayed in my mind. I clenched my eyes tight, as if I could somehow block out the moment my Yoshido fell to the ground or the feeling of my own dagger as it pierced my stomach.

Someone touched my shoulder, and I was snapped from my memory. I blinked several times before Kim came into focus in front of me, his eyes wide with alarm.

I nodded to let him know I was okay. This wasn't Japan and we were prepared this time. No one was going to die.

I repeated the phrase over and over inside my head—*No one's going to die*—hoping the more I thought it, the truer it would become.

Kim waved his hand and motioned us forward. At once, we were on the move. And even though more than 500 years had passed since our last battle, we moved as if we'd fought only yesterday. We were no longer a group of people but a single organism with many limbs, operating with one mind for a single purpose.

We reached the bottom of the hill and Kim raised his arm. Wordlessly, we fanned out.

Drew ran to the nearest tree, hoisted himself onto a limb, and disappeared within the branches. Michelle and Braden sprinted ahead. When they reached the side of the house, Braden crouched down. Michelle used his back to launch herself onto the roof of the porch, where she landed with barely a sound. Next, she reached over the side, grabbed Braden's waiting hand, and hoisted him up beside her.

Meanwhile, Q and I followed Kim as he darted behind a large, silver truck in the driveway. I peered over the truck bed and watched as Braden and Michelle tiptoed around the roof, pausing long enough to glance inside each of the second-story windows. When they finished their circle, Michelle gave me a thumbs-up.

I crouched beside Q and Kim, who lay on their stomachs peering at the house from under the truck. "Michelle gave us the all clear," I said.

Kim nodded. "All right. On to phase two."

Q glanced between us. "What's phase two?"

"It's a surveillance mission," Kim answered. "So now we watch. We don't want to alert Sumi to our presence, but at the same time, we need to know if she has her memories back—as well as her powers."

I nodded and slid down to my belly next to Kim, trying not to flinch as a jagged-edged rock dug into my skin.

"How long do we wait like this?" Q hissed.

"As long as it takes," Kim answered.

And I knew from past experience that "as long as it takes" translated into a very, *very,* long time. I propped my elbow on the ground and let my head fall against my hand. I'd always thought graduation would be a new beginning for me—no more following orders, no more being told what I *had* to do. It was supposed to be my opportunity to finally take charge of my life and decide for myself how I wanted to live.

Considering it hadn't been quite twelve hours since I'd received my diploma and I was belly-down under a truck in the middle of the night—the whole taking charge of my life thing was not going so well.

The three of us remained silent as we watched. My body began to ache from not moving, but each time I tried to find a more comfortable position, the sharp edge of a rock dug into my skin. I cursed under my breath. How long had we been lying here anyway? An hour? Two?

I shifted again and this time a stone jutted against my hip bone, making spots of pain erupt behind my eyelids. I opened my mouth to tell Kim we should maybe find a new hiding place when an uneasy feeling crawled along my skin.

I snapped my mouth shut and tried to make sense of the feeling. It wasn't exactly a danger premonition, but it definitely felt like a warning of some kind.

Kim looked at me. "What's wrong?"

"I'm not sure." I dug my fingers into the gravel to the dirt below, hoping the cold earth would balance the sense of unease spreading through my body. No such luck. "I can't explain it. It's not the electric jolt I get from a danger premonition, but... "

I licked my lips and motioned to the house. "Something's not right."

Kim followed my gaze, his eyes searching the windows. "We haven't seen any movement."

"I know." So why was the creepy-crawly feeling growing more intense by the second? I shuddered as another wave rippled over me.

After several minutes of silence, Kim gave a sigh. "You're not going to be satisfied until we check things out, are you?"

I gave him my most brilliant smile. "You really do have your memories back."

He chuckled softly. "Fine. We'll go in for a closer look. Just remember I'm still in charge of this mission. We are to remain unseen at all times, and if I say we run, we run. Got it?"

"Got it," I said.

"Got it," Q echoed.

Kim turned to him. "Listen Quentin...maybe you should stay here. It's dangerous enough with just Rileigh and me going in—"

"Kim." I placed a hand on his shoulder. "He goes. He's our secret weapon. Besides, if Sumi has her powers back, Q's the only one who can fight off her mind control. There's no way we can leave him outside."

Q leaned past Kim and smiled at me.

Kim sighed. "Fine. Just stay behind us and keep quiet."

He nodded.

"All right. Let's move." Slowly Kim slithered out from under the truck. Q and I were quick to follow. Michelle and Braden watched from the roof as Kim signaled to them that we were heading inside. They glanced at each other warily before unsheathing their swords and backing into the shadows. Better to be prepared than not.

Another icy wave spiraled down my spine, and I clenched my teeth together to keep from crying out. The feeling grew stronger the closer we moved to the house—not a good sign.

The three of us tiptoed onto the porch and stood on either side of the door. Kim reached for the knob and, when it refused to turn, he motioned me forward. "I believe this is your department?"

Right. I closed my eyes and fell inside myself, to where my ki power sat nestled within my core. With a gentle nudge, I released a small amount from my fingertips. What felt like the rustle of a breeze swirled around my body, flipping the ends of my hair before blowing away. A second later, I heard the faint click of a lock being turned. Mentally I drew my ki back inside my body, feeling a slight tug in my stomach like a ball of yarn pulling tight, before closing it off. I opened my eyes with a smile. Controlling my ki had sure become a lot easier now that I no longer had Sumi screwing with my mind.

I reached past Kim and twisted the handle. The door swung open soundlessly. "After you."

He unsheathed his sword, and I gave him a sideways glance as he stepped past me. "I thought you said this was an observation mission only."

"We should still be cautious."

"Agreed." I unsheathed my own sword, relishing the feel of the eelskin-wrapped handle in my grasp. I glanced at Q. "Ready?"

He shrugged. "I don't have a weapon."

"You *are* a weapon," I reminded him.

"Right." He frowned and lifted his hands in the air like a witch about to conjure a spell. "Do I look just like a superhero?"

"Um…absolutely." I grabbed his arm and together we followed Kim deeper into the foyer, where he stopped in front of a large wooden staircase. The house remained silent except for the ticking of a nearby grandfather clock.

"The bedrooms are upstairs," Kim whispered.

"How do you know?"

The muscles in his jaw flexed. "Sumi," he answered simply. He didn't need to say more. Given the look of disgust on his face, I knew he was remembering the time he spent with her after she'd brainwashed him into being her boyfriend for several months. I'd never asked him about it—I hadn't had the chance before he'd lost his memory. But now seeing him stand here clenching and unclenching his fist, I was pretty sure I didn't want to know. But I also knew Kim had a nasty habit of letting his guilt get the best of him.

I placed a hand on his shoulder. "It doesn't matter," I whispered in his ear. "She had control of your mind—you weren't yourself."

He closed his eyes for a moment and nodded. "There are things we should probably talk about—but now's not really the time." He reopened his eyes. "Let's do what we came to do."

"Okay," I agreed.

Kim inhaled sharply and started up the stairs before stopping suddenly. "Since Q is resistant to Sumi's power, I'm going to trust you two to search her room. It's the first door on the right. Being here…my emotions are unbalanced." He glanced at his sword and tightened his grip. "I don't really trust myself right now. Can you handle that?"

Kim rarely lost his cool like this. It stunned the words right out of me. I could only nod.

"Good. I'll check her parents' room at the end of the hall on the left. If they're sleeping and all looks okay, we'll head back outside and resume our watch until morning."

I nodded again. I sincerely hoped we wouldn't find anything.

"Let's go." Kim climbed to the top of the stairs, his cautious steps barely registering on the antique wood. Q and I followed closely behind. I motioned for Q to step exactly where I did to avoid any squeaky or loose boards. When we reached the top, Kim turned left and disappeared into the shadows of the darkened hall. I grabbed Q's arm and pulled him to the right. I stopped when we reached the white, paint-chipped door. The cold tremors twisting through my body amplified, forcing me to clench my teeth to keep them from chattering.

"Remember my trick with the shadows?" I whispered.

His eyes never left the door. "Where you turn us invisible?"

"Better safe than sorry." I sheathed my sword and held out my hand. Q clasped it firmly within his own.

"Let's do this," he said, licking his lips.

I lifted our entwined hands to the shadow cast by the door and watched as they disappeared. "Here we go." I stepped against the door and pulled Q along with me until we'd vanished from sight. With my free hand, I slowly turned the doorknob and gently pushed the door open with my shoulder. My muscles twitched in anticipation. Whatever warning I was experiencing, I was about to find out what it was for.

I couldn't see Q, but I could feel the heat from his palm against my own. Together, we moved quietly into Sumi's room, where I hoped to find her sleeping soundly on her bed. But that wasn't the case. In fact, given her still-made bed, it appeared she hadn't been here all night. The buzzing sensation inside me remained.

"Huh." I released Q's hand, and he appeared beside me.

He lifted his hands in front of his face, examining both the fronts and backs. "I'll never get used to that."

Now that it was obvious there was no threat in Sumi's room, my knotted muscles gradually unwound. "Where do you think she is?" I stepped out of the shadow, revealing myself next to her bed. I spun a small circle. For belonging to a seventeen-year-old girl, her room was unlike any teenager's I'd ever been in. The blank walls held no pictures of friends or posters of bands. Ribbons and soccer trophies were absent from her shelves. The bookcases beside her bed contained only a few worn paperback novels, but nothing more that would let a visitor know a teenage girl lived here.

Her bed was made simply with a plain gray comforter. And stranger yet—especially for me—not a single stuffed animal sat against her pillow begging to be squished in a hug.

Q stepped beside me, repeatedly glancing at the door behind us. "This looks like the bedroom of a serial killer."

He wasn't far off.

I grabbed his arm, spun on my heels, and pulled him to the door. "C'mon."

"Where are we going?"

"To see if Kim's found anything. And then … " I honestly didn't know. If Sumi wasn't here—that couldn't be a good sign. What if she'd regained her memory and was out looking for a way to exact her revenge? Or worse, what if Whitley had changed his mind and decided to go after Sumi alone? He wouldn't have any qualms about killing her. And since she was Kim's inyodo, any attempt on her life put Kim in grave danger.

We emerged in the hallway in time to see Kim shut the door to Sumi's parents' room with a soft click. "Well?" he asked.

I gripped my arms, trying to suppress the tremors coursing through me. "Sumi's gone."

His hand fell from the doorknob. "Gone? Her parents are in their room sound asleep."

The feeling of unease coiling around my chest suddenly squeezed so hard I staggered back.

"Rileigh?" Q reached for me.

I held up my hand to stop him. "I'm okay." But I wasn't so sure about Sumi's parents. I looked at Kim. "They're really sleeping?"

He frowned. "Well, they're in bed. And they're not moving."

"Care if I check?"

Kim motioned me forward. I walked past him and pushed the door open. The pressure inside my chest intensified. I had an awful hunch, one I just had to follow. I fumbled my hand along the wall for the light switch and flicked it on.

"Are you crazy?" Q ran to my side. "You're going to wake them up!"

I stared at the two bodies on the bed. "No." My throat went dry as I took in the scene before me. Reflexively, my hand fell to the handle of the katana at my hip. "Look."

Kim stepped inside the room. A low hiss escaped his mouth as he surveyed the bed before him. In the dark, it was easy to understand how he could have thought Sumi's parents were asleep. They lay side-by-side underneath the covers, their heads nestled deep into their pillows. It was the stain of deep crimson pooling between their bodies that let me know they would never wake again.

Kim approached the bed and lifted the tattered edge of the blanket so he could examine their bodies. "Sumi. She stabbed them in their sleep." He swiped his finger across the bloody sheet before letting it fall once again. He rubbed the blood with his thumb. "Cold," he muttered. "But there's not enough discoloration in the skin for it to have been more than a couple of hours."

Now that I knew the danger, the uneasy waves rolling through my body subsided, replaced instead with a sense of dread. "So about the time you met me on the roof of my condo?"

He wiped his blood-smeared fingers with a corner of his T-shirt and nodded. "That's a good assumption."

"Son of hibachi," I muttered. "She's got a pretty good jump on us."

"Yes." Q stepped inside the room with us. "But at least one of our questions has been answered."

Puzzled, I turned to face him. "And what question is that."

"Her memory." Q motioned to the dead couple on the bed. "I think it's safe to assume Sumi the kunoichi is back and she has a plan."

8

D r. Wendell hung up his cell phone and sank onto the couch in my condo. The grim lines on his face grew deeper by the minute. Not that we looked any better. After Kim had updated Michelle, Braden, and Drew, no one had spoken more than a couple of words since leaving Sumi's house. And now we sat limp, scattered around the living room like a bunch of deflated balloons.

Dr. Wendell pinched the bridge of his nose. "Okay. I've called in a clean-up crew. They should arrive at Sumi's house within the hour and erase any traces of you being there."

"What about the bodies?" Michelle asked.

"I spoke to the Network about it, and we've decided to leave them for the police to find."

"What?" Drew's head snapped up. "Since when do we let outsiders become involved in Network affairs?"

"Usually we don't," Dr. Wendell agreed. "But this is a

time-sensitive situation. We can assume Sumi has her memory and that makes her extremely dangerous. Especially since we have no idea where she's hiding or what her next move will be. This is one of those rare times when a little media exposure might be a good thing."

I had to admit having the public aware a psycho was on the loose might make finding her a little easier.

"When is the truck due to arrive?" Kim asked.

Dr. Wendell sighed and folded his hands on his lap. "It's been dispatched from New York so we probably have at least"—he glanced at his watch—"another eight hours."

"Great," Drew muttered from where he sat on the floor. "You can kill a lot of people in eight hours."

Michelle shivered, and Braden put an arm around her and squeezed her close. "How do you know she's going to try to kill us, anyway? Maybe she's going to lie low or—better yet—leave town."

"Doubtful." Kim pushed off the wall and walked to the middle of the room. "If she wanted to lie low, she wouldn't have killed her parents. Obviously she felt they were an obstacle in whatever plan she's about to implement—a plan she knew there'd be no going back from."

"He's right." I climbed to my feet and joined him. "This is the girl who vowed to kill Whitley in every reincarnated life because he killed Kim in the last one. She's obsessed with revenge and even more obsessed with Kim. Her targets are either going to be Kim—in an attempt to alter his mind again; me—because she thinks I stole Kim from her; or Quentin—because he was able to defeat her in our last fight."

Quentin's jaw clenched but he said nothing.

"She's had a head start," I continued. "There's a good chance she is already nearby."

No one spoke for several minutes as tension settled across the room like a heavy wool blanket, hot and smothering.

Finally Michelle said, "We need a plan."

"Right." Dr. Wendell stood. "Like I said, the truck is going to be here in eight hours. We need to find Sumi by then—before she finds us. Our main objective will be to capture her and transport her back to New York. In the meantime—"

"We need more weapons," Kim cut in.

Dr. Wendell tilted his head, considering. "It certainly couldn't hurt."

"And we need to stick together," Kim continued.

Michelle bit her lip. "That's going to be a problem for me. If I'm not home before my dad wakes up, I'm going to get grounded. He needs to think I've been asleep in my bed. I have to be there for breakfast. After that, I can meet up with you guys again."

Kim frowned. "This is a dangerous time. No one should be alone."

"She won't be." Braden slid an arm around Michelle's shoulder and squeezed her against him. "I'll go with her."

"But won't her dad kill you if he finds you?" I asked.

"Yes." Braden nodded. "But he won't find me. I have mad stealth skills."

Michelle smiled and dropped her head against his shoulder.

"All right." Kim nodded. "Braden will go with Michelle until she can meet us back here." He looked at me. "I wonder if you should go too. Michelle's dad wouldn't have a problem with you there."

"No way." I shook my head. "If Sumi comes after me first, there's no way I'm leading her to Michelle's house. I'm not going to risk anyone's safety on my account."

"I think that's wise," Dr. Wendell agreed. "And with Debbie in a hotel, she'll be safe should Sumi decide to attack here. I'm going to have to leave soon to meet up with your mom before she gets suspicious. But don't worry, I'll tell her I received a call from the hospital and have to leave. I should be gone no longer than twenty minutes."

I forced myself to nod, even though it bothered me how easily Dr. Wendell lied to my mother. Every time I'd brought up his true feelings about Debbie, he'd managed to change the subject. Even now I couldn't be sure if he really cared for her or only pretended to in order to keep tabs on me.

"All right." Kim clapped his hands together. "I guess that means the rest of us should head to the dojo to collect weapons. If Sumi's coming after me first, it's possible she's already there."

Dr. Wendell frowned. "I don't know, Kim. Yes, there's a chance that Sumi could be there waiting for you, but there's also a pretty good chance she could be coming here. We need to locate her as quickly as possible. I think the best way to do that is to make sure there are people here if she shows up."

"He's right," I added before Kim could protest. "If she shows up at the condo and there's no one here, that's a wasted opportunity. We can't afford that. Once she catches on that we're trying to find *her*, she could run and we might lose our chance altogether."

He scowled at me. "What are you suggesting?"

"I'm suggesting we split up—but we do it smart by partnering so no one is alone if we're ambushed. I think you and Drew should run to the dojo for weapons, and Q and I will stay here and watch the condo."

Kim scowled. "I don't like it."

"I know. But you have to admit that together, Quentin and I make a pretty good team."

Q winked at me.

"It's a good plan," Dr. Wendell said.

Kim folded his arms across his chest. "Once upon a time, I thought of myself as the leader of this group. I guess I was only deluding myself. It's pretty obvious who's in charge." He sighed and shook his head. "If we go with Rileigh's plan, I'm adding a stipulation. This is the twenty-first century. There's no reason we shouldn't stay connected. Starting the moment everyone walks out this door, we are to text each other every fifteen minutes until the moment we meet back here. Failure to do so will imply you are under attack and the rest of us should come to your aid. Is this understood?"

Everyone murmured their agreement.

"Good. And one more thing." Kim pulled his cell phone out of his back pocket and held it up. "If one of us does get attacked, we need to be able to locate each other quickly. I want everyone to turn on your phone's GPS."

Everyone pulled out their cell phones except for me—mine was in my bedroom—and turned on their GPS.

"Let's move out," Kim ordered.

Braden and Michelle were the first out the door, followed by Dr. Wendell, who promised to be back no later than a half hour.

Drew stood in the open doorway with his hand resting on the knob. "Ready, brother?"

Kim nodded. "Just a moment. I need something."

Before I could ask him what he'd forgotten, he crossed the floor in several long strides. He slid a hand into my hair and tilted my head up to his. "Be safe," he said, his words so soft they bordered on a prayer.

I placed my hand over his and leaned into his touch. Pain formed in the back of my throat, and I had trouble swallowing. Had it really only been several hours since I'd sat on my rooftop longing to have Kim in my life once again? And now that he was, I was terrified I'd lose him all over again.

I turned my head and placed a kiss against his hand. "One of these days, Gimhae Kim, I won't have to kiss you goodbye anymore."

He tilted his head so his forehead rested against mine and all I could see were his eyes, dark pools I wanted to throw myself into and drown in. "I, too, look forward to that day. But just remember, there is nothing Sumi can do to break us apart."

I knew he meant his words to be comforting, but I couldn't help cringing the moment they left his mouth. If fate loved a challenge, there was nothing more enticing than breaking a promise made in love.

9

Japan, 1491

Chiyo sat huddled against the back of a tent within the bandits' camp. She'd lost count of the hours she'd spent alone inside the dark tent. She didn't dare try to escape. A man with a katana stood guard outside the door. Every so often he would stick his head through the flap and Chiyo would flinch. The man would laugh and disappear again, allowing her to breathe.

She wondered how long it would take Yoshido to receive news of her capture. Surely he'd come for her the moment he heard. He'd ride fast and hard through the night until he'd killed the entire camp. And then he'd carry her safely back to his village atop his horse.

Chiyo's chest heaved, and she stifled her sobs against her shoulder. She'd be brave for him. Courage was expected of a samurai's wife. And when he arrived, he would find her waiting for him, fearless. And he'd be so impressed, he'd fall madly in love with her. And they'd be so happy, this entire nightmare would be forgotten.

Hot tears spilled over Chiyo's cheeks as the gnawing ache inside her grew. It was a lovely thought—one she had to cling to in order to survive. *Just a few more hours,* she told herself. *I must be strong a few hours more—until my samurai comes for me.*

Voices approached from outside, and Chiyo jerked upright. She quickly wiped the tears from her cheek. She would be strong. For Yoshido.

The flap to the tent was pushed aside, and three men entered. Two of them Chiyo recognized as the men who'd killed her servant and best friend before abducting her. The third man wore a gray silk robe and his hair was neatly tied on the back of his head. He had a scar that ran at a diagonal across his face, starting at his left eyebrow, crossing his nose, and ending at his chin. He glanced at her disinterestedly. "This is the girl?"

The man with the katana nodded. "Yes, Ryuu. Chiyo Sasaki. As you requested."

Ryuu frowned. "And how many men did we lose retrieving her?"

The two men exchanged nervous glances before the man with the katana answered. "Four."

Ryuu spit on the ground, inches from where Chiyo huddled. "Do you hear that, girl?" He sneered at her. "You cost me four men. Now I will have to double the price of your ransom. Do you think you are worth it?"

Chiyo tried to scoot away, but her back met with the tent wall, leaving her no escape.

Ryuu's eyes flew wide and he lunged for her, grabbing a fistful of her robes and yanking her to her feet. "Answer me! Do you think you are worth it?"

Chiyo's heart pounded furiously against her chest. She opened her mouth, but her words tangled in her throat. Only a whimper escaped.

Behind him, the two men chuckled. Ryuu, however, stared at her with unblinking eyes. "I understand. You think you are too good to answer me because I am a lowly bandit, is that it?"

"No!" Chiyo shook her head. Despite her earlier vow to remain strong, tears once again sprang from her eyes.

Ryuu jerked his head back. "If it is not because I am a bandit—perhaps it is my scar you do not care for?"

She gasped and shook her head harder. "No!"

"Oh, but I think it is." Still holding her with one hand, he used his other to withdraw a dagger from his obi. He caressed her cheek with the edge. "You see, most people look at scars in disgust. But not me. I find each gash, each tear, beautiful. Pain is art, and I am the artist."

Chiyo's pulse thrashed inside her ears. Where was her samurai? When would he come to save her from this madman?

Ryuu clamped his hand around her neck and pulled her roughly against him. "I can make you beautiful in a way you have never imagined."

"No, please, no!" Chiyo's whimpers turned to sobs. If the bandit disfigured her, would her samurai still want her or turn away in disgust?

But the bandit didn't listen. He pressed the blade against her cheek and pain like fire erupted beneath her skin. Chiyo screamed and tried to break free, but the bandit only tightened his grip.

Blood, hot and sticky, ran down her face and then fell to the ground in fat drops. She screamed until her voice broke and all that remained were ragged gasps. Burst of white light spotted her vision, and Chiyo was sure she would pass out from the pain—she prayed for it.

But awake she remained. Enduring every agonizing moment until she was sure every inch of her face had been carved. Only then did Ryuu pull away the dagger.

"There." He threw her to the ground and she buried her face in her hands. Her bloodied flesh burned fire hot beneath her fingers. "Now," Ryuu said, "you truly are a thing of beauty."

Already the blinding pain had ebbed to a numb throb. Maybe she really was going to pass out. *Please,* Chiyo thought. Because she couldn't endure anymore. "Just kill me," she whimpered through her closed fingers. There was no way her samurai would want her now. And with all of her loved ones dead, what else did she have? "Just be done with it," she whispered.

Ryuu laughed. "And lose my ransom? Not a chance. When I offer your life in exchange for money, they will get just that— your life. So alive you must remain." His footsteps drew near. "Look at me, girl. I wish to see the beauty of my art."

That was the last thing Chiyo wanted to do. But she also knew if she didn't obey, Ryuu would make her suffer—and she couldn't bear anymore. She pulled her shaking fingers from her face and dropped them onto the grass. She blinked several times to clear her eyes of the blood before she dared to look up.

Ryuu gasped and took a step back. "How—I do not understand."

The archer's mouth dropped, and the man with the katana clutched his own throat.

Chiyo frowned. She'd done nothing more than look at them—so what would make them so afraid? Perhaps her face was worse than she could have imagined. Terror squeezed her chest as she brought her hands to her face to explore the damage for herself. But instead of finding torn flesh, she was met with only smooth skin.

She blinked several times, certain she'd felt wrong. She ran her hands across her cheeks over and over again, searching for a cut, a scratch, or even a nick. But there was nothing to be found.

The man with the katana pointed a shaking finger at her. "She is a s-s-sorceress!" he stammered.

"No." A slow grin unfolded on Ryuu's lips. "She is a healer. And she is all mine. Finally, I have found a canvas worthy of my art."

Horror dug sharpened claws into Chiyo's chest. Surely she'd heard him wrong. "B-but my ransom! If you do not sell me, you will not get your money."

Ryuu knelt down and cupped a hand against Chiyo's face. She flinched when their skin touched. "My dear," he said, "one does not sell their prize possession."

Acid burned up her throat. "But my future husband is a samurai. He will come looking for me!"

"Hmm." Ryuu frowned and placed his hand against his chin. "You are right. He will come looking for you. Unless ... " His eyes lit up. "Unless he thinks you are dead!"

Dead? A whimper escaped her throat. Was Ryuu right? Would Yoshido give up the search if he thought her to be dead?

Before she could move, Ryuu reached out and plucked the kanzashi from her head—the same kanzashi Miku had placed in her hair what felt like a lifetime ago. "Here." Ryuu tossed her hairpin to the man with the katana. "Take a girl from a nearby village and burn her body. Make sure this hairpin is found on it. We want the samurai to have no doubts that his lovely bride-to-be is dead."

The man nodded. Together with the archer, the two of them left the tent.

"No!" Chiyo begged. She couldn't spend the rest of her life with a monster. "Sell me, *please!* They will pay anything you want. I am sure of it."

Ignoring her begging, Ryuu wiped the blood off his dagger with the edge of his robe until it gleamed. When he finished, he turned to her with a grin. "Now, where were we?"

10

After Drew and Kim left the condo, I shut the door behind them and sagged against it. The exhaustion from a night without sleeping, along with the stress of Sumi being back, slammed into me with the force of a Metrobus. My head pounded, and every muscle in my body screamed for me to climb into bed and pull the covers over my head.

Quentin dropped onto the couch. "You look exhausted. Why don't you take a quick nap until everyone gets back? I can keep up with the texting."

"Thanks for the offer, but there's no way I could sleep knowing Sumi is out there, probably planning our deaths as we speak." I rubbed my burning eyes. "But I would love some coffee." I pushed off the door and started for the kitchen when Q jumped up.

"Let me." He darted in front of me. "I can't keep sitting around doing nothing."

I didn't have the strength to stop him. "You remember where the coffee is?"

"First cabinet next to the refrigerator." He stepped behind the bar dividing the living room from the kitchen and snatched the coffeepot.

"Great. I'm going to head to my room and grab my cell phone." I plodded down the hallway, each footstep heavier than the one before as exhaustion threatened to topple me over. I really hoped Sumi didn't attack before I had my caffeine fix. Unless she wanted a nap-off. In which case I'd totally kick her ass.

But *after* I'd had my coffee, now that was different story. I cracked my knuckles against my palm. I was actually looking forward to our eventual encounter. After everything she'd done to Kim and me, I had more than a little thirst for revenge. Not to mention I was tired of her trying to come between Kim and me. I wanted this score settled once and for all so Kim and I could finally get on with our lives.

I only hoped it would be that easy. What was it about Kim and me that attracted opposition? No matter the years gone by or the battles fought, why did the ghosts of our past continue to resurrect?

I opened the door to my bedroom and flipped on the light only to jerk back, my hands flying to the handle of my sword. "Oh, son of hibachi!"

From his perch on my bed, Whitley continued to browse the screen of my phone in his hands. "Is that any way to greet an old friend?"

"You're not a friend," I snarled. I released my sword,

marched up to him, and snatched my phone out of his hands. "What are you doing here?"

He yawned. "Well, I *was* reading the most boring emails ever written. Seriously, don't you have a life?"

I switched the GPS on before tucking the phone inside my pocket. I was *not* going to take any chances. "The only one without a life will be you if you don't tell me what you're *really* doing here."

Whitley rolled his eyes and sat up. "Always so dramatic. I'm not here to start any fights with you—that would be stupid considering we're inyodo. Just like it's stupid for you to threaten me. Then again, if my life was as boring as yours, I'd be suicidal too. "

"What. Do. You. Want?" I growled between clenched teeth.

Whitley smiled and clasped his hands. "There's that famous Rileigh Martin hospitality I've grown to love. So glad you asked. I'm here for your help."

"I already told you I'm not going to help you kill Sumi. I won't do anything to put Kim's life in danger."

The smile melted from his face. "No. Of course you wouldn't." He waved a hand in the air. "But I'm not going to ask you to do that. Rumor has it Sumi regained her memory and she's out for blood—*your* blood specifically."

A sour taste burned the back of my throat, and my fingers reflexively grasped the handle of my sword. "How do you know that?"

He laughed. "Because I'm not stupid. I'm not content to go about my life oblivious to the threat of potential danger like some people I know." He gave me a pointed look.

"I'm not oblivious—"

He held up his hand to silence me. "Doesn't matter. What does matter is I know Sumi has her memory back, I know she killed her parents, and I know she's coming after you next. And since we're connected by this annoying inyodo, any attempt she makes on your life would be an attempt on mine. I just can't have that."

I dropped my sword's handle. "We're taking care of it. We're working on finding Sumi as we speak. And once we do, we're going to transport her to the Network security office in New York where she'll be locked up for good."

He cocked his head to the side. "And just how are you going to find her? In her last life, she was one of the most powerful ninjas to ever live. She pretty much wrote the book on evading capture."

I frowned. I guess I hadn't really thought about it like that.

Whitley's grin widened. "And remind me, how did you fare against her in your last life? Oh yeah, I remember— you all died."

Angry heat burned through my body. "It would be wise of you not to bring that up. Because if I remember correctly, Sumi had help." Sumi had hired Whitley to betray us and lead an army of ninja over our walls. It was by Whitley's hands that Kim had died trying to save me. My Yoshido's sightless eyes staring up at me as he lay on the ground still haunted my nightmares.

"Now, now." He lifted his hands in mock surrender. "I didn't come here to get you all riled up. Quite the opposite, actually." He swung his legs over the side of the bed and stood. "I'm here to offer my help."

It was my turn to laugh. "Just what makes you think I need your help?"

"You don't know where Sumi is," he said simply. "And *I* do."

I jerked back as a sudden chill settled into my core. If Whitley wasn't lying and he really knew where Sumi was, we could sneak up on her undetected. That would mean our mission just became a lot simpler as well as safer. Still, Whitley was my sworn enemy. I had a hard time believing he'd want to help me out of the goodness of his heart. "What's the catch?"

He pressed a hand against his chest and feigned shock. "Rileigh Martin, I'm hurt you think there'd be one. Haven't we moved beyond our petty differences? We're connected, you and I. The sooner we dispose of this little threat, the sooner we can go back to living our lives."

"What's the catch?" I repeated.

He laughed. "Well, since you asked. There is one *tiny* thing."

"Spit it out."

He smiled widely. "I want to go."

"You?" I laughed loudly. "You're the biggest coward I know. Why on earth would you want to go anywhere you might be put in harm's way?"

His face darkened. "Because I'm tired of running. I'm tired of looking over my shoulder, wondering if every shadow that falls across my path is her coming to kill me. I want my life back." He clenched his hands into fists. "And I will take it by force if necessary."

Maybe it was because I was overly tired, but Whitley made a lot of sense. And considering I felt the same way, I couldn't help but feel a tad sympathetic toward him.

"Besides," he continued, "we have your healer friend now, and he's proven himself to be very formidable. I think the odds are greatly in our favor."

"True. But Kim has his memory back too. He doesn't know you helped us defeat Sumi before. And since you helped her kill all of us in the past, I don't think he's going to take too kindly to your presence—let alone your help."

"Which is why you aren't going to tell him."

"Tell him what?" Q asked, walking into my room with two steaming mugs of coffee. If he was surprised to find me chatting it up with Whitley, he didn't show it. After handing me a mug, he sipped his own coffee, keeping his eyes on Whitley.

Whitley smirked. "She's not going to tell Kim the three of us are teaming up again!" He rubbed his hands together. "Isn't it exciting?"

Q looked at me with raised eyebrows. "That's not exactly the word I would use to describe it."

"I have a few choice words myself," I agreed. "But Whitley here says he knows where Sumi is hiding. He'll tell us only if we take him and don't tell Kim where we're going."

Q snorted. "Do we look like idiots?"

"Fine." Whitley shrugged. "Then I guess you can hunt down Sumi on your own." He walked to the door. "Hopefully you'll find her before she finds you."

Son of hibachi. If Whitley was telling the truth, having him lead us to Sumi would save us a lot of time and trouble. If we could add the element of surprise to our attack, it just might give us the edge needed to defeat her. "Wait!" I called out before Whitley passed through the doorway.

He turned around with a smile. "Yes?"

"What are you doing?" Q hissed into my ear. "You can't be seriously thinking about going with Whitley and not telling Kim?"

"That's exactly what I'm thinking about doing." But for an entirely different reason. As long as I *didn't* call Kim, he would know something was up and come looking for me. With the GPS enabled on my phone, he'd also know exactly where I was. I gave Q a pointed look. "No one is going to *call* Kim."

Q blinked several times before his eyes lit up. "Oh. *Oh.* We're not going to *call* him."

"Nope."

Whitley crossed his arms and leaned against the door frame. "But what if he calls you?"

"I won't answer it." I pulled my phone out of my pocket and set it to vibrate before exchanging a quick glance with Q. It had almost been fifteen minutes since Kim walked out the door, which meant he would be calling at any minute. When I didn't answer, he was sure to come looking for me. So he wouldn't be far behind us, wherever Whitley planned to take us.

"Good." Whitley narrowed his eyes. "I just know if we invited your little boyfriend along, he'd want to imprison me along with Sumi."

I dropped my phone into my back pocket. "What makes you think *I* don't?"

He laughed. "Oh please. You wouldn't do that. You need me."

I snorted. "Yeah, like I need a shuriken to the head."

He shook his head. "When are you going to admit that we make a great team?"

"Uh, *never.*"

"That's a little unfair, don't you think?" he asked.

"Is it?" I took a step toward him. "I let my guard down once. Once! And you led a group of ninja over our castle walls.

You killed our Lord Toyotomi. You killed Yoshido. In order to be a team with someone, you have to trust them, and I don't trust you. I will *never* trust you."

He grinned. "Fair enough. But if you don't trust me as much as you say you do, why agree to go with me in the first place?"

I stepped up to him with my hands balled into fists. "Because if you screw me over, so help me Whitley, I'm going to have Q alter your mind so you'll never hurt anyone again. The only thing you'll be able to do is stare out the window and drool. Do you understand?"

A flicker of fear passed through his eyes. "He can do that?"

Q shrugged and flexed his fingers. "Never tried before, but I'm willing to give it a shot."

Whitley swallowed, his eyes darting nervously between me and Q. "All right, point taken. So let's put the brain damage on hold for right now. We should probably get going before Sumi makes her move."

I glanced at Q to make sure one last time he was on board with the plan. Any situation involving Sumi was a dangerous one. And throwing Whitley into the mix didn't make it any better. By going along with me, I was asking Q to risk his life. But instead of hesitating or showing any signs of doubt, Q locked eyes with me and gave a curt nod.

"All right." I pulled my jacket from my desk chair. "Let's go find Sumi."

Together, Q and I followed Whitley out of my condo, down several flights of stairs, and into the parking garage where his BMW waited.

Just as I was about to climb into the front passenger seat, my phone began to vibrate from my inside my pocket. I smiled and settled back into the seat. When I didn't answer, Kim would surely come looking for me. Sure, Whitley would be pissed. But after all the times he'd double-crossed me, I definitely owed him one.

11

Whitley pulled into a remote shopping plaza and parked his car outside a twenty-four-hour gym.

I frowned at him. "Not really a good time for a workout, don't you think?"

He rolled his eyes. "We're not here to work out, you dummy. Sumi is here." He pointed to the blue Honda parked a row over. "I followed her here earlier. And since her car is still here—it's safe to assume she hasn't left yet."

In the backseat, Q unbuckled his seat belt and leaned forward. "Are you sure? I don't see anyone inside."

He was right. With the early morning light yet to break through the purpling horizon, the rows of treadmills, elliptical machines, and weightlifting equipment sat unused. But dawn was quickly approaching, and the gym would soon be full of people wanting to get a quick workout before work. If Sumi was in there, we needed to find her before the innocent bystanders arrived.

Whitley pulled the keys from the ignition and placed them inside his pocket. "She's in the locker room. What better place to clean up undisturbed after a murder? If you can somehow get inside the gym without swiping your membership card, the police would never think to look for you here. Meanwhile, you can rest and clean up, and all that DNA evidence goes right down the drain. It's genius, really."

I made a face. "I guess you have to be a psychopath to really appreciate the achievements of another psychopath." I opened the car door and stepped out into the chilly spring air. "Let's get this over with. The sooner we do, the sooner I don't have to see you ever again."

Whitley followed me out of the car. "Fair enough."

I quickly glanced at the road behind us. How long would it take Kim to arrive? Since climbing into the car with Whitley, my phone had buzzed five different times over the course of our fifteen-minute drive. He had to be on his way, and I'd sure feel a lot better taking Sumi on with Kim by my side.

Q exited the car and approached the gym door. After trying unsuccessfully to pull the door open, he tapped a gray box beside the door. "You need one of those magnetic key cards to get inside."

"On it." I marched to the door and placed my hand on the card reader. Closing my eyes, I opened myself enough to allow a small ribbon of ki to uncurl from my fingertips into the box beneath my fingers. A second later, the box beeped and the door clicked as the lock receded.

Q smiled before pulling the door open. "That never gets old."

Whitley snorted. "It's a cheap trick—one that any ninja

could do. What would be really handy is if you could do that thing where you make us all invisible." He gave me a hopeful look.

"Sorry." I shook my head. "That only works if I'm standing in shadows and this place"—I gestured to the brightly florescent lit room—"is seriously lacking in shadows."

Whitley sighed. "So much for that idea. Guess we'll just have to face her head-on." He removed a long chain from his pocket. A blunt weight dangled from one end and a gleaming hatchet from the other. A kusarigama—the perfect weapon for both bludgeoning your enemy to death and cutting them into ribbons.

I slid my sword free from its sheath at my hip and spun it in several slow arcs in front of me to loosen my muscles. I glanced at Q. "Ready?"

He nodded, his mouth tight. "Ready."

We quietly stepped inside the gym and shut the door softly behind us. Immediately, I was assaulted by the smell of stale sweat and rubber. As I approached the front desk, an electric current jolted through my body, raising the hair on the back of my arms and constricting my lungs. Definitely a danger premonition—which meant someone was on the verge of trying to kill me. *Awesome.* I tightened my grip on my sword. "We're definitely in the right place," I whispered.

Whitley rolled his eyes. "I *told* you we were. Why would I lie?"

I directed a scowl at him as I brushed past. Why *wouldn't* he lie? He'd killed me in my last life, and it had only been a year since he tried to kill me in this one. I'd have to be an idiot to put my trust in him now.

I glanced at the clock on the wall. *Hurry, Kim!*

Slowly, we made our way to the back of the gym. I scanned every corner of the room but still didn't see any signs of Sumi. As we approached the locker rooms, I became aware of the hissing sound of water from a shower. I dropped my gaze to the floor, where I noticed tendrils of steam curling out from under the women's locker room door like reaching fingers.

If Sumi was in the shower, we definitely had the element of surprise on our side. But it also meant I couldn't afford to wait for Kim. I motioned for Q and Whitley to stay close as I pulled the door open.

A hot wall of steam rushed out at me, blasting me in the face. There was no way one hot shower could have created the mass of steam blanketing the locker room. And the loud hissing coming from the shower stalls confirmed my suspicions—all the showers were running full blast. And that could only mean one thing.

I tightened my sweaty grip on my sword.

Sumi knew we were coming.

"What do we do?" Q asked. I glanced over my shoulder and could barely make out his features through the blanket of white.

"We fight!" Whitley hissed. "We're never going to get another chance like this again. If she slips through our grasp now, she'll only attack again when we're not expecting it. It's now or never."

As much as I hated to admit it, Whitley had made a good point. If Sumi knew we were coming for her, then she might also have known about the Network's arrival and how we planned to imprison her.

Besides, Kim was sure to be here any minute. If anything,

we could stall her until reinforcements arrived. I pulled the boys closer to me and said, "If we want to defeat her, we need to keep our backs together so she can't sneak up on us. Got it?"

"Got it," both Whitley and Q answered.

"Okay then. Let's move out." I lifted my sword in front of me so that it arched over my shoulder and slowly made my way deeper inside the locker room. Q and Whitley followed, and the door shut behind us with a soft click.

Steam beaded along my skin and ran in lines down my neck. Immediately, I wondered if I had just made a huge mistake. I'd walked into a fight where two of my senses were crippled. The fog distorted my vision and made the room appear hazy and distorted. And it was nearly impossible to hear over the hiss of rushing water.

A shot of pain jolted through my leg, and I looked down to discover I'd bumped into a bench. "Son of hibachi," I growled.

"I'll fix that." Q offered his hand, and I knew if I took it he'd use his powers to melt away the pain.

"No. I'm good." I waved his hand away. I wanted the pain—needed it. Somehow it helped me focus.

"Do you think she's still in here?" Q asked.

If the electric current zipping through my veins was any indication, she was definitely close. "Oh, yeah. Let's cover our backs."

"Right." A second later, Q's back pressed against mine.

I kept my eyes trained on the row of lockers in front of me. "Whitley?"

He didn't answer.

I twisted my head around, unable to see him through the fog. "Whitley?" I hissed again. "This isn't funny."

"Uh, Ri-Ri?" Q's voice held a waiver of fear. "Whitley's gone."

"What?" I grabbed Q's elbow and whirled around, forcing him to stay behind me as we moved. Sure enough, Whitley was nowhere to be seen. "That traitor!" I growled through clenched teeth. I should have known he'd bolt. He was a coward, after all, and I shouldn't have doubted for a second that, once faced with the threat of danger, he'd abandon us.

I sucked in a deep breath in an attempt to calm my rapid heartbeat. "It's fine, it's okay," I muttered, only I wasn't sure if I was saying it for Q's benefit or my own.

A girl's laughter filled the room around us, echoing off walls and reverberating against the locker doors.

Sumi.

My muscles coiled and I raised my sword. I whipped my head around, hoping to discover her hiding spot, but I was unable to see more than a few feet through the fog. Behind me, Q's breathing quickened and I could feel small shudders rippling down his spine where it pressed against my back.

I transferred my weight to the balls of my feet, readying myself to spring in any direction. "Why are you hiding, Sumi? Afraid we'll defeat you like last time?"

"Hardly." She stepped out from behind a row of lockers. Unlike the last time we'd encountered her, she hadn't bothered with the ridiculous geisha dress. Instead, she wore a pair of black spandex running capris, a green tank top, and black Nikes. She would have looked like an average gym-goer if it weren't for the splatters of blood staining her shirt.

Q spun around so we stood side by side. He folded his arms across his chest and lifted his chin. For someone who'd been so tense with fear only moments ago, he sure knew how to exude confidence when it counted. "What's the matter, Sumi? Your stripper outfit at the dry cleaners?"

She narrowed her eyes and stepped forward. "I'd watch my tongue if I were you. You cannot begin to imagine all the ways I could kill you. But this fight does not belong to you. This is a feud spanning more than five hundred years. Leave with your life while you can."

Q's fingers curled into fists. "This fight became mine the moment you tried to kill my best friend."

"Have it your way." Sumi lifted her hand and blue bolts of electricity bled from her fingertips, striking Q in the chest. He sailed backward and slammed into the lockers behind him with a sickening thunk.

"Q!" My sword wavered in the air, but I knew better than to turn my back on the enemy in front of me.

Q groaned and placed a hand against his forehead. "It's all right. I'm fine."

"Impossible." Sumi's eyes fluttered wide. "Your healing powers are stronger than I thought." She waved a hand dismissively. "Doesn't matter. You're still no match for me."

"What the hell do you think you're doing?" Whitley called out.

He came back? I whirled around to find him standing in the locker room doorway. Relief loosened the ropes of anxiety pulling tight around my chest. He hadn't abandoned us after all.

Whitley strode into the middle of the steam-filled room and faced Sumi head-on. "Our deal was you wouldn't hurt him."

Sumi snorted. "I seem to recall you made me a similar deal centuries ago, resulting in the death of my betrothed."

Son of hibachi. We'd been double-crossed. Again.

My stomach quivered. Q and I exchanged furious glances. As much as I wanted to be surprised, the emotion wouldn't surface. I knew all along that trusting Whitley was like bathing in a pool of electric eels—it was only a matter of time until I got stung.

Whitley threw his hands in the air. "How many times do I have to tell you? That was an accident!"

"So you're working with Sumi now?" I asked him. "I thought she was trying to kill you."

"I was," Sumi answered for him. "But then I realized the old saying is true—the enemy of my enemy is my friend."

I looked at Whitley. "And you believe her? Who's to say she won't kill you the moment your back is turned?"

"She wouldn't." Whitley said, but his eyes flashed with uncertainty. "We came to an arrangement that benefits both of us."

Quentin used the locker door to pull himself to his feet. Sumi was right—his powers had to be growing. It was a miracle he was even alive, let alone able to stand after her attack. "Nothing she could offer you will help," he said. "Especially when you're both rotting in a Network security cell."

Sumi grinned. "That's what we're counting on."

She wanted us to throw her inside a cell? "Well, uh... *good*? Because it just so happens I have my phone's GPS turned on and Kim will be here any minute."

Sumi whirled around and glared at Whitley.

He shrugged and took a tentative step backward. "I didn't know."

"Doesn't matter," she said, even though the look on her

face was less than thrilled. "We'll have to work fast. Do you still have the bracelet I gave you?"

He pulled a long, braided cord out of his jeans pocket. Woven throughout the leather were a multitude of colorful stones and what appeared to be fragments of bone. "Are you sure this will work?"

"There's one way to find out." She turned to me with a smile.

Okay, I was really confused now. "You're going to accessorize us to death?"

Sumi rolled her eyes. "Of course not. We don't want to hurt those precious bodies of yours."

Now she was concerned about our well-being? Q and I exchanged a confused look. This was by far the strangest fight I'd ever been in.

Sumi pulled a dagger out of her waistband. The razor edge winked under the light, like it was also in on the joke Q and I couldn't figure out. Sumi spoke to Whitley. "It's time."

He nodded and lifted the sharpened edge of the kusarigama.

A fight. Now *this* made sense. My muscles tensed and I licked my lips in anticipation of the attack to come.

But it never did.

Instead, Whitley and Sumi lifted their blades to their own palms and drew the edge across their skin. Whitley made a hiss of pain but Sumi barely flinched.

I lowered my blade a fraction and blinked. *Well, this is new.*

Quentin sidled up beside me. "I haven't been in a lot of fights," he whispered. "So can you explain what's going on?"

"Not a clue," I answered. "The bad guys usually throw the sharp, pointy things at your head. They don't use them on themselves." A growing sense of unease bloomed inside me, making my stomach quiver. Fights made sense—bad guys tried to kill you. And in return, you tried to kill them. But this? My pulse quickened. Something was up, something dangerous; I could feel it like poison in my blood—dark, undetectable, but dangerous all the same.

Sumi balled her hand into a fist and fat droplets of blood fell like rose petals against the floor. She lifted her head and looked at me. "Now."

Whitley lifted the sickle and lunged for me.

12

Whitley ran at me, his blade aimed at my head.

I knew I couldn't waste much time or energy on Whitley—especially with Sumi in the room. With only seconds until he brought the blade down on me, I ducked low and lashed out with a side kick.

My foot connected with his gut, sending him stumbling backward. He toppled against the bench behind him and fell over it with a grunt. The kusarigama slipped from his hands and clattered to the floor.

"Idiot," Sumi hissed. She raised her arm, and streaks of electricity leapt from her fingers.

The static charge in the air pulled the hairs on my arms and neck to attention as the bolts arched toward me. My heart quivered. I knew I wouldn't be able to dodge them in time, so I closed my eyes and braced for impact.

But no sooner had I done so when Q's hand tightened on my arm. "Hold on!" he shouted.

A second later, the electricity tore through me, convulsing my body and fluttering my eyelids. But miraculously, I didn't feel a thing.

When the spasms ceased, I opened my eyes and looked at Q. "Did you do that?" I asked between gasps for air.

Before he could answer, Whitley attacked him from behind and they both collapsed on the ground in a heap. I started for them when I was kicked just below my ribs. I cried out as pain exploded inside me. Losing my grip on my katana, I hit the ground, forcing myself into a roll to cushion the impact.

I propped myself up on my elbows in time to see Whitley descend on Quentin with his blade. "NO!" I screamed.

Q threw his hands in front of his face and Whitley's blade sliced through his palm.

I tried to scrambled to my feet when Sumi lunged at me, wrapping her hand around my neck and screaming, her eyes wild. "You think you can take everything away from me and get away with it? Let's see how you like it when I take everything away from you!" Her fingers tightened around my neck, her nails ripping into my skin. "You will have nothing!" With her free hand, she raised the dagger over her head.

I curled my fingers into a fist and swung. Sure, it wasn't exactly a *traditional* technique, but it was effective. My fist connected with her cheek in a satisfying crack. Her head snapped back, and she cried out. I thrust her off me, frantic to get back to Q. I climbed to my feet just in time to see Whitley clasping Q's bloody hand within his own, frantically tying the cord around both their wrists as Q stared, his eyes wide.

"What the hell, dude?" Q placed his free hand on Whitley's forehead. A second later, a light flashed from his palm. Whitley's eyes rolled into the back of his head and he crumpled to the ground. The cord he'd wrapped around their wrists unraveled and fell onto his chest.

I rushed over to him. "Are you okay?"

"I'm—" The words died on Q's tongue. "Rileigh, behind you!"

Before I could turn around, a jolt of electricity slammed into my back and coursed through my body like razor blades. I opened my mouth and a scream tore from my throat.

Q's fingers were a brush away when another arc of lightning smashed into his chest, sending him flying across the room. As soon as he hit the floor, the electric current stopped tearing through my body. I fell to my knees, swaying for a moment before falling forward. I tried to stand, but my body refused to listen as my muscles continued to spasm.

A hand grabbed my shoulder and roughly flipped me over. Sumi kneeled beside me and snickered. "That looked like it hurt."

I glared at her, forcing words through my chattering teeth. "If—you—kill—me—Kim—will—kill—*you*."

She laughed. "Like I said before, I'm not going to kill you. You are more useful to me alive." She lifted my trembling arm and pressed her dagger against my palm.

Pain burned white-hot where the dagger ripped through my skin. I pressed my teeth together to keep from crying out—I wouldn't give her the satisfaction.

Sumi took my bloody hand and placed her own bleeding

palm against it. I tried to wrench my arm from her grip, but my body continued to spasm.

With a grin, Sumi set aside the knife and pulled out a long leather cord woven with bits of rock and what appeared to be bone. It was identical to the one Whitley had used moments ago. She proceeded to wrap our wrists together. "Say goodbye to your life, Rileigh Martin."

My mind raced to make sense of the situation. What the heck was going on? Sumi could have easily killed me with her electricity. Instead she kept me alive for—well, I wasn't exactly sure what this was. My best guess was a demented friendship bracelet ceremony.

After she'd finished wrapping our hands together, a tingling sensation pushed through the numbness inside me. Finally! I pressed my teeth together and growled, "Get off me." I brought my shaking legs against my chest and kicked out, striking her in the gut. She flew into a plastic trash can, denting its side.

She struggled to climb to her feet. "You're too late." She raised her hands as sparks danced along her fingertips.

Son of hibachi. There was no way I was getting fried again—especially without Q nearby to deflect the blow.

I slid across the concrete until my hands grasped the handle of my sword. My pulse thundered loudly in my ears as I pushed my ki into the blade and held it in front of me as a bolt of electricity streaked toward me. My sword intercepted the blow and, with a scream, I used my ki to push the lightning back the way it had come.

Sumi's eyes widened just before the lightening struck her chest. The electricity sent her spinning backward. Her head hit the floor with a crack, and her eyes blinked lazily before rolling back into her head. I couldn't be sure, but I thought I saw the faintest smile cross her lips.

I pulled my ki back inside of me and closed it off with a shiver.

Q stepped over Whitley's unconscious body and moved beside me. "So, is that it?"

I nodded—with both Whitley and Sumi knocked out cold, it certainly appeared that way. So why did I feel a gnawing sensation within my gut?

A battle cry rang out from the other side of the locker room door. I raised my sword and whirled around in time to see the door kick open.

The showers must have run out of hot water during the course of our fight, because the steam had dissipated enough for me to watch as Kim and Drew burst inside the locker room with their swords extended. Kim's eyes swept over Whitley's and Sumi's bodies and the angry lines on his face melted into confusion. Gradually, he lowered his sword and studied me. "You did this?"

I smirked and sheathed my katana. "You say that as if you're surprised."

"I am. And not because you defeated Sumi and"—he glanced at Whitley's body in disgust—"that *traitor*. I am only surprised at how quickly you were able to do it."

Drew nodded, his eyes wide. "It *is* impressive."

Quentin draped and arm over my shoulder. "It's easy when you know how."

I laughed. "Q is pretty badass. And I think I'm really starting

to get the hang of this ki thing." I shrugged. "Still, thanks for getting here so quickly."

Kim shrugged and nudged Whitley's thigh with his toe.
"Not sure how helpful we were."

"It helps to know I can count on you to come if I'm in
trouble."

Drew grinned and elbowed Kim in the side. "You're moral
support, dude."

Kim smiled at me. "Keep it up, and maybe I can put in for
early retirement."

"Dork." I laughed. Still, his words stirred a flutter of hope
inside me—hope that maybe Kim would someday give up
his work with the Network. Hope that we could have a life
together of our own, and not one dictated by others.

"Is she really out cold?" Drew pointed at Sumi's unmoving body.

Q walked over to her and bent down, placing his hands on
her head. "She's a healer like me. She won't stay down for long.
But I can give her a little boost to ensure she stays asleep—at
least until the transport gets here." A flash of light burst from
his fingers, flickered along Sumi's temples, and disappeared as
quickly as it came. "There. That should hold her."

"And what about him?" Kim motioned to Whitley.

"Oh, he's out cold." I laughed. "It's one of Q's specialties.
He can alter brain serotonin levels. When Whitley wakes, he'll
feel almost drunk. You won't have to worry about him getting
very far."

Kim's eyes widened as if impressed. "That's handy."

Now that I was no longer moving, the blood from my

hand trailed like ribbons from between my clenched fingers and fell onto the floor in fat, crimson drops.

"You're hurt." Kim's gaze narrowed, and he strode across the room.

"It's nothing." I hid my hand behind my back only to have Q grab it.

"I'll take care of that," he said. A second later, a tingling warmth flooded my hand. "Good as ne—" But his words trailed off. "Huh."

"What's wrong?" I pulled my hand out of his grasp and glanced at my palm. Just like before when Q had healed me, the gash had closed and was no longer bleeding. *Unlike* before, a faint shining scar remained in its wake. "It scarred…"

"I don't understand." Q scratched his head and looked at his own cut palm. "The same thing happened when I tried to heal my cut." He held up his hand, revealing the jagged pink line across his palm. "I usually don't leave scars."

The knot of uncertainty inside me pulled tighter. "It *was* a deep cut," I offered.

He frowned and traced the line with his finger. "I guess."

I tried to push the worry from my mind. After all, I'd just survived a pretty epic battle with my arch enemy—it only made sense that I would still be on edge.

Kim placed his hands on the side of my face, electrifying my skin beneath his fingers. "Are you okay?"

I forced a smile to my lips. "Of course. We stopped Whitley and Sumi from whatever crazy plan they'd concocted. And better still, you have your memory back. I've never been better."

He nodded, his eyes locked on mine, and giving me the uneasy feeling he was trying to read the truth in them. "You would tell me if there was something bothering you, wouldn't you?"

"Of course." And because I could think of no reason why something should be bothering me, I added, "I think I'm just tired."

"Of course you are." Kim wrapped an arm around my shoulder, tucking me against him. "I'll take you home so you can get some sleep. You'll feel better when you wake."

"You're probably right." I rested my head against his shoulder so he wouldn't see the uncertainty in my eyes. For just a moment, I wanted to pretend that the worst was over. I didn't want him to know about the tangles of worry twisting across my body, pulling so tight I had to strain against them just to breathe.

It was a feeling I knew all too well—a feeling that danger lurked just around the corner.

13

Together, Kim, Drew, Quentin, and I dragged Sumi and Whitley out of the locker room just in time to see Dr. Wendell pull up in his black Audi sedan.

We watched from inside the gym as he climbed out of his car with a roll of police tape in hand. Within minutes he'd taped off the front entrance. He tucked the roll back inside his pocket and joined us inside. "That should keep people away long enough to get the truck here." He glanced at Whitley and Sumi. "Good job taking care of this so quickly. Everything go okay?"

"For the most part." I rubbed my freshly healed hand against my leg. A strange tingling sensation tickled along the pink edges of the scar—probably the result of having it healed so quickly. I made a note to ask Quentin about it later.

"Rileigh? Are you okay?"

I glanced up to find Kim frowning at me.

I quickly shoved my hand inside my pocket. "Yeah. Why?"

"Because I said your name two times and you didn't respond."

Oh. "Sorry about that." My vision blurred at the edges, and I blinked several times until my sight refocused. What was wrong with me?

"You look exhausted," Kim said.

Dr. Wendell shook his head. "Not only has she been awake for twenty-four hours, but she also executed a surveillance mission as well as fought and captured our targets." He looked at me with lines of concern etched across his brow. "I honestly can't believe you're still standing."

"Well now that you mention it … " My knees wobbled together, and I grabbed onto Kim's arm to keep myself upright.

"Whoa there." Kim slid an arm around my waist to steady me. "I think it's time we got you home to bed."

"No!" I shook my head. "I'm not going anywhere until these two are loaded onto the truck."

"*Rileigh.*" Dr. Wendell folded his arms. "You can barely stand. Kim's right. You need to get home and get to bed. Besides, thanks to Quentin, Sumi and Whitley aren't going anywhere."

"But—"

He shook his head. "If you're still concerned, I'll have Drew stay with me, and Michelle and Braden are on their way. We've got this covered."

"But—"

"Maybe they're right." Q rubbed his eyes with the heels of his hands. "All of a sudden I'm feeling pretty exhausted too."

Kim nodded. "Adrenaline crash."

Q yawned. "Has to be. I wouldn't mind going home and going to bed myself."

"But—"

Kim squeezed my shoulder and steered me toward the door. "Come on, sleepyhead. Let's get you home before you collapse. We wouldn't want the Network to accidentally take you too."

"No, we wouldn't," Dr. Wendell agreed. "Their technology is quite impressive. Their cells and transport trucks are inescapable."

A faint chill whispered along my spine, raising the hair on my neck. I was scared, but for the life of me I couldn't figure out why I should be. "All right, you win." I sighed. "I guess a little sleep couldn't hurt."

"I'm glad you've come to your senses," Kim said. He motioned Q to follow us. "Come on. I can drop you off before I take Rileigh home."

I felt myself being pushed forward as my eyelids grew heavier by the second. It was all I could do not to fall into the depth of unconsciousness as Kim led me out of the gym. He must have realized I wasn't going to make it much farther because the next thing I knew, I was swept off my feet and carried by a muscular pair of arms.

My head rolled lazily against his chest. "Don't let me fall," I teased, my voice barely a whisper.

"Never." His breath was warm against my neck. "It's like I said before, now that I have you back, I'm never letting go."

I wanted to tell him it wasn't him I was worried about. Second by second the darkness behind my eyes pulled me deeper into unconsciousness. But instead of guiding me gently along, this darkness ripped into me, tearing at me with claws, wanting to devour me whole and leave nothing behind.

I tried to weave my fingers into Kim's shirt, to keep from being pulled away. But my tired fingers fell from his chest and dangled limply as I fell deeper inside myself. Instead of feeling my heart racing inside my chest, I heard it echo around me, ringing inside my ears. I tried to scream but no sound came forth.

This wasn't right. Sleep, no matter how exhausted I was, should never feel like this. I fought against the darkness, digging my nails into the side of it, trying to claw my way out of the pit, but all I managed for my efforts was a single word.

"Kim."

"Yes?" His voice sounded miles away.

"Don't," I muttered before succumbing to a wave of unconsciousness barreling over my head. I tried to scream the rest before it was too late. Even then, I wasn't sure if I actually spoke the words or if they merely circled through my mind.

"Don't let me fall."

14

He wasn't coming. It'd been a year since her capture and her samurai had yet to show.

Chiyo sat on the ground whimpering as she pulled the arrow from her shoulder. It was bad enough being Ryuu's *canvas*, but even worse when he loaned her out to his men for their amusement. Today she'd been the target in archery practice.

She breathed deeply as pain washed over her in hot waves. *Just two more.* She cried out as she pried another arrow from her stomach, and a final one from her upper thigh. She threw the arrows over her shoulder and fell onto her back, panting as the ache dulled to a throb—a sign her wounds were healing.

She blinked back tears as she stared at the blue, cloudless sky above her. She was supposed to be married to a handsome samurai and living within the village walls. If things had gone according to plan, maybe she'd even be a mother. She never imagined she'd end up the play thing for a camp of violent bandits.

But maybe, just maybe, that could change.

Someone tsked and Chiyo sat up to find Ryuu standing before her. He folded his arms across his chest. "We are going to have to get you new robes *again*. Look at you. You are a mess."

Chiyo glanced down at her bloody and tattered robes. They could be washed and mended, but she knew Ryuu wouldn't allow that. He kept all her blood-stained clothing in a chest, collecting them the way her father had collected calligraphy when he was still alive.

"No matter." Ryuu waved a hand dismissively. "Am I to understand you were looking for me?"

Chiyo inhaled, hoping to slow her rapid breathing. Since her previous attempts at escape had ended in severe beatings, she normally spent her days hiding from him. Today was the first she'd gone looking for him. The spark of an idea had come to her when the first arrow pierced her shoulder, an idea she had no choice but to implement if she hoped to survive. "I noticed—" Her voice broke and she was forced to swallow before continuing. "I noticed you have not taken a wife. I thought, given the situation, I might make a suitable match."

Ryuu's eyes flew wide and he laughed. "What is this? You wish to *marry* me?"

Actually, Ryuu was the last person Chiyo wanted to marry. But couldn't bear to continue on as she was—with every day bringing more torture than the day before. And hadn't her father always told Chiyo that a husband's duty was to care for and protect his family? Surely if Chiyo were to become Ryuu's wife, he would end his daily "art" sessions and no longer allow his men to abuse her.

Chiyo nodded. "I do."

Ryuu scratched his chin. "What an entertaining idea." He looked at her, *really* looked at her, as if seeing her in a new light.

Could her plan actually be working? A shiver of delight traveled through her body.

He held out a hand for her, the first gentle touch he'd offered in the year she'd been with him, and helped her to her feet. "I must say, Chiyo," he said as he escorted her through the camp, "your proposition is an intriguing one. We must discuss this more in depth." He stopped in front of his tent and brushed the flap aside, ushering her inside.

Waves of nausea rolled through her stomach as she stood in the middle of the room where most of her torture took place. She swallowed the bile burning up the back of her throat and squared her shoulders. If she had any hopes of convincing Ryuu, she must appear sincere. "It makes perfect sense. Surely you want children to carry on your legacy. And I have proved myself to be more than obedient and loyal to you." Her eyes drifted to a patch of dried blood on the grass below her feet. Perhaps *too* obedient...

"I rather like this idea." He smiled and walked a slow circle around her. "But I do have one concern. How do I know this is not a trick? How do I know you would pledge your love and loyalty to me forever?"

A tremor danced down her spine. She'd been prepared for this, and she knew she had no choice but to offer. "M-my body." With trembling hands, she began to untie the sash at her hips. "I offer it to you." For as much as the men loved to hurt her, none of them had ever touched her in *that* way. And the thought of allowing Ryuu to do so made her gut clench. But still, if it kept her alive and safe, she would gladly give herself away.

"Wait." Ryuu grabbed Chiyo's wrist, stopping her from pulling open her robe. He licked his lips and Chiyo fought the urge to shrink away from him. "I have a better idea." He released her hand and pulled his dagger free from his obi.

No. A pit of ice formed inside her gut. This was not how her plan was supposed to play out.

"If your body truly belongs to me, then I should be permitted to place my name on it?" He grinned. "Would you not agree?"

Tears burned Chiyo's eyes, but she quickly blinked them away. After all she'd endured, she could be brave one last time, if that's what it took to make him happy. "Of course. Where would you like to put it?"

He licked his lips. "The place it deserves to be—that is, if you really love me. I wish to write my name on your heart."

Chiyo's throat tightened to the point she nearly choked. "You cannot be serious. T-t-that would kill me." She started to back away, but Ryuu snagged her wrist.

"Would it?" He pulled her against him. "We do not know the extent of your healing abilities because they have not been fully tested. Let us do that now." He brought the dagger to her chest and pressed the tip of the blade into her skin.

The pain blinded her, flashing spots before her eyes. Chiyo screamed and thrashed in his grip. She didn't have to be tested to know a dagger to the heart would kill her. She twisted in his arms and clawed at his face. But he struck her against the temple with the handle of his blade, making the world around her spin.

"Hold still," he hissed in her ear as she tried to maintain her balance. "This is a delicate procedure and we would not want any accidents, would we?"

A sob escaped her lips. She pushed against him but he snatched her wrists with one hand and placed the blade against her chest with the other.

"No!" Chiyo cried. Fear jolted through her like an electric current. Her fingers tingled. "Please." She pressed her palms together to plead for her life when a streak of blue electricity arched from her fingers and struck Ryuu in the chest.

His eyes fluttered wide and he cried out. The blade fell from his hand and he stumbled back, his body jerking awkwardly before he fell to the ground with a moan.

Chiyo blinked at him, her chest heaving, as she tried to figure out what had happened. After all, she'd barely touched him. But when she lifted her hands, she saw the blue waves crackling between her fingers like lightning. She sucked in a sharp breath. What was going on?

Ryuu gasped and Chiyo realized her questions would have to wait. She dropped her hands and looked at Ryuu to find him grasping wildly for the dagger just beyond his reach. Chiyo knew that once he claimed it, he was sure to finish what he'd started. If she wanted her nightmare to end, she wasn't going to have a better opportunity. She reached down and grabbed the dagger.

Ryuu's eyes widened in terror as she gripped the blade with both hands—the same blade that had been used to carve her skin every day for the last year. With her pulse racing, she raised the dagger over her head.

Her samurai wasn't coming to rescue her.

Sometimes, Chiyo realized, as she slammed the knife into Ryuu's neck, *you have to rescue yourself.*

15

I sat up with a gasp, sure I'd just woken up from the world's scariest nightmare. Only now that I was awake, it appeared the nightmare had bled out of my dreams and followed me into consciousness. *Where the heck was I?*

My pulse leapt inside my throat, so heavy and thick on the back of my tongue I could almost taste it. Unable to see, I used my hands to feel around the pitch-black room I found myself in. But there was a noise—the hum of an engine? And then a bump as the floor lurched underneath me.

Oh, God.

I wasn't in a room—I was in a vehicle.

My head swam as a thousand questions raced through at once. Where was Kim? How long had I been asleep? How did I get inside this vehicle? Where was it going?

I found a padded rubber wall and used my hands to guide me into a standing position. My breathing came in short gasps, making me lightheaded. If I didn't watch it, I was going to hyperventilate and pass out again—which would *not* be very helpful in figuring this out.

"Just calm down, Rileigh," I muttered to myself. I sucked in a deep breath through my nose, held it for the count of five, and slowly exhaled. After I'd repeated the process several times, my head finally stopped swimming.

"Better," I sighed. But I couldn't relax too long—I had to figure out where the heck I was, or, more importantly, how to get out. I grasped for the katana at my hip only to find it missing, sheath and all.

Perfect.

The darkness was so complete I couldn't see my own hand in front of my face—so how was I supposed to assess my surroundings for an escape? The vehicle hit another bump, and I was thrown forward. I rubbed my aching shoulder where it had collided against the wall. *Think, Rileigh. Think!* Obviously, I wouldn't be able to stand up in a trunk—so I had to be in something bigger...like a truck...like a *Network* truck.

Impossible. My throat tightened, and it took several tries before I was able to swallow. Was this the transport truck meant for Sumi? And if so, how did *I* get inside it?

With my heart racing, I felt my way along my enclosure. In order to get inside something, you would need a door—so finding it was the first step to getting out. I'd only just felt my way into my first corner when someone groaned from within the darkness.

I whirled around and pressed my back against the corner. "Who's there?" My voice sounded foreign—probably from the tight grip of fear around my throat.

"Where am I?" the voice asked.

Son of hibachi. I'd recognize that voice anywhere. "Whitley?" Anger sparked through my veins like a spark burning through a fuse. I should have known he had something to do with this, and I'd make him pay.

"Whitley's here?" the distinctly Whitley voice asked.

"Funny, *really* funny." Fueled by rage, I pushed off from the wall and took several steps forward in the hopes of locating him. "Don't even bother with your stupid games. I don't know how you and Sumi pulled this off, but you won't have to worry about her killing you anymore—because I'm going to do it!"

"What are you talking about?"

I ignored his question. I didn't have time for his games. "I'd love to know how you pulled it off—not that it matters. As soon as the truck stops and they realize I'm in it, they're going to let me out."

"Who *are* you?" the voice demanded. "Because you're not making any sense. I'm *not* Whitley, and I have no idea what I'm doing in this truck."

I laughed. "For someone who's not Whitley, you sure sound exactly like him."

"Well, I'm *not.*"

I took another step until I was sure he was just in front of me. My fingers curled into fists. I didn't need light to fight. My past-life samurai training would help my foot locate his face just fine. I shifted my weight to my back leg and lifted my front leg in the air. "If you're not Whitley, then who are you?"

There was a long pause before he answered. "Quentin."

What felt like a ball of ice slammed into my core. I lowered my leg to the ground. "*What?*"

"My name is Quentin," he repeated. "Now who are you?"

"Not funny," I growled. I clenched my hands so hard my knuckles ached. What game was he playing? "I'd have to be an idiot to not recognize the sound of my own best friend's voice."

"*Ri-Ri?*"

I jerked back at his use of my nickname. How had Whitley known that's what Q called me? "Of course it's me," I said.

"You don't sound like you."

I folded my arms across my chest. "Then who do I sound like?"

"Sumi."

My blood boiled through my veins. What the heck was Whitley trying to pull? If this was a game, I definitely didn't understand the rules. "Listen to me, because I'm only going to tell you this once. I am not Sumi!"

Something beeped and the scratchy sound of an intercom filled the space around us. "What's going on back there?" a man's gruff voice asked. A second later, a fluorescent light flashed overhead and the back of the truck flooded with a blue light.

I raised my hands, shielding my eyes until the black dots in my vision stopped flashing. When I dropped my hands, the guy sitting on the floor in front of me was exactly who I thought it'd be.

"Whitley." I growled his name through clenched teeth. "I knew it was you, you lying snake."

His visible eye—the one not hidden behind a curtain of hair—flashed wide as the color drained from his face. "Sumi," he muttered. "I knew it." He scrambled backward on his hands and knees until his back hit the opposite wall. "When Rileigh finds out what you've done to me, she's going to kill you."

I groaned. "Oh give it up already. The light is on. I can see you and you can see me. I know you're not Quentin and I know I'm not Sumi."

"*Really*?" Whitley narrowed his eye. Then why do you look *exactly* like her?"

I lifted my hands to my face. "I don't look—" But the words died on my tongue. My hands—they didn't look anything like my hands. Their color was more olive than pink, the fingers were longer, and there was a trace of chipped black polish on the clean nails.

"Oh my God," I whispered as my stomach clenched in horror. There had to be a logical explanation—maybe my eyes hadn't adjusted to the light yet.

"Your *hair*," Whitley prompted.

With shaking fingers, I reached to the top of my head and pulled the rubber band free from my sloppy bun. A second later, a curtain of black hair fell to my shoulders. My knees buckled, and I slid down the wall until I sat on the padded floor.

Across from me, Whitley held a strand of his own long blond hair in front of his face. He let go of the hair and slowly his good eye met mine.

"Quentin? Is it really you?" I asked, my voice tight.

He nodded. "Rileigh?"

We locked eyes. One of us screamed, I couldn't be sure who started it, but the other joined in until our voices filled the back of the truck and I thought my ears would rupture from the noise of it.

The intercom clicked on again. "Settle down back there or we'll turn on the gas!"

The lights flickered once before turning off and leaving us bathed in darkness. For me, this was a good thing. It calmed me to no longer see the body that didn't belong to me. The scream faded and I snapped my mouth shut. Quentin fell silent as well.

My mind spun in an attempt to make sense of it. Obviously, Sumi had done this with her knife and bracelet ritual. But the question was, how had it worked? Was there a way to reverse it? Or were we stuck like this forever? And if so, did that mean Q and I would spend the rest of our lives locked up inside Network headquarters as Sumi and Whitley?

A whimper escaped my lips.

"Are you okay?" Whitley's voice asked.

I flinched upon hearing it. If my best friend was really trapped inside Whitley's body, would I ever be able to get used to the fact that he looked and sounded like one of my worst enemies? "I'm okay." But the quiver in my voice betrayed my words. "I'm just—"

"Yeah, I know." Q sighed. "Every question that you have, every worry that's racing through your mind, I can assure you I'm thinking the same thing."

I laced my fingers together in an attempt to get them to stop trembling. "How do I know it's really you?"

"Ask me something only I would know."

I chewed on my lip. Sounded simple enough. "Okay, what's my favorite store in the mall?"

He snorted. "That's easy—the candle store. You like to smell things."

I smiled and, even though I couldn't see it, I knew it was a sad smile. Yes, I was glad to have my best friend with me, but it also meant he was in the same mess I was.

"My turn," Quentin said. "What did you buy me for my last birthday?"

"Also easy," I answered. "A subscription to *Psychology Today* because you're going to be the world's greatest psychologist."

He sighed. "Well, that was the plan ... you know, before this ... " I heard the scratchy sound of a hand rubbing over face stubble.

"Do you think we're trapped like this forever?"

"I don't know. I'm not sure how this works. I know Sumi's a healer like me, but she uses her powers to hurt instead of heal. I only recently figured out how she altered minds. This? To switch bodies with someone? This took a lot of power, and I don't know if it can be undone."

"What?" I jerked forward as an invisible hand curled fingers into my heart. "Of course it can be undone!" There had to be a way. I couldn't spend the rest of my life trapped inside my worst enemy's body.

"Okay," Q said, sounding weary. "Let's say you're right. Let's say this switch Sumi performed *can* be undone. The only way I see that as being possible is if we perform the same ritual on them."

A flicker of hope eased the tension inside me. "Okay. Let's do that."

Quentin sighed. "Yes, well. In order to do that we'd have to find the *real* Whitley and Sumi—who I imagine look like us right now."

"Oh, God." I pressed my hand against my head. I hadn't

even considered the other aspect of this switch—that they were in *our* bodies. "They're going to be living in our houses, with our parents, and hanging out with our friends. Sumi will finally have—" Acid burned the back of my throat, and I struggled to swallow it down.

"Kim," Quentin answered. "Yes. I know."

I jumped to my feet as a wave of hot fury washed over me. "I'm going to kill her."

"Don't forget she's still Kim's inyodo. If you kill her, Kim would die as well."

I cried out in frustration. "You're a healer, right? How about I *almost* kill her? You could heal her, and we can repeat the process over and over again." I twisted my hands in the air like I was strangling an invisible neck.

"There's just one problem with your plan."

I stopped strangling the air and let my hands fall to my side. "What?"

I heard a sliding sound as Q moved closer. "In order to do those things, we first have to get out of this truck. And if I remember correctly, didn't Dr. Wendell say it was built so no one could escape?"

"Crap. I hadn't—wait a sec." I placed my hands against the wall. "The wall is covered with rubber—probably to absorb any attempts Sumi would make to use her electricity. This truck has been designed to hold Sumi—*not* Rileigh Martin."

"*Rileigh*," I could hear the warning in Q's voice. "Let's not do anything too hasty, okay? Maybe we could wait until the truck stops and explain who we are."

I snorted as I felt my way along the wall. "You really think they'd buy that load of crap? There's no way they'd believe

110

us. Our only chance to get home and stop the *real* Sumi and Whitley is to break out of this truck."

"And how do you plan to do that?"

Finally, my fingers brushed over what I was looking for—a seam, barely noticeable since the rubber covering the doors was so tightly pressed together. If there was a way out of this truck, it was here. "The doors are right here." I smacked my hand against the rubber.

"How exactly does that help us if there are no handles?" Q asked.

"I don't need a handle." I transferred my weight to my back foot, spun around, and kicked my heel against the seam. The rubber muffled the clang of metal as the doors reverberated against my foot.

"Did that do anything?" Quentin asked, sounding hopeful.

"Not yet—but maybe if I keep going ... " I lashed out over and over again, landing blow after blow with both my foot and my elbow. The walls around us shook as I continued to pound against the seam.

The crackle of the intercom clicked on. "Cease what you are doing at once. This will be your only warning."

"*Rileigh,* maybe you should stop." Quentin's voice drew nearer in the dark.

I snorted and wiped away a line of sweat trickling along my temple. "I'm not stopping until we're out. What's the worst they can do to us, anyway? Even if they were to stop the truck and come back here, once they open the doors that would provide us with another opportunity to break free."

"I don't know ... "

I pounded harder. With the walls as padded as they

were, it was unlikely I was doing much damage to the door at all. But if it got the truck to stop, maybe we stood a chance of escaping.

The intercom clicked on again. "Have it your way."

"What do you think he means by that?" Q asked.

"Who knows?" I backed away from the door and braced my hands against my knees to catch my breath. "Hopefully it means we won and they're going to stop the truck. If they do, be ready. When they open the door, I'll attack. Your job is to get to the driver's seat and be ready to drive this thing the second you get inside. Got it?"

"You really think—" His words were cut off abruptly by a hissing sound. "What is that noise?"

Oh, crap. The small burst of hope inside of me vanished. *Please don't let that be what I think it is.* I jerked upright and spun a circle hoping to locate the source of the noise, but it was impossible. The hissing surrounded us.

"Ri . . . I don't feel . . . right." Quentin's words were thick, as if he spoke them through a mouthful of cotton.

"It's gas!" I pulled my T-shirt over my nose, knowing it would buy me an extra minute at most. My plan failed. Tears burned behind my eyelids, and I quickly blinked them back before they could fall. They really had created an inescapable truck—one in which they could incapacitate their prisoners without even leaving the cab.

The gas filled my head, making me sway on my feet. I knew I should have been afraid, but with the gas swirling inside my lungs, I found I couldn't muster up any emotion other than exhaustion. I fell forward against the door. The rubber wall pulled at my cheek as I slid slowly to the ground. "Son...of...hibachi."

"I...can't...fight..." But Quentin never finished his sentence. A second later, I heard the soft thump of what I could only assume was his body hitting the floor.

Without light, I couldn't tell if the inky black of unconsciousness had already begun to bleed into my vision. My eyelids lowered, pulled down by a force too strong for me to fight. From somewhere far away, I was vaguely aware of my heart beating a panicked rhythm, as if it knew we were losing valuable time. Once we arrived in New York, our chance of escape would be lost.

The floor smacked against my cheek. I hadn't even been aware I was falling. Sleep pulled at me. Unable to fight it, I fell deeper until even the hissing of gas drifted away, leaving me alone in silent night.

16

A strong hand reached through the darkness and grabbed my hand.

My eyes fluttered open. "Kim?"

"Rileigh, it's me—Quentin." Only it didn't sound like Quentin.

I blinked in groggy confusion as the pieces of what had happened to us after we'd been gassed gradually came together. "Oh. Right. How long have I been out?"

"I don't know. I only woke up a little bit ago—there's no telling how much time has passed."

I sat up, immediately regretting it when a rush of dizziness swirled through my head. "So we could be anywhere?"

Quentin's hand slid from mine. "Yeah."

"Son of hibachi." I crawled through the darkness with a hand stretched out in front of me until I met the wall. If we were drawing closer to New York, then time was running out.

Once the Network imprisoned us inside their headquarters, there would be no escape. And I wouldn't spend the rest of my existence in a cage while Sumi lived *my* stolen life.

"What are you doing?" Quentin asked, his voice full of alarm.

I braced against the wall and guided myself onto my feet. "I'm getting us out of here before it's too late."

"What?" I heard the soft pad of hands and knees scuttling across the rubber floor as Quentin drew near. "You already tried to do that, and it got us gassed. If you do anything like that again, who knows how much gas they'll use on us? We might just wake up inside our cells."

He was right. I couldn't lash out like I had last time—I needed a plan. I braced my back against the wall and tried to recall everything Dr. Wendell had told me about this truck. "Dr. Wendell said this truck was designed specifically for Sumi, right?"

"Well, yeah. But I don't understand—"

"So let's break down Sumi's powers." I felt my way along the wall, searching for the door seam. "She can manipulate minds, which is why they designed the truck to keep her isolated. It's covered in rubber so she can't use her lightning ... so let's think about what it *doesn't* have."

"Door handles?"

Just like that, a flicker of an idea sparked inside my mind. "Quentin, you're a genius!"

"That's been established a long time ago. But I don't understand what it has to do with getting us out of the truck."

Just then my searching fingers brushed over the slight

dip in the rubber indicating the seam of the adjoining doors. "Sumi can't open a locked door without a key—but I can!"

"Your ki!" Q whispered so close to my ear I jumped. "Do you think it will work in Sumi's body?"

My hand fell to my side. "I hadn't thought about that."

His fingers grasped my shoulder and squeezed. "You have to try. It could be our only chance."

He was right. I cracked my knuckles. Even if it didn't work, I had to try. "Okay. Let's do this." Even in the pitch dark, I closed my eyes and tried to fall inside myself as I'd done so many times before. But this time, something was different. I could still sense the white-hot energy that was my ki. I felt the heat pulsing from inside me, and yet each time I reached out to it, it slipped beyond my grasp.

"Oh, God," I muttered, letting my forehead drop against the door. "Something isn't right—I can't reach it."

Quentin's hand squeezed my shoulder again. "I was afraid of this. I noticed something similar when I tried to use my healing powers to revive you."

I turned my head toward his voice. "What do you think it means?"

He sighed. "I think it means that because these bodies don't belong to us, our powers won't stay inside them."

"But I can feel my ki!" I protested. "I just can't … reach it."

"Right. I think when we switched bodies we took our powers with us, but they're slowly bleeding away."

I turned and placed my palm against the door. "So you're saying we have a fraction of our power now—but soon we won't have any at all?"

He was silent a moment. "Yes. That's exactly what I'm saying."

As if we weren't in enough trouble. "In other words, if I'm going to use my ki to break us out of here, I better do it while I still have ki left."

"I'm afraid so."

I sighed. "But how can I use my ki power when I can't reach it? I can feel something blocking me—like a wall. I can't touch it."

"Hmm." His hand slid from my shoulder. "If I were to make a guess, I would assume the only thing blocking you is you."

"What?"

"You know you're in Sumi's body, and it's messing with your mind. Just try to imagine that you're in your own body. Don't think about Sumi. You know who you are. You're Rileigh Martin. Senshi, reincarnated samurai. A body doesn't make you that."

"No. But it sure helps." I didn't bother to hide the sarcasm from my voice. "So what do I do? Think happy thoughts? Aim for the second star on the right?"

He sighed. "Your attitude isn't helping us get out of here any faster. Just close your eyes and *do* it."

I huffed loudly. "All right. I'll try it your way. But if it doesn't work, make sure you hold your breath while I pound the crap out of the door."

"Right. Because that worked out so well for us last time."

I scowled at him despite knowing he couldn't see me through the darkness. "Now who has the attitude? Are you sure you're not turning *into* Whitley?"

"Just try it!"

"All right. All right." I closed my eyes and sucked in a deep breath. Luckily, I'd trained with Lord Toyotomi in my past life in the art of meditation. I inhaled deeply through my nose and exhaled through my mouth. I repeated the process several times until I felt myself gradually relax.

"You are Rileigh Martin," Quentin whispered—only it was Whitley's voice, so my eyes fluttered open despite themselves.

"Q?"

"Yes?"

"I love you, but your voice—Whitley's voice—it's not helping."

"Oh. Right. Sorry."

"That's okay." I closed my eyes and tried again. This time, I imagined myself not inside the truck, but on the recon mission with Kim the night before. I pictured myself on Sumi's porch, and the way Kim looked at me as I stood before her locked door. I was Rileigh Martin. I was Senshi. A locked door meant nothing to me. "I am Rileigh Martin," I whispered.

My ki stirred inside me.

"I am Rileigh Martin," I repeated.

My ki flared within me like a match dropped onto a pile of kindling.

"I am Senshi!" This time my ki burst through the wall holding it back, spilled through my veins, and ignited my blood. My eyes fluttered wide—only now, instead of seeing darkness, I could see the inner-workings of the door in front on me. I pressed my palm against the seam and willed my ki to spill from my fingers, where it bled into the seam and flooded the lock beyond. A second later, I heard the whine of metal being retracted right before the door swung wide open.

After so much time spent in complete darkness, the sunlight spilling into the back of the truck blinded me. "Grab the doors!" I caught the edge of the metal door closest to me and pulled it inward, all the while trying to blink the sun spots out of my eyes.

Q dropped to the ground and grabbed the bottom of the other door, keeping it slightly ajar. Through the gap, I could make out a lush green forest on either side of us.

"I thought you wanted the doors open," he panted.

"I do. But if the doors swing wide and bang against the side of the truck, they'll know what we've done and stop the vehicle. First we need to figure out where we are."

"Got any ideas?"

I looked at him and, even knowing it was my best friend trapped in another body, I still couldn't help but wince when I saw Whitley staring back. I returned my attention to the road and the trees surrounding us. "None," I finally answered. "I have no clue where we are."

We crested the top of a hill, and the view spreading before us took my breath away. Tree-covered mountains reached for the cloudless, blue horizon like the lacey edge of a bridal gown.

"Which states between Missouri and New York have mountains?" I asked. "Illinois doesn't." I tried to recall the map of the United States posted on the wall in my history class. "And Ohio doesn't."

"No," Quentin agreed. "But Pennsylvania does."

"Pennsylvania!" I tightened my grasp on the door the wind desperately tried to wrench out of my hands. "Please tell me you're joking."

He frowned. "You know I never joke about geography."

I sighed and surveyed the rolling landscape. "That doesn't give us much time to escape before we get to New York." My fingers were already beginning to burn from the strain of hanging on to the door—I wouldn't be able to hold on much longer. "There's nobody behind us. We're going to have to jump, and we're going to have to do it before another car comes along."

Quentin stared at me, not blinking, as Whitley's long hair whipped around his face. "Jump? Are you crazy? At this speed, the fall would kill us."

"I think I might be able to brace our impact with my ki."

"*Think?*" He shook his head. "That doesn't really inspire a lot of confidence. Aren't you worried you used up most of your ki opening the door?"

I bit my lip and looked away before he could read the doubt on my face. Of course I was worried about that—but I was even more worried about spending the rest of my life locked inside a cell. "Look, you don't have to go with me. I can't ask you to risk your life like that. But I'm going to jump."

Quentin was quiet a moment before finally answering. "I have to come with you."

"No, you don't." I tried to readjust my grip on the door to ease the ache in my fingers. "Once I make it back home, I'll tell the others what happened. I'll make sure Sumi switches our bodies back, and then I'll get Dr. Wendell to call the Network and release you."

"It's not that." He looked at me. "I ... there's something I haven't told you."

My gut clenched, and I almost lost my hold on the door. "What is it?"

He shook his head. "I'm a healer. This means, when it comes to the body, I can feel things that other people can't."

I nodded for him to continue even though I was sure I wasn't going to like what he had to say.

He licked his lips. "And I can feel this body latching on to me. Its hold is becoming stronger by the minute."

I frowned, trying to make sense of his words. "Its hold? I don't understand."

He sighed. "Look, there's no easy way to explain this, but if what I think is true, we have to get out of these bodies as soon as possible, before ... " He shook his head, and the look on his face tightened my throat.

"Before what, Q?"

He was quiet, and for a moment, I worried he might not answer me. But then he looked at me and swallowed hard. "Before we get trapped inside them permanently."

17

W hat?" The door slipped from my fingers and hit the side
of the truck. The resulting bang was loud enough to
bounce my heart against my ribs.

The truck slammed on its brakes, the tires squealing in
protest as Quentin and I were thrown to the floor. We scrambled to our feet and I heard the distinct squeak of vehicle
doors opening before slamming shut.

"C'mon!" A voice ordered. "They couldn't have gotten far."

"Son of hibachi," I muttered. I ran across the padded
floor and grabbed Q's arm. The bombshell he'd just delivered
would have to wait. If we had any hopes of escaping, now was
our moment.

I pulled Q beside me and pressed us into the corner of the
truck by the door hinges. Not even several heartbeats later, a
shadow fell across the crack of light created by the door seam.

"You check the woods," another voice said. "I'll check the back of the truck."

Quentin tensed beside me, but I held him steady with my arm. We had one chance—we couldn't blow it.

Fingers grasped the edge of the door, but before they could pull it open, I moved out of the corner and kicked the door as hard as I could. The man didn't have time to cry out before the door clanged against his head. A second later, he crumpled to the ground.

"Now!" I grabbed Quentin's arm, and together we jumped from the truck, landing beside the dazed man on the asphalt.

Quentin knelt next to him. The man was dressed in all black, and his cracked sunglasses hung at an awkward angle across his face. "Look," Quentin began. "I'm sorry we had to do that to you. I'm sure you're just trying to earn a living—but we're not who you think we are."

"Q!" I grabbed his arm and motioned to the line of trees. If I hadn't been convinced he wasn't Whitley, his apology to the Network official certainly did the trick. "We don't have time for this. We have to go!"

He nodded and reluctantly followed me as I bolted into the woods. Brambles and twigs pulled at my clothes and scratched across my skin as I sprinted through. But I didn't dare stop. I knew the other man had to be close by.

"Hey! Come back here!"

I chanced a glance behind me just as something whizzed past my face and lodged into the tree in front of us.

Quentin pulled it out as we ran past, looked at it, and chucked it over his shoulder. "Tranquilizer darts," he said between huffs. "If they get us, we're screwed."

My heart felt on the verge of exploding. Another series of pops exploded behind us and I lunged behind a tree, grabbing Quentin by the arm and pulling him with me. Three soft thwacks sounded as the darts sank into bark. "Okay, let's go!" I shoved him forward and together we sprinted ahead.

The farther we ran, the more the ground sloped downward. I had to slow my pace to keep my footing sure as the incline steepened.

"You can't hide from the Network!" a voice shouted behind us. "So you might as well surrender now!"

Fat chance of that happening.

"Watch out!" This time it was Quentin who pushed me aside as a dart soared over my shoulder.

"I don't understand." I shook my head before leaping over a log. "My danger premonitions usually allow me to sense things like that."

"Yeah, well." He ducked under a low-hanging branch. "You better get used to not relying on your ki so much. You're probably not going to have it much longer."

I swallowed hard. "Awesome."

"Speaking of which." Q placed a hand against his ribs and grimaced. "I'm starting to get a stitch in my side—something I've never had. I guess my healing ability kept me from cramping before. I'm going to need to stop soon."

I peered over my shoulder one more time. I couldn't see the man following us, but that didn't mean he wasn't out there. "Just a little bit farther until I know we're safe." We ran for several more minutes until I could no longer hear the distant rustling of footsteps behind us. "This is good," I whispered, ducking behind a boulder and indicating for him to join me.

Quentin collapsed on the ground beside me, heaving ragged breaths with his hand pressed against his side. "Do you think he's still out there?"

"Yeah." I nodded, trying to calm my own erratic breathing. "He wouldn't give up so easy. In fact, he's probably called for backup."

"Great." He leaned his head against the rock. "So what's our plan? We can't just sit here."

"No," I agreed. "After we rest for a minute, we need to put more distance between ourselves and that truck."

He frowned. "But we don't know where we're going. We're in the mountains! We could get eaten by a bear."

"We won't be eaten by a bear," I hissed.

Quentin opened his mouth to respond, but a twig snapped nearby and I clasped my hand over his mouth. Leaves rustled as our pursuer pushed through the brush. Quentin's skin paled as footsteps drew nearer. He looked at me with Whitley's one good eye as if to ask, "Now what?"

My muscles tightened with the urge to bolt. Normally I might try to fight. With my ki, a weapon of any kind wouldn't faze me a bit. But now that my powers had faded, I needed to be more careful—especially since I had Quentin to look after too.

The footsteps shuffled closer until they stopped on the other side of the boulder we crouched behind. If the man took even one step closer, we'd be discovered for sure. And then what? I could attack, but I couldn't guarantee I wouldn't get hurt in the process.

Think, Rileigh, think!

Before a solution came to me, the grass rustled and the tip of the man's boot appeared from the side of the rock.

Quentin pressed himself deeper against the rock until his body was covered by shadow.

Wait a second... Rock. Shadow. *That was it!*

I only prayed I had enough ki energy to pull it off.

The man wasn't looking in our direction when he stepped past the rock. Like the man we'd struck with the door, he, too, wore a skin-tight black T-shirt that prominently displayed all the bulging muscles underneath as well as a pair of black, baggy cargo pants. His eyes swept over the scenery in front of him, and I knew we had seconds before he turned in our direction.

Q reached for my hand and squeezed so hard I almost cried out.

Instead, I swallowed the yelp, closed my eyes, and tried to fall inside myself. But like earlier inside the truck, my access was blocked. Only a few wisps of ki reached out to me, and I grabbed onto them with everything I had.

When I opened my eyes, despite the fact that Q was still squeezing my hand to the point of bringing tears to my eyes, I could no longer see him sitting beside me.

I'd done it. I'd used up the last of my ki in the process, but I'd made us invisible.

Without thinking, I let out a sigh of relief.

The man standing before us snapped his head in our direction and scowled. He tilted his head and took a step in our direction, the dart gun aimed at where my chest would be if it were visible.

I held my breath, afraid the slightest noise might set off his index finger, which twitched against the trigger. Already I could feel the ki inside me slipping away like unraveling spools of ribbon. I knew I couldn't keep us invisible much longer.

The man slowly lowered his gun, reached for the walkie-talkie clipped to his belt, and brought it to his lips. "I don't see any signs of them. I'm going to head back to the truck and check on Agent Ross—he might need medical attention. The bitch got him good."

I stiffened, but Quentin's hand on mine kept me from standing up and giving him his own reason for needing medical attention.

"Roger that," a voice answered through the walkie-talkie. "Your orders are to remain with the truck until backup arrives."

He brought the walkie-talkie back to his lips. "Tell them to bring the dogs."

"Roger," the voice answered.

A knot formed inside my gut and pulled tight. I couldn't hold on much longer. I watched in horror as Quentin and my clasped hands flickered in and out of view.

The man snapped his walkie-talkie back on his hip and set off toward the road. I let go of Quentin's hand as we both appeared in view. Still, I didn't dare make a sound until I could no longer hear the man's footsteps trudging through the brush.

"Are you all right?" Quentin asked, lightly touching my arm. It was so strange to see him looking at me through Whitley's good eye with a look of genuine concern.

I shook my head. "Not even close. And to make matters worse, I think I might have used up the last of my ki."

He frowned. "I was afraid of that. I don't think I have much of my healing powers left, either."

Awesome. So there we were, lost in the woods, running from Network agents, without food, powers, money, or even a map. I stood and brushed the leaves off my pants before carefully peeking over the boulder to make sure the coast was clear. "We need a plan."

He nodded. "We need to get home. You know, before—"

I snapped my head in his direction. "Do you really think that could happen? That we could get stuck like this *forever*?"

He used his hands to help himself into a standing position. "Yes. The only thing I'm not sure about is how long we have. A couple days at the most, I think."

A newly formed headache throbbed beneath my temples, and I squeezed my palms against my head to ebb the pain. "Son of hibachi," I groaned.

He nodded grimly. "So what do we do?"

I dropped my hands and tried to come up with a solution. I couldn't spend the rest of my life in Sumi's body. We had to get home—and fast. I checked to make sure the coast was clear. When I didn't spot anyone coming, I pointed deeper into the woods. "We have to go that way."

He shielded his eyes and surveyed the forest in front of us. "How do you know that's the right way?"

"I don't." I motioned for him to follow me as I marched ahead. "But we have to keep moving, and we certainly can't go back in the direction of the road. That's where the Network will be setting up a search team."

"But"—Q sidestepped a tree—"what if we get lost? What if we come across a bear?"

"You're really worried about that bear, huh? Don't. With the mood I'm in, I'd feel pretty sorry anything that decides to cross our paths." I cracked my knuckles together.

He frowned at me before pushing through the branches of a bush. "That doesn't seem like much of a plan."

"It's not." I shrugged. "But we can't sit there and wait for the Network to catch us. I also can't wait around doing nothing while Sumi steals my life—possibly forever." In a fit of desperation, I'd been forced to kill myself in my last life. There was no way I was going to let this one be taken from me as well.

"You're right. We're running out of time." He was quiet a moment before adding, "You'll get us out of this. I know it."

"Of course I will." I gave him a reassuring smile but quickly turned away before it had the chance to slip. I didn't want him to know how scared I really was. The odds were stacked against us. We were lost, outmanned, and outgunned.

I licked my lips and leapt over a fallen tree. If only Kim were here. In our past lives, he was the leader of our samurai army. I could always count on him to know what to do in any situation, and to always lead us in the right direction. But now that responsibility had fallen to me, and the burden of being the one to make sure we made it home felt like a noose around my neck.

"There sure are a lot of trees," Q mumbled.

My throat constricted and I said nothing. I hoped the trees weren't an omen of what was to come. Because when you walked with a noose around your neck, all it took was one branch to end it all.

And a million stretched out before me.

18

D o you see that?" Quentin asked. He stepped to the ledge of a rocky cliff and looked at the tree-covered valley below.

I walked up beside him, trying to ignore the ache in my legs from a full day of hiking. Not to mention the hundreds of cuts and scrapes we'd accumulated by pushing our way through thistles and thorny bushes. I pushed a sweat-soaked lock of black hair from my eyes. "See what?"

The sun had begun its decent into the valley. I'd followed its path throughout the day, knowing that as long as we headed west, we traveled toward home. But now its orange glow was barely visible over the tops of the trees. Shadows elongated at our feet like a thrown blanket. Before long, we wouldn't be able to see anything at all.

"I think"—he squinted his eyes—"I see a cabin up ahead."

"Really? Where?" Hope bloomed inside me.

He pointed at a line of trees. "Through there, I think."

I tried to follow the direction of his finger, but the only thing I spotted beyond the trees were more trees. Still, I wasn't about to squash the hope in his eyes, especially as tired, hungry, and dirty as we were. But I also knew we couldn't stop—not with the Network on our tails. But maybe the cabin would have supplies or, better yet, a car. I figured since Sumi was already a murderer, it wouldn't matter much to add auto theft to her rap sheet. "Let's go. You lead the way."

Q nodded, and together we made our way down the rocky embankment. By the time we reached the valley, the entire forest floor was bathed in shadow, making it impossible to see the foliage clearly. Branches and thorns pulled at my hair and raked across my skin until every inch of me bled or burned.

Quentin ripped a twig free from his hair and pushed forward. "Just a little bit farther."

I said nothing. I didn't want to tell him that my hope in the so far "unseen" cabin was fading fast. After all, it had been getting dark when Quentin first spotted it; maybe he mistook it for a cluster of trees. Even if the cabin did exist, I wondered if we'd be able to find it in the growing darkness.

I was on the verge of suggesting we give up on the cabin and instead locate a spot to rest when he stopped in front of me.

"There!" He pointed. "Just past those trees. Do you see it?"

I squinted my eyes. "Q, I don't see—" But before I finished my sentence, I spotted it. It was nestled within a grove of evergreens. It wasn't what I would have called a cabin by any means, as it was barely more than a stack of logs with a moss-covered roof. Still, my heart swelled in the hopes we'd find something useful inside.

"C'mon!" I grabbed his hand and sprinted forward. "Maybe

they have a car or a four-wheeler—we need to get mobile fast."
I pulled him along as I ran through the valley, darting around
trees and leaping over fallen branches until we arrived at the
door.

That's when my heart sank.

There was no car parked outside. In fact there was no
road, just an overgrown animal trail that wound to the door.
One of the windows was busted. Leaning in, I saw the jagged pieces of glass strewn across the dirt-covered floor. It was
obvious no one had been there in a very long time.

As if sensing my disappointment, Q placed a hand on
my shoulder. "We should still check for supplies."

I didn't have the heart to tell him I doubted the cabin held
more than raccoon turds. Instead, I walked to the mostly rotten door and shoved it open with my shoulder. I peered into
the darkness. "Hello?"

Something small and furry scurried across the back of
the room. I shuddered and withdrew my head. "I don't think
we're going to find anything useful."

Quentin made a face and stepped around me, into the
cabin. "Let's just look around real quick. Just in case. There
could be something helpful."

I followed him and wrinkled my nose at the smell of rot
and mold. "Squirrel poop helps no one, Q." I leaned against
the wall but jumped up when I thought I felt something crawl
across my shoulders.

"No." He stepped over a fallen chair and opened a cabinet. He withdrew a can and held it out to me with a grin.
"But canned chili does!"

I made a face. "And how is that better than squirrel poop?"

Quentin sighed. "There's nothing else in here, Ri. Oh wait." He pulled another can out of the cabinet, squinting as he read the label. "Unless you want … ALPO."

I couldn't deny I was starving. And if I had to choose between dog food and chili … "Chili," I replied glumly.

He grinned. "Coming right up." He stuck his head back into the cabinet but stepped away a moment later with a frown. "Um, there's no can opener."

I sighed. "Of course not. Because that would have meant that one damn thing would have gone our way."

"I know that's your hunger talking." Q gave me a stern look, which looked hilarious on Whitley's face. "There's no need to get so cranky. Let me just search over here." He closed the cabinet and rummaged through the drawers beneath the counter. "No can opener here" he muttered. Then, a second later, "Aha!" He pulled a tarnished knife from a drawer and held it over his head like a warrior charging into battle. "This will work." He brought the tip of the blade down against the can and it barely made a dent in the lid. He glanced at me. "You might want to wipe off two spoons while you're waiting. This is going to take a while."

"Yeah." I walked past him and pulled open a drawer. Something squeaked in the back of the drawer when I stuck my hand in, so I pulled out the first two utensils I could find and slammed the drawer shut.

Quentin raised an eyebrow as he continued working the knife into the lid of the can.

"Poisonous snake." I walked around him and picked up the fallen chair, turning it over so I could sit.

He made a face. "Oh yes, the squeaking snakes are especially deadly."

"Do you always mock the person who just saved your life? That's pretty rude." I examined the two utensils in my hand, pleased to find one of them was a spoon and the other a fork. With the light fading fast outside, we needed to scarf down our food so we could get a little more distance before it became too dark to travel. Who knew? We might find a cabin that wasn't just an outhouse for woodland creatures.

The spoon was gross, spotted and covered with some sort of green film, so I set about rubbing it vigorously on the edge of my T-shirt. After several minutes of rubbing so hard I thought the fabric would catch fire, I was happy to find it shining and silver. I held it up to the light, and that's when I saw dark eyes reflected back at me.

I gasped and the spoon fell from my fingertips, clattering against the filthy floor.

"Rileigh?" Quentin stopped working the knife into the can and eyed me with concern.

I shook my head. "Sorry. I'm fine. My reflection … it's not my reflection. Seeing her eyes staring back at me … " I swallowed the bitter taste in my mouth. "It startled me."

"I know." He nodded. "But don't worry. We won't be stuck like this much longer."

I bit my bottom lip to keep it from trembling. As much as I wanted to believe him, without a phone, money, or transportation I didn't see how we'd make it home in time to switch back our bodies, let alone avoid capture by the Network. I set the spoon on my lap and rubbed my hands over my face—only it wasn't my face. Even without seeing my reflection, the bridge of the narrow nose and high cheeks felt foreign under my fingertips. "What are we going to do?"

Quentin walked the can of chili over to me and set it in front of me. A thick crust of orange-speckled fat sat on top. Quentin took my discarded spoon and sank it into the can. "You're going to eat."

I made a face. Our only other option had been dog food, but if both cans were open in front of me, I wasn't sure I would be able to tell the difference. "That looks revolting."

"Sure does." He scooped the layer of fat out of the can and flung it through the broken window. Next, he scooped a spoonful of chili and lifted it in front of my face.

Despite the appearance of the disgusting slop before me, my stomach roared to life.

"We haven't eaten in over twenty-four hours." Q waved the spoon. "There are a lot of things out of our control right now. But we can control eating. We need to keep up our strength. We have a long journey ahead of us."

Reluctantly, I took the spoon and swallowed the chili. Despite the greasy texture and dog-food-like appearance, I half-expected my stomach to sing with joy the moment the food slid down my throat. "Thanks." I handed the spoon back to Q who took his own bite. "Do you always have to be right all the time?"

He shrugged. "It's just my cross to bear."

I took the spoon from him and fished out another heaping spoonful. "Do you think the others have noticed that we're—I mean *they're*—not us?" The idea that Kim would think for a second that Sumi was me made me sick to my stomach. Surely he would know something was up. Then again, I never believed in body swapping before it happened to me. How could I expect Kim to?

"I don't know." Q took the spoon from me. "It's going to be tricky. It's not like we can go running to Kim and the others to tell them what happened."

I narrowed my eyes. "Why *not*? They deserve to know what's going on. Besides, we're going to need all the help we can get to stop Sumi and Whitley!"

Quentin chewed thoughtfully. "After the body switch, we both had access to our powers, right? At least for a little bit."

I nodded.

He continued. "Then it only makes sense that Sumi has access to her power too. And since her powers are ridiculously strong, I bet hers last a lot longer than ours did. If Kim or the others became even a little suspicious that something wasn't right, she could have easily manipulated their minds so they don't question her."

The meaning of his words hit me like a fist to the stomach. I gripped the edge of the chair so hard my arms shook. "If killing Sumi wouldn't hurt Kim, I would do it, Q. I swear! Just like we did in the old days. I'd cut off her head and mount it on a spiked board."

"Easy, killer." He touched my arm, sweeping me from the fantasy I'd concocted of facing Sumi on the battlefield with my sword in hand. "You can't go around beheading people in this lifetime. The law frowns on that sort of thing."

I sighed, blinking away the images of hoof-trampled fields and blood-stained corpses. "Sometimes I really miss the old ways."

"*Yeah.*" He took another bite of chili. "Sometimes you can be a little scary—did I ever tell you that?"

A bark of a laugh escaped my lips as I ripped the spoon from his hand and dug into the chili. "You're friends with me, so what does that say about you?" I'd meant the words as a joke, but the second they left my mouth I wished I could take them back. There was a truth to them that burned through my heart like acid. If Quentin hadn't been friends with me, he never would have fallen under Sumi's radar. He'd be planning what to pack for college—not living in the wrong body and running through the woods from a secret government agency.

"What's wrong?" Q asked. "Your face just got really pale. You're not going to throw up, are you?" He glanced at the can. "I have no idea how old this stuff is."

I shook my head and swallowed hard. "It's not the chili. It's just . . . do you think you'd be better off if you'd never met me?"

He jerked back. "How could you even ask something like that?"

"Q! Look around!" I motioned to the dark shack. "Look where we are! Are you telling me if you'd been friends with somebody else you'd be in the same situation?"

He reached out and touched my hand. "If I didn't know you, I never would have found out about my powers. Besides, I like to think of these situations as . . . adventures." He grinned. "Life with you is never dull."

I snorted. "You're the only person on the planet who would look at it that way."

He shrugged. "I take that as a compliment."

"We'll see how cheerful you are when we're captured by the Network and locked in a cell for the rest of our lives."

137

His smile wavered. "How about we try really hard not to let that happen?"

"That's the plan." I yawned. Now that I was sitting, the exhaustion that had been chasing me all day finally had the chance to crash over me. I rubbed my burning eyes with my palms. "You think this shack has an espresso maker?"

He laughed. "No. But you know how many Starbucks are in the world, right? I bet there's one in a cave nearby."

"Oh man, wouldn't that be great?" I dropped my head into my hands. "I could sure go for a triple-shot caramel macchiato right about now."

He nodded and pushed the empty chili can aside. "Or a chai tea latte. That would be amazing."

"Well, we can't stay here. Let's go look for that Starbucks." I stood, only to have my legs buckle from exhaustion. I fell back against the chair.

Quentin frowned. "You know, you look really tired."

I made a face. "I hate it when people say that—that's just a nice way of telling someone they look like crap."

"Okay then, you look like crap."

I narrowed my eyes.

He held up his hands in defense. "All I'm saying is maybe we should rest for a few—just long enough to gather our strength."

I shook my head and used the table to help myself stand. "We don't have that kind of time, not with the Network catching up to us." No sooner had I spoken the words than a tingling sensation prickled my skin. I jerked toward the window, straining to hear any unusual sounds from outside. And that's when I realized it—I didn't hear *anything*. None of the usual night noises, like an owl's screech or a coyote's howl, could be heard.

And that could only mean one thing. The animals were hiding from something.

Quentin stiffened. "What is it? What's wrong?"

The sound of my own heartbeat thrashed in my ears. "I'm not sure..." I closed my eyes and tried to concentrate on the feeling—like the softest brush of a finger down the back of my neck. I opened my eyes. "I think I'm having what's left of a danger premonition."

He glanced wildly around the cabin. "What does that mean? Are they close? How long do we have?"

I shook my head as my pulse rocketed through my veins. "I don't know. If I was in my body with my ki at full strength, I could tell you. But now... I don't know."

Quentin rushed to the broken window and leaned his head outside. "I think... yes, I definitely hear something."

I darted beside him. "What do—" But I didn't bother to finish my sentence because at that moment I heard it too—the sound of barking dogs. A second later, a flashlight beam broke through the tree line and confirmed my worst fear.

The Network had found us.

19

What do we do?" Quentin hissed.

I dashed to the cabinet, squinting in the darkness until I located the can of dog food. "We have to get out of this cabin. We're basically sitting in a trap." I snatched the knife from the table and slammed it into the lid, working it furiously around the can until I was able to pry the jagged lid open.

He leaned back from the window. "What are you doing?"

"Insurance." I handed the can to Quentin, and motioned for him to follow me to the door. "Stick by me. We don't know what these guys are packing. They could have night vision for all we know."

"Night vision?" he squeaked.

"Well, yeah, along with the dogs and tranquilizer guns."

"Right. And to combat all that you've decided to go with ... " He looked at the can in his hand. "Dog food? Are you sure the exhaustion hasn't made you delirious? Can we at least take those jagged can lids and use them as throwing stars?"

I shook my head. "Weapons won't help us now. We're horribly outnumbered and outgunned. We can't fight them. Our only option is to run. So stick close, understand?"

He pressed his lips into a thin line and squeezed the can into his pants pocket. "Okay."

I pushed open the cabin's door with my shoulder and glanced out. The barking grew louder by the second. I motioned Q to follow and sprinted in the opposite direction of the approaching flashlight beams. My stiff muscles screamed in protest. I could only clench my teeth and push through the pain.

Quentin matched my stride. Together, we forged through the dense brambles and tree branches blocking our escape. But no matter how fast we ran, the barking continued to draw closer.

A voice called out from behind us. "Over here! I see them just up ahead."

Quentin glanced at me. Even in the moonlight I could see the terror in his wide eyes. "Do we throw the dog food now?"

I shook my head. "No," I answered, panting. "Not yet."

His breathing came in rapid bursts. "I don't know how much longer I can keep this up."

I knew exactly how he felt. My legs felt like rubber bands on the verge of snapping. Every muscle inside my body screamed at me to stop. I tightened my fists and pressed on. "Hang on."

Just then, a pop sounded behind us.

I grabbed Quentin's arm and yanked him toward me just as two darts sailed over his shoulder and sank into a tree. When we reached the tree, I paused long enough to yank the darts from the bark before I continued on.

"What are you going to do with those?" Q panted.

"I have an idea."

"Good. Because they're getting closer."

Something snarled behind us.

I glanced over my shoulder to see a dark shape push through the brush and hurtle toward us. Its bared teeth glowed an almost ethereal blue under the moonlight.

Cords of fear tightened around my chest, and I skidded to a halt. There was no way we could outrun it.

The dog slowed its pace. Its lips rippled as a deep growl emanated from its chest.

I sucked in several ragged breaths, but no amount of air could quench the fire burning in my lungs. I'd never fought a dog before—but I had to assume the same principles I'd learned in hand-to-hand combat would apply. And being small, I relied on one lesson above all else: use your opponent's energy against them. I squared my shoulders and balanced my weight on my back foot.

"Rileigh?" Quentin called nervously behind me.

Before I could respond, the sleek brown dog lunged for me.

"Rileigh!" Quentin screamed. "Look out."

There was an old samurai saying that the greatest opponent a warrior had to overcome was himself. Because if you doubted your abilities for even a second, you'd lost the battle before you even drew your sword.

The dog's lips curled back, revealing all of its sharp teeth. I tightened my sweat-slick grip on the tranquilizer dart. I had to believe I could do this. My heart pounded against my ribs with so much force I thought it might burst through. "You can do this," I muttered to myself. I had no other choice.

The dog's mouth widened, its eyes locked on my face. With its teeth inches from my neck, this was my moment.

I dropped to the ground just as the dog's jaws snapped shut over my head. Before the animal could complete his arch, I jabbed one of the tranquilizer darts into its soft belly, thrusting upward as I did.

The dog somersaulted through the air before landing on its side with a grunt.

I took a step back, preparing to bolt if my plan hadn't worked.

The dog raised its head and blinked sleepily. It growled once before its eyes rolled back and its head dropped to the ground.

I couldn't help but feel a pang of guilt. "I'm so sorry, doggy," I murmured before turning back to Quentin.

"You're sorry?" Q asked. "That thing tried to rip out your throat!"

I shrugged. "Technically, it tried to rip out Sumi's throat. That makes him a very good dog—my favorite dog in the world, actually. Remind me if we ever get out of this alive to send him a steak."

Before he could answer, the pop of a dart gun sounded behind us.

"Duck!" Q cried, and we both hit the ground as several more darts sailed overhead.

"Don't move!" a voice screamed.

But not just any voice.

"No." My voice was barely a whisper. "It's impossible."

A dark silhouette walked toward us. As he approached,

the moonlight gradually revealed his features, like a mask pulled from his face.

Kim stood before us, dressed in the black uniform of the Network. He held a tranquilizer gun, which he aimed at my head. "Don't move," he growled.

My lungs seized from the shock of it, and I struggled to breathe. For a brief moment, hope blossomed inside me. Now was our chance to explain what had happened. Once we convinced him what Sumi and Whitley had done to us, we'd finally be safe.

"Kim! Thank God!" Q took a step toward him and Kim jerked the gun in his direction.

"I said don't move!" he screamed again.

"But Kim," Q continued, "it's me, Quentin. And that"—he pointed at me—"is not Sumi. That's Rileigh. Sumi performed some sort of ceremony during our fight and switched our bodies."

Kim's eye's narrowed. "You expect me to believe something so crazy?"

"It's the truth," I added. "You have to believe us. We don't have much time to switch our bodies back. Please, help us!"

He gave me a disgusted look. "This is one of your mind tricks, isn't it?" He aimed the gun's muzzle at my chest. "Save it, Sumi. Everything that comes out of your mouth is a lie."

The venom in his words stomped the hope inside of me flat. "Kim, please!" My voice wavered as hot tears welled inside my eyes. If I couldn't convince Kim, what chance did I have? "We're telling the truth."

"Enough!" He took a step closer, his eyes bright with fury. "We've all suffered enough because of you. I'm not going to let you hurt anyone ever again. I don't want to hear another word out of your lying mouth!"

The first hot tear burned a trail down my cheek because I knew that no amount of convincing would make Kim believe I was Rileigh.

"Ri?" Q whispered in my ear. "What are we going to do now?"

The only thing we could do—leave without Kim. I discreetly reached for Q's hand and pressed my remaining dart into his palm. "I need you to tranq him when I give the signal," I whispered back.

His eye bulged. "I'm going to what?"

"Both of you, stop talking!" Kim ordered. He pressed the walkie-talkie on his shoulder and spoke into it. "I've apprehended the fugitives. Once I have them secured, I'll meet you back at the truck for transport." He dropped his hand and looked at us. "I mean it. One word, one funny movement, and I'll use the gun. Got it?"

I glanced at Q and he gave the slightest shake of his head, as if silently begging me not to do what I was about to.

Unfortunately, if we had any hope of escape, I had no choice.

Kim pulled a zip tie from his pocket and motioned me forward. "Give me your hands."

I lifted my hands and took a step forward. A jagged lump pushed up my throat. Kim and I were so evenly matched, there was no telling who would win an actual fight between the two of us. Luckily, I didn't have to beat him—I just had to catch him off guard.

He reached for me, and I knew I wasn't going to be given

a better opportunity. The moment his fingers closed around my wrist, I stepped back while simultaneously grabbing his wrist and pulling him toward me. With my free hand, I pushed his shoulder forward and sent him tumbling to the ground.

"Now, Q!" If Kim regained his balance before Q struck, we were sunk.

"Q?" Kim glanced at me even as he fell, a question in his eyes.

"I'm so sorry!" Quentin added before he jabbed the dart into Kim's back.

Kim cried out and pulled the dart from his back before falling back to the ground. He blinked lazily up at the night sky.

"Son of hibachi," I muttered, clasping my hand over my mouth. Even though he'd tried to apprehend us, I still hated to see him put down this way.

Kim's eyes rolled in my direction. "*What* did you just say?" he slurred.

I opened my mouth to answer him when the bark of another dog sounded behind us.

Q's hand tightened around my arm. "Now what?"

I placed my hand over his. "We're going to have to run." But before I could pull him with me, he yanked out of my grasp.

I blinked at him. "What are you doing? We have to go!"

He shook his head. "No. We can't keep doing this. I think— I think it's time to split up."

"What?" I took a step back. "That's a horrible idea. We need to stick together."

Q gave me a sad smile. "As long as we're together, they can keep tracking us. But I can lead them in the wrong direction. That should give you enough time to get away."

I couldn't speak as I tried to process his words.

"Don't worry." Q pulled the can of dog food from his pocket and proceeded to smear the greasy slop across his boots. "The person with the greatest chance of making it back is you—so you're the one who has to continue on. I'll be fine. All that matters is you get back home in time to switch our bodies. I'm certain it has something to do with the bracelets they used."

"Q, I—" But I couldn't finish. His plan was a good one. Still, I didn't want to let him go.

He drew me in for a hug and squeezed tightly. "You can do this," he whispered. "I know you can."

Before I could argue, he pulled back and screamed into the forest, "Hey! I'm right here!" He ran past me, only to stop and glance at me over his shoulder. "What are you waiting for? Get out of here!"

Right. I cast one last look at Kim's now-unconscious body. A pang of regret shot through me. If only I had more time. Maybe I could have convinced him...

"Rileigh!" Q shouted. "Go!"

I took off running in the opposite direction. I jogged at a pace fast enough to keep covering ground but not one that would tire me out quickly. It wasn't long before the sound of Q's shouts and the barking dogs faded into nothing. And then I knew our plan had worked. He'd successfully led them away.

But at the same time, I knew something else.

I was completely on my own.

20

'm going to drop dead," I muttered as I slogged through the shin-high stream.

Despite the warm morning sun filtering golden rays through the gaps in the trees, the icy water surrounding my bare feet had my teeth chattering and limbs trembling. My body ached from exhaustion, not to mention that a black haze had gathered around the edges of my vision and threatened me with unconsciousness each time I blinked.

I'd decided to wade through the creek to keep the dogs from scenting my path, but it'd been hours since I last heard a bark. Assuming I'd shaken my pursuers for the time being, I climbed up the embankment and collapsed against the soft mud. The desire to lay my head down and succumb to the fatigue pulling at me was overwhelming. But Q hadn't sacrificed himself so I could take a nap—he was counting on me to get home and get our bodies back.

And it wasn't just Q I had to protect. I knew Sumi would never hurt Kim, but that didn't mean she wouldn't kill Braden, Michelle, or Drew if they suspected something wasn't right. A hot wave of fury rolled over me, providing me with a second wave of energy. I withdrew my dry shoes from my waistband and tied them on my feet. I couldn't let that happen.

I trudged up the embankment, occasionally using small trees and vines to keep my footing in the slippery grass. It appeared nothing on this journey would be easy.

Or at least that's what I thought until I reached the top of the hill.

At first I thought it was my imagination or a trick of the dim morning light. I shielded my eyes with my hands and blinked several times to make sure.

Just ahead, through a part in the trees, it beckoned me. A road.

I barely held back a squeal of joy as I plowed through branches and brush. Thorns raked across my skin, but I barely felt their sting. A road! I emerged from the forest and stood at the edge of the dusty road. I fought the urge to fall to my knees and press my lips to the gravel. It wasn't a paved road, which was a good thing. That meant it wasn't a main road, so the odds were slim the Network patrolled it. But it also wasn't overrun with weeds, and that meant it was a used road. And a used road had to lead somewhere—hopefully, to a place with food, supplies, or better yet a vehicle.

So all I needed to do was find where that somewhere was.

After about fifteen minutes of walking, the wall of trees surrounding me opened up to reveal a clearing. My heart leapt, forcing me to pause long enough to pinch myself to ensure I wasn't dreaming. There, just ahead, sat a faded brown trailer surrounded by the carcasses of three rusted pick-up trucks. Behind the trailer stood a sun-bleached wooden barn.

Even from a distance, I could tell the vehicles in the yard were worthless. One had been stripped nearly to the frame, while the other two were tireless and propped up on cinder blocks. Still, I quickened my pace to a trot. I'd come too far to give up so easily. Besides, there had to be something drivable here, otherwise there wouldn't have been tire treads in the gravel road.

I set my sights on the barn. If there was a running vehicle here, that was where I'd find it. Normally, I would have performed a quick sweep of the property to determine if the occupants were at home. But without the luxury of time, I had no choice but to barge in.

As I approached the barn, I noticed the overgrown lawn contained more than rusted-out cars. Several large metal barrels were scattered about in the tall weeds, like rotten Easter eggs waiting to be discovered. Also among the barrels were the deflated remains of a kids' pool, a red cooler missing a lid, and a splintered shovel—nothing that would do me any good.

When I reached the barn, I breathed a sigh of relief. I'd been worried I'd find the doors padlocked shut. Lucky for me, nothing but a simple hook latch held the doors in place. I glanced around to make sure no one was looking, pulled the latch free, and slipped inside.

The musty air inside the barn pressed against me, hot and humid. A strange, sour smell I couldn't identify burned my nostrils with each breath I inhaled. It took me several seconds of blinking before my eyes adjusted to the dim lighting. Even then, I still couldn't make sense of the device before me.

In the middle of the barn sat two metal barrels joined by tubes. One barrel rested on the dirt-covered ground while the other hung over a wood-burning stove. A crate filled with empty glass jars was positioned nearby.

What in the world?

I took several steps closer to inspect the contraption when something else caught my eye. Several yards away in an open horse stall, a polished handlebar protruded from beneath a dust-coated tarp.

Hope squeezed my ribs in a too-tight embrace. I ran to the tarp and yanked it off, revealing the shining motorcycle beneath. To make things even better, two helmets dangled from the handlebars and the keys were already stuck in the ignition.

I clasped my hands over my mouth to keep from squealing out loud. This was it—the answer to my prayers. Now if only I could figure out how to drive it.

As I reached for the handlebars, I heard a click behind me. I glanced over my shoulder to find the muzzle of a double-barreled shotgun pointed at my chest.

I froze, a scream lodged inside my chest.

"What are you doing on my property?" a scowling woman demanded through nicotine-stained teeth. The lines on her face from a lifetime of sun and cigarette use made her age impossible to determine. Inch-long black roots bled into peroxide-bleached hair that hung limply to her shoulders.

Instinctively, I threw my hands in the air. "I-I'm sorry. I was, um, hiking. I got lost and found your barn. I thought there might be a phone in here." It was a weak lie, but it was the best I could come up with as my mind searched frantically for a way out of this mess.

Without my ki, I couldn't make a shield. And I was willing to bet this woman's gun wasn't loaded with tranquilizer darts like the Network's. Since I couldn't fight a bullet, my only chance was to lure her close enough to make a grab at her gun.

"Lost?" She snorted and spit out a greasy wad beside her feet.

My stomach convulsed, and I did my best to nod.

"You're lying." The woman narrowed her eyes. "The trails don't come around here."

"I'm not lying." My gaze darted from the barrel of her gun to the open door behind her—it was too far to make a run for it. "I've been wandering the woods all night. I haven't eaten or slept. I'm exhausted and there are people looking for me." That much was true. "If you'd just let me use your phone, I could call someone to come get me."

The woman's lips puckered in disgust. "Do you see any phone lines?"

I shrugged helplessly. "Then your cell phone—"

She let out a guffaw. "You think a cell phone would get reception way out here?" She snorted again. "But you already know that, don't you?"

"What?" The hair prickled along the back of my neck. Something dangerous was happening; I could hear it in the woman's voice. "I don't know what you're talking about."

She took a step closer. The smell of tobacco rolling off of her burnt my nostrils. She thrust the gun at my chest. "You're not fooling me if you think I'm gonna buy your *hiker* story."

My heart hammered against my ribs. With the motorcycle

behind me, I had nowhere to run. "I-I have no idea what you're talking about."

"Don't play dumb with me, Missy!" she roared. "I know who you really are—what you came here to do!" Her face burned crimson, her eyes wild.

It was apparent I was losing control of the situation and fast. "Listen, I think there's been a misunderstanding. Maybe we could just take a deep breath and calm down for a minute."

"Calm down?" She snorted. "How do you expect me to calm down when the ATF shows up on *my* property?"

She wasn't making sense. "The AT-what?"

"Ha! You must really think I'm stupid." She took a step closer. "I know you guys have been after me for months. But I don't care about your goddamned government regulations! After Danny died, with me out of work, making shine is the only way I survive. And I'm not going to let you take that away from me. The way I see it, Missy, it's your life or mine." She licked her lips. "There's an awful lot of mountain to cover. If you went missing for real, they'd never find you."

My breath caught inside my throat. Of all the mountain folk to stumble upon, I had to find the psycho! I couldn't believe I'd survived the night running from Network agents only to die at the hands of a lunatic. I searched frantically for a way out but came up with nothing. The woman was still too far away for me to attack, and without my ki, I had nothing to protect me.

The woman grinned. "Looks like the bears won't be going hungry tonight."

I sucked in a quivering breath. I couldn't believe this was the end. After everything I'd done to stop her, Sumi would win,

Whitley would die, and Q would forever be stuck inside Whitley's body. And there wasn't a damned thing I could do about it.

A bitter taste burned up my tongue. I closed my eyes and braced myself for the blow.

The bang that followed was loud enough to rattle my bones. I gasped, and my eyes fluttered opened. I ran my hands along my body and searched for the warm spot where blood was sure to be spilling. Nothing hurt, and that was always a bad sign. Little to no pain almost always signaled a mortal blow.

But as I continued to search my body for the bullet hole, something hit the ground at my feet. I looked down and, no matter how many times I blinked, I couldn't make sense of the sight before me. The woman, who only seconds ago was on the verge of shooting me, now lay at my feet with a tranquilizer dart protruding from her flannel shirt.

"Prove to me it's really you."

I looked at the person standing inside the barn door, blinking to ensure my eyes weren't playing tricks on me.

Kim walked inside the barn with the dart gun raised.

I opened my mouth, but the words tangled in the back of my throat. Every muscle inside my body strained to run to him. Yet the dart gun aimed at my chest kept me locked in place.

Kim stopped several feet away. "Tell me…" He pressed his lips together and glanced at the ceiling as he thought. But then his eyes lit up and he looked at me, and I knew he'd found his question. "In our past life, I made you promise me something the night before we died. Do you remember what that was?"

My body sagged with relief because I did know. The memory of that night was engraved into my memory like a firebrand. "You made me promise to never go where you couldn't follow."

He flinched as if I'd slapped him and slowly lowered the dart gun. "I thought you were lying, playing another one of your mind games. But then, before I passed out, I heard you talking. How Quentin offered to lead the other agents astray." He shook his head. "That's something Whitley never would have done for Sumi."

My heart threatened to beat through my chest. "You believed me?"

"Not at first. But after I woke up I trailed you here." He nodded to the woman on the ground. "The real Sumi would have killed that woman on the spot. But you—" He cocked his head. "You don't have Sumi's powers, do you?"

I shook my head. "I also don't have my ki manipulation powers, either. They won't work in this body."

He walked closer until he was an arm's length away. From this close the smell of his sandalwood cologne enveloped me, bringing with it memories of long ago. "The Network called me when you escaped. I told Rileigh—or at least the person I thought was Rileigh—that I was going to look for you. She was acting so strangely. She demanded I didn't go. We had a fight." He holstered his gun and ran a hand along his face. "I'm such an idiot. How could I not have known?" He stared into my eyes, but what he was searching for, I wasn't sure. "How are you ever going to forgive me?"

I fought to stand my ground as everything inside me strained to close the distance between us. "Shut your eyes," I whispered.

He frowned. "What?"

"You can't get something for nothing, Gimhae Kim. If you want my forgiveness, you have to give me something first."

"I will give you anything you want."

"Your trust, then."

He closed his eyes.

I lifted a trembling hand and placed it over his heart. I wanted to feel the beat of it beneath my fingers, to prove this wasn't a dream. "On the roof of my condo, you promised you wouldn't let me go, remember?"

He made a pained noise and his eyelids twitched.

"Don't!" I warned. "Please don't open your eyes."

"Why?"

My hand fell from his chest. "Because I don't want you to see me like this. I want you to picture me as Rileigh, not Sumi. Especially when I do this." I slid my arms around his waist.

Kim wrapped his arms around my shoulders and pulled me tight against him, his chin resting on the top of my head. "I'm so sorry," he murmured. "God, I'm so sorry."

I pressed my cheek against his chest, letting the beat of his heart bleed through me, until my own pulse matched the rhythm. For one shining moment, the world fell away and nothing remained but Kim, me, and our hearts beating in time.

Kim's fingers wound through my hair. "How do I get you back?"

"Quentin thinks it has something to do with a bracelet that both Sumi and Whitley are wearing." I murmured the words against the cotton of his T-shirt.

Gently Kim pushed me back and opened his eyes. "I remember a bracelet. Leather? With beads?"

I nodded.

He made a disgusted noise and raked his hand through his hair. "I asked Ri—I mean, Sumi—about it because it was so unusual. She told me they were friendship bracelets." He shook his head. "How could I be so stupid?"

"How could you have known?" I asked. "I certainly had no idea Sumi was capable of something like this. We just have to get back home and cut those bracelets off."

"Then let's do that." He reached for the walkie-talkie on his shoulder, but I grabbed his hand before he could hit the button.

"What are you doing?" I asked.

He frowned at me. "I'm following protocol. I've got to call the Network and alert them to the situation."

"And you think they'll believe you? What if they think I'm using Sumi's mind control on you?"

He was quiet a moment. "Good question. I guess they would want you to come to New York to prove you were Rileigh. It would probably take a couple of days at most."

A couple of days? I shook my head and took a step back. "I can't do that, Kim. I don't have time."

His forehead wrinkled in confusion. "What do you mean?"

"Q thinks that we only have three days at the most before we get stuck in these bodies forever. Even if the Network believes me, the delay would cost me my body!" I glanced at the motorcycle behind me. "Maybe . . . maybe you could go back to the Network and explain the situation. You could convince them to stop chasing me."

His frown deepened. "That would never work. They'd want to see for themselves that you're Rileigh. If I went without you, they'd assume I'd been brainwashed." His eyes followed mine to the bike. "Besides, I made a promise."

I was sure I heard him wrong. "What are you saying?"

He snapped the walkie-talkie off of his shoulder and dropped it onto the ground. Next, he walked over to the motorcycle and picked up the two helmets lying on the seat. He tossed one at me before straddling the bike and patting the empty seat behind him. "I'm saying you better hurry. We're burning daylight."

I hugged the helmet against my body. "But the Network... you do realize if they think I've brainwashed you, they're going to come after you too."

"Let them." He turned the ignition. The bike roared like a beast, making me gasp. "Let them send an entire ninja army after me." He extended a hand toward me, and I slipped my fingers inside his. He pulled me onto the bike behind him and revved the engine.

After we put our helmets on, he glanced at me over his shoulder. "No one is going to take you away from me again. Not the Network, and definitely not Sumi." With that, he kicked the bike into gear with his foot, and together we shot out of the barn.

When we hit the gravel road, I tightened my arms around his waist and rested my head between his shoulder blades. In both lifetimes, Kim and I had been torn apart. He seemed to think this time things would end differently.

I only hoped he was right.

21

It wasn't until the winding inclines of the mountainous roads gave way to level interstate that I loosened my white-knuckled grip around Kim's waist. In fact, if we weren't in a race against time with Network agents on our tail, I might have actually enjoyed myself. Cruising along on the motor-cycle brought back fond memories of riding horseback in my previous life. Sure, our current speed was ten times greater, but the thrill of the wind pulling across my face while the ground blurred beneath me was just as exhilarating.

We crossed a bridge and Kim pointed a finger at a large, white billboard welcoming us to Ohio.

I nodded my chin against his shoulder.

"We're making really great time!" he shouted, his words barely making it to my ears before being carried away by the wind. "Maybe eight or nine hours tops. We'll be home by nightfall."

By nightfall? I closed my eyes and allowed myself one glorious moment to bask in the warmth of hope that flooded through my veins. After everything I'd been through in the last twenty-four hours—everything that had gone wrong—it was almost too much to hope I'd actually caught a break.

"We have a slight problem," Kim said, interrupting my thoughts.

And apparently I was right. "What's wrong?" I screamed.

He pointed to the gas gauge and the needle falling deeper into the red.

"Do you have any money?" I asked.

He shook his head.

"Son of hibachi." I spit the words through clenched teeth. That was what I got for thinking things were finally going my way. There was no way we'd make it all the way back to St. Louis on the little gas we had. I doubted we'd make it more than another fifty miles—if that.

As we continued to fly past mile markers, I wracked my brain for a possible solution. If we ran out of gas, not only would we lose valuable time, but we'd be stuck should any cop or Network official find us. Maybe we could make up a story about Kim losing his wallet and convince someone at a gas station to give us money. It might work...or it might get the police called on us. Either way, it was our best bet for getting home.

I leaned forward to tell Kim to take the next exit with a gas station when I caught site of a familiar black truck barreling toward us in the side mirror.

It couldn't be. My fingers curled like claws into Kim's shirt. He glanced over his shoulder and gave me a questioning look.

It took me several swallows before the lump inside my

throat loosened enough to allow me to speak. "I think we're being followed!"

He frowned and checked the side mirror. At that early hour, only a few tractor trailers dotted the road around us. The black truck stuck out like a thorn on an otherwise smooth stem.

Kim's frown deepened into a scowl. He twisted the handlebar and the bike growled as we shot ahead. My head swam as I watched the scenery whirl past in dizzying waves of color. I couldn't be sure if the pounding inside my head was from the rush of wind or my own heartbeat. "Kim!" I cried out, but his name was ripped from my throat before it ever touched his ears.

He pointed a finger at the side mirror for the briefest second before placing his hand back on the handlebar. Keeping my head pressed against his back, I slowly turned to look behind us. The wind ripped lines of tears from my eyes, but even through my blurred vision, I could see the truck closing the gap between us as we continued to accelerate.

"We can't outrun them," Kim shouted. "But we might be able to outmaneuver them."

"What?" I didn't like the sound of that.

"Hang on!" Kim swerved sharply onto an off ramp, forcing me to bury a scream into the cotton of his T-shirt. Behind us, the truck squealed its tires and struggled to cross two lanes in time to make the exit. Even then, it kicked up gravel and swerved dangerously as its back tires caught the shoulder.

When we reached the top of the ramp, Kim jerked to the right, causing the bike to tip dangerously on its side. I thought for sure we would fall until the last second, when Kim put his foot to the ground, balancing us, as we turned and sped down the country highway.

"Kim!" I screamed, curling my nails into his shirt. "Please tell me you know what you're doing!"

He shook his head, a sly smile reflected back at me in the side mirror. "When don't I?"

My heart beat against my ribs like a hammer. I wanted to believe him, but at the breakneck sped we were traveling, I couldn't help but wonder if facing the men with the guns was a safer option.

We raced along the empty road. Nothing but fields and pastures passed on either side of us. Each time Kim made a turn, we would jump ahead only to have the black truck catch up within seconds.

I bit my lip as I watched the truck close the gap between us yet again. We couldn't keep this up forever. First of all, we were running dangerously low on gas. Second, I knew the truck behind us had probably radioed for backup and it would only be a matter of time before more trucks and more men showed up. And while we might be able to outmaneuver one, I didn't think we'd be able to escape them all.

No sooner had I thought this than a tranquiller dart sailed over my shoulder. Kim jerked the bike to the left, nearly tossing me from my seat in the process. I tightened my hold around his waist as he sped up. What the hell were they thinking shooting darts at us when we were on a bike? If one of us was hit, odds were we wouldn't survive the fall. I assumed their orders were to bring me back alive. But maybe because I'd escaped them so many times, they no longer cared.

Anger burned through my blood, melting away my fear. I was not going to let them kill me or anyone I cared about.

I unlocked my hands from Kim's waist and slid my fingers

under his jacket until I found the cold piece of steel protruding from his waistline.

He glanced at me before turning his attention back to the road. "What are you doing?"

I wasn't entirely sure. I'd never used a gun, let alone a tranquilizer gun, before. I much preferred the comforting grip of a katana in my hands. But since I didn't have a choice, I prayed my aim would find my target.

"You've got to let them get a little closer," I shouted.

After a pause, Kim let off the gas and the truck closed the gap between us. The man in the passenger seat leaned out his open window and fired several more darts. Kim swerved the bike and the darts sailed close enough to my head to tug at my hair whipping from underneath my helmet. If my plan was going to work, I had to act now before I became one with the pavement.

"Brake on my signal," I screamed in Kim's ear.

Even though I couldn't see him, I could hear the grin in his voice. "Say when."

A dart speared my seat cushion, inches from my body. "Now!"

The bike's tires squealed angrily against the pavement, kicking up smoke as well as filling my nostrils with the smell of burnt rubber.

The truck also slammed on its brakes. But it was too big a vehicle to stop so suddenly, and it swerved dangerously from side to side as it tried to stop. When the front of it skidded past our bike, I aimed the gun and fired.

The first dart sank into the metal door. But the second met its target. The tire exploded with a bang that rang inside my ears several seconds after it was over. The deflated rubber spun around the rim several times before it tore free and landed on the road in shredded black strips. The truck careened off the shoulder and into the ditch. The sound of shrieking metal pierced my ears as the truck rolled onto its side, where it remained crushed and smoking.

"We did it!" I wrapped my arms around Kim's chest and squeezed.

He nodded. "Yes. But that was only one truck out of the many probably headed this way." He twisted the handlebar, revving the engine before peeling out. We lurched down the country road. "Now they know we're headed home," he shouted over his shoulder. "We're going to have to travel side roads to keep them off our trail."

My stomach sank. Traveling the side roads would take us longer to get home—and we didn't have much time to spare. Not to mention, what would happen when Sumi got news I escaped and was heading her way?

We drove on, and the farmland gradually gave way to woods. I rested my head against Kim's back, trying to fight away the exhaustion that pulled at me with velvet fingers. At least I had Kim with me, believing in me.

Kim, as if sensing how overwhelmed I felt, let go of a handlebar long enough to squeeze my arm reassuringly. That was my samurai—always so confident and determined. Once upon a time I'd been confident as well. But that was before I died. Now I knew how fragile life really was, and how easy it was to lose everything you loved.

No sooner had the thought crossed my mind than we

rounded a sharp corner to discover a man and his dog walking in the middle of the road.

I screamed, but it was too late.

The brakes squealed as Kim wrestled with the bike for control. He turned the wheel sharply, avoiding the man by inches. We skidded onto the shoulder. I tried clinging to Kim's arms, but it was useless. Once the bike met with loose gravel, it slid out from beneath us, sending us airborn.

I wasn't sure what part of me hit the ground first. One minute I was flying through the air, the next there was an explosion of pain, followed by nothingness as the world around me went dark.

22

A cool, leathery hand touched my face and my eyes shot open.

I gasped. "Get back!" I scrambled backward, convinced a Network agent had been moments from choking the life out of me. Instead, I found myself staring at Sumi's wide eyes reflected back at me in the old man's black glasses.

"Easy there." He lifted his hands. "I'm sorry for frightening you. But your crash sounded pretty bad, and I wanted to make sure you weren't dead."

"Dead?" I pulled off my helmet and felt along my torn clothing. I winced every time I brushed a cut or scrape. Luckily, none of the gashes appeared too serious. And while every bone in my body throbbed with a gnawing ache, nothing inside me screamed it was broken.

After my self-examination, my head snapped up in realization. "Kim!" I climbed to my feet on wobbling legs. I spun a quick circle as the old man stood beside me. The sideways motorcycle sat several yards away, but Kim was nowhere to be seen.

Panic ripped through my chest, and I fought to breathe.

"Kim?" The man dropped the tip of his cane against the ground. "There was somebody else on the motorcycle with you?"

"Yes! Didn't you see him?" I whirled around, and that's when I realized the dark glasses, white cane—*duh, Rileigh.* The man couldn't see *anything.* "Never mind," I added before he could answer. "Kim is my boyfriend. He was driving the motorcycle and now he's ... " My voice cracked as I scanned through the woods. "I don't know."

"I bet Rosie does," the man answered.

Fear pulled tight across my chest like the laces of a corset. "Who's Rosie?"

"Rosie!" The man patted his thigh.

A second later, a large golden retriever lumbered out of the woods. She met my gaze with a whine, bobbing impatiently on her feet before turning and disappearing back into the brush.

"If you follow Rosie, I bet you'll find your friend."

I didn't have to be told twice. Despite the burn of my screaming muscles, I sprinted into the brush after Rosie. I only had to tear through two thorn bushes before I found her on the other side of a fallen log. She stood over Kim's unmoving body with a look of concern I'm sure mirrored my own.

"Oh, my God." I clapped my hand over my mouth to stifle a scream and fell to my knees at his side. His helmet was still on—a good sign. But there was a trail of blood twisting along his neck to the ground below.

I lifted a trembling hand to touch him, but it only hovered above his chest. I was too frightened to discover the truth. "Please, please, please," I muttered. I couldn't lose him—not again.

"Now don't you worry, young lady."

I looked up, startled to find the man standing beside me. I briefly wondered how he'd managed to maneuver through the woods with only his cane to guide him.

He kneeled beside me. "He's not dead. Probably just a concussion."

I glanced back down at Kim's unmoving body. "How could you possibly know that?"

The man shrugged. "I can hear him breathe. And the sound of a person's breathing can tell you an awful lot about what condition they're in."

Reluctantly, I tore my gaze away from Kim. *Who was this guy?* "Are you a doctor or something?"

He chuckled softly. "Definitely an *or something*." He grabbed Kim's arm and slung it around his shoulder.

"Wait." I stood and hugged my arms across my body. "What are you doing with him?"

The man shook his head. "We can't just leave him in the woods. Help me take him back to my place—it's not far from here."

I chewed on my lip as I considered my options. Kim was hurt, and the man was right. I couldn't let him sit in the woods, especially with the Network hot on our trail. But the other part of me couldn't help but be suspicious of the blind man—maybe because my run-in with the moonshine woman was still in the front of my mind, or maybe because there was really something to be suspicious of. What was he doing in the middle of the road, anyway? On the other hand, I had to get Kim someplace safe and hidden until he recovered. Time was ticking away, Q was counting on me, and I couldn't afford to be caught in the woods again.

I had no choice but to go with the blind man.

I slipped underneath Kim's dangling arm and hoisted it over my shoulders. "Lead the way," I said, though I immediately cringed when I realized how my words might sound to a blind man. "I'm sorry. I didn't mean—"

The man's chuckle interrupted my words. "The world cannot be seen through something as simple as eyes, young lady." With one hand gripping Kim's arm and the other guiding his cane in front of him, he moved through the brush. "A person's true self isn't something that can be seen, but rather how the world around them is affected by their presence. So despite this"—he lifted his cane—"I can see just fine, thank you." He smiled and continued on.

I stared at him a moment before concentrating on the path ahead of me. He sure was philosophical for a random stranger out for a walk. He kind of reminded me of … I shook my head, dismissing the thought. No. It was simply a weird coincidence.

The old man was right about one thing, though. He really didn't need to see. He carefully guided us around thorn bushes and trees until we emerged at the road with his golden retriever happily bouncing along behind us.

Still, the thought nagged at me as we walked along the side of the road. I swallowed before asking, "What you said about a person's true self—did you just make that up? Or did you hear it somewhere?"

He smiled and shrugged, not appearing burdened at all by Kim's weight. My own muscles, however, burned with strain. "Oh, I suppose I read it in a book somewhere. I'm always reading this or that."

"Right." I tried to shrug back my disappointment. The man's explanation made perfect sense. It was my own wishful thinking that Lord Toyotomi would be here, the one man who always knew how to fix any situation. Still, as we continued to travel along the road, I couldn't help but sneak glances at the blind man, hoping to spot any similarities between him and my long-lost daiymo.

As if reading my mind, the man smiled. I quickly turned my attention back to the road. The hair on the back of my neck prickled for no reason that I could determine.

"See the clearing up ahead?" he asked, the smile still on his face. "We're going to follow that to my house. Once we get there, we can call an ambulance for your friend."

"Ambulance?" I jerked back, my throat suddenly dry. "That won't be necessary."

"Of course it is." The man's smile faded and his brows furrowed. "After a nasty accident like that—you should both be looked over."

I shook my head before realizing he couldn't see it. "No. That's okay—really." My mind raced in search of a believable explanation. "We don't, um, believe in modern medicine. Going to a hospital would be going against, uh....our religious beliefs."

The man's frown deepened. "Religious beliefs, huh?"

The golden retriever glanced at me from over her shoulder. Even she appeared to roll her eyes at my pathetic excuse.

As soon as we reached the edge of a gravel driveway, the man stopped short, forcing me to do the same. He didn't look at me as he spoke. "Before we go any farther, I need you to be honest with me about something. Do you think you can do that?"

A solid lump rose inside my throat, and I struggled to swallow around it. Could I? I didn't know anything about this man, and he didn't know anything about me. What would prevent him from calling the cops if he learned I was a fugitive on the run? But at the same time, a niggling in the back of my head told me I could trust him. He had helped us this far, and I certainly couldn't help Kim on my own. "Okay."

He nodded. "Are you and your boyfriend in some sort of trouble?"

I sucked on my bottom lip before answering. That was definitely a loaded question. And if I told the truth, would that be enough to turn us away? But at the same time, didn't I at least owe him the courtesy of finding out?

"Yes. We're in a lot of trouble, actually." I held my breath and waited for him to tell me to get off his property.

Except he didn't. He inclined his head to the little white house at the end of the drive. "Let's get him inside and set up on the couch. I'd prefer he go to the hospital, but since you can't, I'll see what I can do."

"Thank you." My words, so heavy with relief, were barely a whisper.

Together we hoisted Kim's body down the driveway with Rosie bounding ahead. Once we reached the house, the man opened the front door and we carried Kim inside.

His house wasn't anything like I'd expected—though I'd never been inside a blind man's house so I wasn't sure what to expect. The shades were open, filling the tiny living room with an abundance of light. On each windowsill sat at least five different potted plants and herbs. Some I could recognize easily as aloe or basil, while others, with yellow flowers and striped leaves, I'd never seen before.

And despite the fact the man was blind, there had been some attempt at decoration at one point. Sun-aged yellow doilies sat on top of a coffee table littered with condensation rings from a lifetime of no coaster use. Dust-coated pictures of the blind man in various stages of his life hung on a far wall. In one, he wore a graduation gown, and in another, he proudly held a largemouth bass in his hands. And in every picture of him from his twenties and beyond, a smiling woman stood by his side with her hand lightly on his arm.

Through the smell of herbs and dust, the scent of something sharp and tangy hung in the air—like overly steeped tea.

Together, we lowered Kim onto the faded floral coach. His head rolled lazily on his neck and a groan escaped his lips. I held his hand tightly within my own. Had I made the right decision not calling for an ambulance? What if Kim's injury was more serious than a concussion? If he had internal bleeding…

But no, I wouldn't allow myself to dwell on the worst-case scenario. He was going to be fine. He had to be.

"Take that blanket over there." The man motioned to a blanket draped across a cracked leather recliner. In front of it, an old tube television quietly played the news. "Get him wrapped tight and meet me in the kitchen. He'll need some ice for his head and steeped cinnamon to combat the nausea he's going to feel when he wakes."

I nodded and the man retreated into the kitchen.

Rosie stayed by Kim's side, watching him with anxious eyes as I grabbed the blanket and tucked it around his body. When I finished, his eyes cracked open before flying wide. "Sumi!"

"No, Kim." I took a step back and glanced over my shoulder, hoping the blind man wouldn't hear. "I'm Rileigh. Remember?"

He blinked several times before his body relaxed. "Rileigh, yes." He started to sink against the pillow before jerking upright. "We were in an accident. Are you hurt?"

"I'm fine. And you will be too." I sat beside him and smoothed his hair off of his face. He hissed softly when my fingers ran over the goose-egg-sized lump on his head. I quickly pulled my hand away. "Sorry."

But Kim snatched my hand and drew it to his face, planting a kiss against my wrist that sent shivers along my back. "If your touch condemned me to a lifetime of pain, I would gladly accept my fate."

"It's good to see you two back together again."

Kim and I turned to find the man standing in the doorway with a steaming mug in one hand and a plastic bag of ice in the other.

"What?" I asked.

The old man chuckled. "I guess that came out wrong. What I meant to say was, it's good to see your boyfriend awake so you can be . . . back together."

"Oh." I gave Kim an uncertain glance, and he shrugged in response.

The man waved dismissively. "Anyway, now that you're

awake, we can be properly introduced. My name is Gene." He shuffled forward and handed Kim the mug and bag of ice. "Put the bag on your head to reduce the swelling. And take small sips of the tea to help with any nausea."

Kim placed the bag of ice on his head and sipped the tea as instructed. "Thank you for your kindness, Gene. My name is Kim, and this is Rileigh." He said my name without hesitation, which only made me love him more. "We are in your debt."

Gene waved his words away. "Life is mysterious in that it always delivers us where we need to be—even if that place is where we least expect."

"Very *mysterious*," I agreed. Kim shot me a questioning look, but before I could say more, the nearby television stole the words from my mouth. The local midday news cut to a picture of Sumi's face—or rather, my current face—with the title caption *Criminal at Large* scrolling across the screen.

My teeth snapped together with an audible click. Kim followed my eyes, his lips parting when he saw the screen.

"Breaking news," the reporter announced as Sumi's face disappeared. The camera cut to a woman wearing a blue blazer sitting behind a news desk. "Seventeen-year-old Sumi Meadows is wanted for questioning in the murder of her adoptive parents, Alice and Christopher Meadows. The middle-aged couple was found brutality murdered in their beds. The teen disappeared from her home in Waterloo, Illinois, and is believed to be in the Ohio area. If you see her, you are urged to call police. Do not approach, as she is considered to be armed and dangerous."

The urge to vomit was overpowering. I took the cinnamon tea from Kim and swallowed a large gulp.

Gene tsked and shook his head. "So sad how some can be lead astray at such a young age."

I placed the mug back into Kim's hands before my shaking fingers could spill the contents on his lap. It was nothing short of a miracle that we had found ourselves in the home of a man who couldn't see—especially when my face was broadcasted on his television.

I ran my fingers through my hair, realizing just how complicated our situation had become. Not only did I have the Network hunting me down, but I also had the police and general public to worry about. There was no telling how many people saw the news broadcast, or how far across the country the coverage ran.

Kim took my hand and squeezed it gently. He pressed his other finger against his lips, as if to warn me about saying anything that might give us away.

"What do you suppose," Gene asked, "would make a girl so young angry enough to kill her own parents?"

"Maybe some people are cursed." The words escaped my lips before I had the chance to censor them.

Gene folded his arms. "What do you mean?"

I licked my lips. "Maybe we're all cursed in that we're destined to relive the same life, over and over again, in every reincarnated lifetime."

Kim's eyes widened with shock in a way that made me wonder whether the thought had never occurred to him before. It was a theory I'd considered more and more when it appeared that no matter what Kim and I did, something was always bound to come between us. And if we were destined to repeat the same life over again, did that mean that not only would Kim and I not be together, but also that we'd die at a young age as well?

Gene scratched the white stubble on his chin. "Hmm. That's an interesting theory, young lady. But one I have to take issue with. I cannot believe fate would be so cruel as to force us to relive the same life over and over again. What is life but an opportunity to learn and find inner peace? No. I believe the same situations might arise as a chance for us to prove we are able to learn from our mistakes."

Kim set his mug on the coffee table. "So you believe in reincarnation?"

Gene smiled mysteriously. "I believe in many things. Some people might find the things I believe in to be ridiculous or absurd."

I snorted. "You won't get that from us."

"I figured as much." Gene walked to his recliner, swiveled it in our direction, and sat down. Rosie wandered over to him and flopped at his feet.

"What do you mean?" I asked. "You hardly know us."

He reached down and scratched Rosie's head. "You might say I'm a good judge of character."

I curled my fingers into the sofa as a sense of uneasiness shook my body. If only I had my ki powers, I would be able to sense if something more unusual were going on other than an old man acting strangely.

Kim must have felt something was off as well. I could tell by the way he sat silent and rigid beside me.

"All right," I said. "What do you think about our character?"

Gene turned his head in Kim's direction. "Kim, is it? Right

away, I could tell you were a strong young man with strong convictions, and an even stronger sense of honor."

Kim swallowed but said nothing.

"Now you," this time Gene inclined his head toward me. "You're a little trickier."

"Why's that?" I asked.

He shrugged. "I don't know. I'm having a hard time getting a good reading on you."

I chuckled nervously. "Must be because I'm so complex."

"No." Gene shook his head. "If I were to guess, I'd say the reason I can't get a good read on you is because you're in the wrong body."

23

Kim ripped the blanket off and climbed to his feet. I tried to stand as well, but the shock rolling through my body kept me planted on the couch.

Kim narrowed his eyes. "How do you know she's in the wrong body?"

The man chuckled. "The same way you can look up and see a blue sky, I suppose. I may not be able to see with my eyes, but that doesn't mean I can't see in other ways. And that's how I know"—he gestured to me with his hand—"you are entirely wrong."

I exchanged a nervous glance with Kim before I asked, "Do you know about this sort of thing? Do you know how to undo it?"

He leaned back in his chair. "I would imagine it was done by some sort of binding, correct?"

"Yes," I answered. "The girl who stole my body cut our hands and bound them together with a beaded cord."

He scratched the stubble at his chin. "Then I would guess you need to sever the cord, but you only have a short time to do so." He reached for me. "Let me see your hand."

I hesitated and looked at Kim, who nodded his assurance. Slowly, I stood and crossed the room, finally letting my fingers fall into Gene's open hand.

He curled his warm, weathered fingers around my hand. He didn't move for several heartbeats until finally he released me.

"Exactly what I thought," he murmured. "You only have twenty-four hours until the change becomes permanent."

Ice flooded through my veins and I began to tremble. "That's it?" I whispered. That hardly seemed like enough time to make it home and cut the bracelet from Sumi's wrist. What if we didn't make it? I promised Q I'd get him his body back. And how could I survive a lifetime trapped inside Sumi's body? Especially since I wore the face of a suspected killer?

Kim wrapped an arm around my waist and hugged me close. His warmth helped quell the shivers coursing through me. "Everything is going to be okay," he whispered in my ear. "I will get you home safely, and together we will stop Sumi once and for all."

"That's right." The old man patted my arm. "Don't you worry about a thing. Just give me a moment to pack my things, and we can all be on our way." He pushed out of his chair and walked toward the kitchen.

Kim's arms fell from my waist. "Excuse me?"

The man stopped. "Of course. You didn't really think I'd let you two go off without me, did you? Especially when it's apparent you're in so much trouble. We can take my wife's car. It's in the garage."

"Wife?" I asked. The doilies and pictures on the wall suddenly made sense. "Is she here?"

"No." His voice softened. "She passed ten years ago."

I placed my fingers against my lips, wishing I could take my question back. "I'm so sorry."

The man smiled. "There's no need to be sorry. We'll be together again. Someday."

"In another life?" Kim asked.

The man was quiet a moment before answering. "I sincerely hope not. I'm an old soul, as I sense you two are as well. And because of the many lifetimes I've lived, I'm hoping this is my last one on this earth. I'm ready for ... " He paused. "What's next."

Gene's words swirled inside my head. Did I want this to be my last life? When I drew my last breath, would I be ready for what was *next*? There was an old saying that samurai were cursed to keep being reborn as samurai. Was that what I wanted? An endless loop of lives spent fighting? Just the thought exhausted me, making me feel tired beyond my years.

The back of my neck prickled, and I glanced over my shoulder to find Kim staring at me with an unreadable expression on his face. Finally, he gave the smallest shake of his head. "I will follow you down whatever path you walk."

I slipped my hand inside his before turning back to Gene. "Thank you for your generous offer, but we can't have you go with us. The body-swapping is only a fraction of our problems. We have people chasing us, people who want to lock up me and my friend forever. Not to mention, the girl who has my body isn't going to give it up easily. Our journey will be a dangerous one, and I can't have you risk your life for us."

He snorted. "My life is my life. I'm the only one who gets a say in whether or not it's put at risk." Rosie snorted in agreement at his feet. "Besides," Gene continued, "it sounds like your life is in jeopardy, and who's to say my life is worth more than yours? I'm going with you."

Kim looked at me with his eyebrows raised, as if to ask, *Who is this guy?*

I could only shrug.

Gene smiled. "Besides, I've waited a long time for you two to show up." Before we could respond, he walked to the door and plucked a jacket off a hook. "How are the others? You've found them all, haven't you?"

My throat went tight and I nearly choked. "Others?"

He waved my question away with his hand. "Yes, of course. Kiyomori, Yorimichi, and Seiko. You five were woven together so tightly in the past, I'm sure those ties followed you through to this lifetime, yes?"

The weight of his words hit me like a punch in the stomach, knocking the air from my lungs. *It couldn't be.* But what other explanation was there? How else could he know about our past lives?

Kim's fingers slid from mine as he took several steps backward. The sun filtering in through the window reflected against his wide eyes. "Are you telling me you're—but you can't be." He swallowed, and added in a soft voice, "Can you?"

Gene quirked an eyebrow. "So my two greatest warriors

think nothing of finding each other. But you would believe it impossible to stumble across your old master?"

The strength I needed to stand bled out of me. I collapsed against the couch with my hand clasped tightly over my mouth. A thousand words spilled up my throat, only to be held back by the fingers clamped over my lips. It wasn't until the shock wore off that I was able to speak. Even then, only one word remained on my tongue. "Lord Toyotomi?"

Gene smiled. "Maybe five hundred years ago. Now? I've happily spent this lifetime as a writer." He gestured to a bookshelf against the far wall and the row of paperbacks bearing the name Gene Landon on the spine. One title in particular caught my eye and confirmed my suspicion about Gene's identity. It read, *Finding Balance through the Art of Meditation.*

Kim made a choking sound and pressed his fist to his chest. "It doesn't matter how many lifetimes have passed— you will always be my Lord Toyotomi."

Gene waved his hands in the air. "Please, that's not necessary."

Kim dropped his hand. The muscles in his jaw flexed as he worked his teeth back and forth. "I understand. It is because I failed you in the past. I have dishonored myself and brought disgrace to you."

"What?" Gene's eyebrows arched in surprise. "Nothing could be further from the truth."

"How can you say that?" Kim asked. "I failed you."

"Yoshido, you did not—"

"You died!" Kim cried. "You died, and I wasn't there to stop it. Not only that, I was unable to kill your murderer to avenge your death. There is no greater dishonor than that."

Without warning Kim spun around, opened the front door, and disappeared outside. The door slammed behind him with enough force to rattle the pictures against the wall.

Rosie stared at the door and whined.

"Kim!" I jumped to my feet, but Gene grabbed my arm before I could go after him.

"This must be a great shock to him. Give him a moment to himself. He'll be fine."

I wasn't so sure. I chewed my lip and stared anxiously at the door.

"Do you want to know how I know he'll be okay?" His hand fell from my arm.

Reluctantly, I turned my eyes away from the door and looked at Gene. "How?"

"Remember the first day you came to me all those years ago? I led you out into the courtyard, where we found Yoshido."

I nodded. How could I forget the moment that had been branded on my heart forever? If I closed my eyes, I could still picture Yoshido kneeling beneath the cherry tree, his fingers curled into the soft earth at his knees as pink blossoms drifted down on him like snow. "He'd been mourning the death of his betrothed."

"Yes. And do you remember what I told you then?"

I blinked away the memory. "You told me true love would never weigh a person down. That there were heavier emotions."

He placed a hand on my shoulder. "Such as?"

I swallowed. "Guilt."

He nodded. "Such a useless emotion, wouldn't you agree? It can't change anything. But our Yoshido, or Kim as he is now called, has an abundance of it. Before you came along, he would spend all his days sulking in the gardens or spilling blood on the battlefield. But meeting you changed him, just as I knew it would. You brought him back to life. You reminded him there is more to the world than grief and guilt. That's how I know he'll be fine. He'll always be fine as long as he has you."

A tight knot rose inside my throat. "And I will always be there for him. But that doesn't change the fact he's right. We were supposed to protect you—and we failed."

"No." He shook his head. "I failed you. I had long suspected Zeami carried darkness inside him. I was the one who foolishly thought I could help him. And by keeping him around, I put the viper in our beds."

I'd found Lord Toyotomi all those years ago, dying with an arrow protruding from his chest. The guilt I'd carried with me since, that I'd disappointed the man who'd been like a father to me, had been an agonizing burden. I couldn't believe he held himself responsible. "But—"

He held up a hand to silence me. "What good is it to argue about yesterday when it doesn't change tomorrow?"

My mouth snapped shut. Leave it to Lord Toyotomi to say something that made so much sense. I rushed forward and did the thing I'd longed to do for nearly five hundred years: I hugged him.

He made a startled sound that dissolved into a chuckle. "Oh, my dear, it pains me to hear you were unsuccessful in your last battle." He shook his head. "I had hoped by making you a samurai, I'd saved your life. Now it looks like I did quite the opposite." He sighed. "How you must blame me for the way things turned out."

I thought about that. If he'd never asked me to be a samurai, then I never would have discovered how to control my ki.

I would have spent my life as a courtesan instead of a warrior. And most of all, I never would have met and fallen in love with Yoshido.

Kim walked back inside before I could answer. Unlike at his departure, he shut the door quietly behind him before jamming his hands into his pockets and bowing his head. "Please forgive my abrupt departure. I was"—he lifted his head—"taken aback."

Gene held his hand out to him. "My dear boy, I couldn't be more proud of you if you were my own son."

The muscles in Kim's jaw tightened and he didn't move. That didn't stop Gene from reaching forward, snagging Kim's wrist, and pulling him into a hug.

"I won't," Kim said, his words tight, "I won't let you down again."

Gene laughed and pulled away. "Do you really want to bring me honor?"

Kim nodded. "Of course."

Gene clapped his hands together. "Well then, do as I have done. Live your life to the greatest of your capabilities."

"But—" Kim began.

Gene shook his head. "You devoted your life to me in the past. You've earned this one. And it looks like you two haven't had an easy time of it." He patted me lightly on the shoulder. "This time, let me help *you*. What do you say? It's been a long time since I had an adventure."

A slow smile crept onto Kim's face as he glanced at me. "What do you think?"

I smiled back. "We *could* use all the help we can get."

"Excellent." Gene rubbed his hands together eagerly. "Rileigh, you should probably drive, as our Kim may still be dizzy from his earlier crash." He pulled keys out of his pocket and tossed them to me. "We can work on a plan for getting your body back as we drive."

I couldn't help but laugh. For the first time since I'd awoken in the wrong body, I felt like everything was going to be okay. And how could it not? Lord Toyotomi was the wisest man I'd ever known. With him on our side, there was no way we could fail.

"Okay then." Gene turned around and walked toward the kitchen. "Just let me grab my wallet and Rosie's leash, and we'll be on our way."

Rosie thumped her tail happily against the floor.

Kim slid his fingers through mine and squeezed my hand tight. "I'm sorry for walking out on you earlier."

I gave him a playful bump in the side. "I wasn't worried."

He arched an eyebrow. "No?"

"Nope. You couldn't get rid of me if you tried, Gimhae Kim." I shrugged. "Like it or not, you're stuck with me."

He brushed a piece of hair from my eyes. "And that's just the way I want it. No matter what lifetime or body you find yourself in, we're meant to be together. I am more sure of that than anything else in my life."

He leaned forward and, as much as I hated having him kiss me in this body, there was a greater part of me that no longer cared.

But before his lips could meet mine, Rosie barked sharply. She ran to the door, jammed her nose against the frame, and gave a low growl.

Kim jerked back and we both looked at Gene, who stood

frozen in the kitchen doorway. The leash in his hands fell to the floor.

Rosie's growl deepened and her lips peeled back to reveal her clenched teeth.

A tremor danced down my spine. "What's going on?" I asked.

Gene held out his cane, using it to push me and Kim back as he marched to the front door. "There's been a change of plans, I'm afraid. You two are going to have to go on without me."

"What?" Kim went rigid at my side. "We just found you! And now you're leaving us? Why?"

Gene moved Rosie back and jerked the door open, startling the Network agent on the other side. Before the man could raise his gun, Gene grabbed him by the arm and flipped him over his shoulder. The man landed with a grunt at Gene's feet. Gene lifted his head in our direction. "I can't go because I have to make sure you aren't followed. It's the only way you'll escape and make it back in time."

"No!" Kim's hands balled into fists. "I wasn't there for you in the last life. I won't leave you on your own again. We'll fight them together."

A blur of color flashed behind Gene. He whirled around and raised his hand, making a fist. He turned back to us and opened his fingers, letting the dart he'd captured fall to the floor at his feet.

I nearly choked. "How did you—"

He shook his head and smiled. "Another time. You need to go."

"We're not leaving you," Kim said.

Gene adjusted the dark glasses on his face. "And I told

you that this life is your own. You owe me nothing, Yoshido. Let me repay your years of faithful service in your past life by making sure you get to live this one. You two need to make it back home before Senshi gets stuck in that body. As you can see"—he gestured to the unconscious man on the floor—"I am more than capable of stalling these men."

Kim folded his arms. "What if I refuse?"

Gene rolled up his sleeves, revealing arms decorated with faded tattoos. "Then I'll make you go."

Rosie whined once before turning back to the open door with a growl.

Kim frowned. "I really don't see how you could possibly—"

"Really?" Gene cocked his head to the side. "You may still be an exceptional warrior, Yoshi, but please remember I also have skills of my own."

Without warning, he raised his hand and what felt like an invisible wall slammed into us, knocking us both to the ground.

Blinking and stunned, Kim and I scrambled back to our feet.

Gene lowered his hand. "Without your true body, my dear Senshi, you are no match for my ki manipulation."

He was right. And even if I had my body, his powers had always been greater than mine.

"Please don't fight me on this. I will push you two from my house if I have to." Gene raised his hand and caught another dart a mere inch before it slammed into his chest. He tossed it to the ground.

Kim and I exchanged another glance. Last time we'd been under attack, our dear Lord Toyotomi had been mortally wounded by an arrow to the chest. If we left him alone, how were we to know history wouldn't repeat itself?

Just then, a black figure crashed through the window. We threw our hands up, shielding our faces as shards of glass exploded into the room as the man landed on the couch.

Rosie yelped and ran for the kitchen.

The Network agent jumped off the couch and aimed his gun at my head.

"Go!" Gene shouted before raising his hand. A blue light pulsed from his fingers and slammed into the man's gut. He fell back onto the coffee table, which splintered under his weight.

Gene raised his other hand in our direction, his fingertips glowing brightly. "Do I have to tell you again?"

Behind him, another man ran through the door while another climbed through the broken window. A fight would only slow us down, and I was running out of time. If I wanted to get my and Q's bodies back, we had to leave. "Come on, Kim!" I looped my arm through his and pulled him into the kitchen.

"Take Rosie with you!" Gene called. "She's a passive spirit and the fighting won't do her any good."

We found Rosie in the back of the small kitchen, shivering against a door. Kim gently pulled her aside by the collar and opened the door, which luckily led to the garage and an old Subaru parked inside.

Kim ran to the passenger door and climbed inside.

"C'mon, girl!" I patted my leg, urging Rosie to follow me. I opened the back door of the car and ushered Rosie inside. After closing her safely in, I opened the front door and climbed in myself.

I stuck the key in the ignition but found myself unable to turn it. The sounds of fighting grew quiet inside the house.

"Rileigh." Kim gently touched my shoulder. "This is what he wants."

"I know." I bit my lip to keep it from quivering. "But we just got him back. I don't know how to leave him again."

"We have to." Kim reached forward and turned the key. The car's engine rumbled to life. "When this is all over, we'll come back for him." He looked over his shoulder at the panting dog in the backseat. "We'll have to get Rosie home, after all."

"Right." I swallowed, my throat tight. "We'll come back."

I muttered a silent prayer he'd still be here when we did.

24

Japan, 1492

Chiyo arrived at the village under the cloak of night. After slitting Ryuu's throat, she'd taken the first horse she could find and fled the bandit camp before anyone realized what she'd done.

Miraculously, her sense of direction had held true and after hours on horseback, she'd arrived at Yoshido's village.

Ryuu's men would be furious with her once they discovered his body. She knew they'd demand her death, so she fled to the only person who'd be able to protect her. Her samurai. Her Yoshido.

She dismounted from her horse and tied the reins to a nearby post with trembling fingers. She hadn't been able to stop shaking since she left camp. She glanced at her hands. Ryuu's blood stained her fingers and darkened her nails. She went to wipe them on her robes, but they, too, were stained crimson.

Chiyo cursed silently under her breath. This was not the reunion she'd imagined. She raked her hands through her hair, trying to untangled the knots. For the last year she'd day-dreamed what it would be like to finally see Yoshido again. Of course, in those dreams she wore silk robes and her hair was styled. Her beauty would take his breath away and he'd feel compelled to open his arms. She'd rush into his embrace and all would be well.

Chiyo sighed at the thought and her lips pulled into a smile. After a year of living in terror, the expression felt foreign on her face.

But that didn't matter. She imagined she would get used to it quickly enough. After all, once she was reunited with her samurai she was sure nothing but a lifetime of smiles awaited her.

Now she just had to find him.

But before she could begin her search, the sound of footsteps approached behind her. She whirled around and found a samurai, with much sharper features than her Yoshido, approaching. He stopped in front of her with his hand resting on the hilt of his blade. His eyes traveled the length of her body, growing larger when they took in the blood stains on her robe. He grinned. "Just what do we have here?"

Her pulse quickening, Chiyo quickly bowed her head. "Please. I have travelled very far in search of someone. Perhaps you can help me find him?"

The samurai folded his arms. "Perhaps I can. Do you have a name?"

"Yes." She looked up eagerly. "I am searching for my be-trothed, a samurai by the name of Yoshido."

He jerked back suddenly, before a bark of a laugh

escaped his lips. "Oh this is too good. *You* are Yoshido's betrothed? I thought you were killed by bandits."

Chiyo fought the urge to scowl at him—she knew better than to disrespect a samurai. Still, how dare he find her suffering amusing! The tingle of electricity sparked between her fingertips and she quickly balled her hands into fists before he noticed. "No. I was merely held hostage. If you do not mind, I have travelled far and I am exhausted from my escape. Could you please take me to him?"

"He is in there." The samurai crossed his arms and glanced at a building over his shoulder. "He is currently *assisting* another samurai." He grinned, and the wickedness of it rolled through Chiyo's stomach. There was *something* this man wasn't telling her—and it filled her with dread. "But I cannot allow you to go wandering through the master's estate by yourself," he continued. "What kind of samurai would I be? Besides, I would not miss this for the world." He offered her his arm.

Chiyo couldn't put her finger on it, but something about him reminded her of Ryuu. Maybe it was the quirk of his smile, or the glimmer in his eye. Regardless of what it was, she was certain the last thing she wanted to do was go anywhere with him. She forced a smile to her face. "Thank you. That is very kind." She reached for his arm and uncurled her fingers. Before they touched, a spark of electricity leapt from her fingers into his body.

He opened his mouth and a strained gurgling emerged. A second later, his eyes rolled into the back of his head and he dropped to the ground. Chiyo waited long enough to make sure his chest still rose and fell with breath before she darted toward the building he'd indicated. After all, she didn't need to be in any worse trouble than she already was.

Chiyo entered the building and a sour smell assaulted her nostrils. She pressed a hand to her nose and took several gulping breaths through her mouth. She'd lived with bandits long enough to recognize the smell of death when it greeted her.

She glanced around the narrow hallway with its rice paper doors. She must be in a house of death. But that didn't make sense. What on earth would Yoshido be doing here?

Perhaps the samurai outside had been playing a cruel joke on her. She started to turn around when she heard the sound of muffled voices from down the hall. One of them sounded female and the other voice had to be her Yoshido!

Her heart fluttered. Breathless, she ran down the hall as fast as her feet would carry her. Finally, after living through a year of hell, the reunion she dreamed about would finally be made real. She wondered if he'd even lose himself in the moment and kiss her. A heated blush warmed her cheeks at the thought. It would be improper of him to do so, but she'd forgive him—just like she'd forgive him for not rescuing her. She'd almost reached the corner, his name on the tip of her tongue, when she heard him speak.

"There is a samurai. His name is Yoshido."

She skidded to a halt just before the corner. That didn't make sense. *Why would he refer to himself in the third person?* She peeked her head around the wall. Yoshido sat in the hallway facing a rice paper door. The slender silhouette of a girl faced him from the other side. *What on earth were they doing?*

"Ah yes," the girl answered from the other side of the door. "The irksome one. I have heard of him."

Yoshido sputtered and the girl laughed, the sound of it twisted a knife into Chiyo's heart. Her legs grew weak and she grabbed the corner of the wall to keep from falling. The samurai outside had said Yoshido was training another samurai. But there was something else going on here—Chiyo could feel it in the air, crushing against her and making it hard to breathe.

"Yes, well, be cautious with him," Yoshido continued.

"I thought you said I was the dangerous one," the girl said.

"You are," he agreed. "Be cautious of his heart. You hold it."

No. Oh, please, no. The pain of his words cut deeper into Chiyo than Ryuu's dagger ever had. She covered her mouth with her hands to keep from crying out. This couldn't be happening. This wasn't how her reunion was supposed to go.

"I-I do not understand," the girl said.

Yoshido paused before he raised his hand and placed it against the rice paper. "I love you, Senshi."

The room tilted on its side and waves of nausea twisted through Chiyo's gut. *No. No. No, no, no!* A moan rolled up her throat and she fled down the hallway before she could give herself away. Only after she exited the building did she allow the sob she'd fought to burst from her throat. Chiyo collapsed to the ground as fat, hot tears spilled from her eyes, only to soak into the dusty ground at her blood-stained fingertips. She was too late. She'd been gone too long and now her samurai loved another—some *Senshi.*

She remained on the ground until the last of her tears had dried. And still, the weight of her grief kept her pinned down. What was she to do now? She had no home. No family. And no samurai to love and protect. She had *nothing.*

Chiyo raised her hand to her face to rub her burning eye,

and that's when she noticed the blue spark dancing along her fingertips.

Well, almost nothing.

Slowly, she pulled herself to her feet and made her way down the path to her horse. She couldn't remain here a moment longer. When she passed the place where she'd jolted the samurai, she noticed he was no longer there. It was just as well. She wasn't staying. She couldn't live in a place where the man she loved loved another.

She formed a plan as she untied her horse and mounted the saddle. With nowhere else to go, and no husband to want her, she would return to the bandit camp and declare herself their leader. And if anyone opposed her? She lifted her hand and watched the blue sparks roll across her fingers. She'd kill them. Because that's what you did when the world turned its back on you.

A numbness settled over her as she kicked her horse into a gallop. She was on her own. It was time she realized that the only person who was going to take care of Chiyo was Chiyo.

25

Several hours later, we entered Illinois.

The knots of anxiety pulling tight across my body finally began to loosen. We'd crossed two state lines, and there'd been no sign of the Network. And our luck hadn't ended there. When the gas gauge fell into the red, Kim found a handful of twenty dollar bills rolled up inside the glove box.

Worried I might be spotted thanks to the news broadcast of my face, I stayed inside the car while Kim led Rosie around a grassy area sectioned off for dogs at a rest stop. We didn't have a leash, but it was soon apparent we didn't need one. Rosie barely walked more than a couple of feet in front of Kim before she'd turn her head anxiously around to make sure he was still there.

When Rosie finished her business, Kim led her back inside the car and I moved the shifter into gear. "Ready?"

He nodded and reached into the backseat to give Rosie a pat on the head.

She grinned, her tongue lolling out the side of her mouth.

"But the second we switch you back—" he began.

"I know." I didn't need him to finish. I could read the emotion radiating off him like I could the pages of a book. "We'll drive straight to Gene's house. I'm sure he's okay." My words sounded hollow, even to me. I couldn't help but worry he might be hurt ... or worse.

I shook my head, as if I could dislodge the thought from my mind. Gene would be okay. Even though he was blind, he was obviously a skilled fighter, and his ki powers surpassed my own. He was fine. He had to be.

Kim said nothing. His eyes continued to flick to the side mirror, scanning the cars behind us.

I licked my lips. "How are we looking?"

"So far so good. There doesn't appear to be anyone following us."

"That's a good thing, right?"

He sighed and brought his eyes forward. "Yes and no. As a former general, I'm familiar with strategy. They *know* where we're going, Rileigh." His eyes met mine and held them for several seconds before I was forced to return my attention to the road. "If they figure they can't catch us during the chase, they're going to cut their losses and wait for us where they know we'll show up."

"Son of hibachi," I muttered.

He nodded. "So you see the problem. I'm sure they've been in contact with Wendell, who is keeping the other samurai updated—including Sumi, who he thinks is you."

A dull ache began to throb beneath my temples as a headache formed. "So Sumi will be expecting us."

"Exactly," he agreed. "She knows we're coming, and she'll have time to prepare."

My throat tightened. I hadn't considered that. "You think we're driving into a trap?"

He was quiet a moment. "I've been thinking about something."

"Do you have a plan?" I asked hopefully.

"Not exactly. Maybe Lord Toyo—" He stopped and swallowed. "Maybe *Gene* was right. We're not in Japan anymore. Maybe, for once, we *should* stop fighting."

I tightened my grip on the wheel to keep from swerving into the other lane. "*What?*"

He turned away from me and stared out the window. "We know if we go home we'll be walking into a fight—possibly one we won't win. So what's stopping us from turning this car around and driving someplace they'd never find us? We could do it, you know. We're warriors. We know how to survive on our own. We could disappear, just the two of us."

I blinked as I stared at the road ahead of us. Never in my life would I have expected Kim to suggest we turn away from a fight. "Is that . . . what you want?"

"It's not as easy as what I *want*." From the corner of my eye, I could see his lips pressed into a thin line. "I'm a warrior, Rileigh. Every bone inside my body is telling me to fight for what is right—even if it means we don't win. But then there's you. We suffered so much in the last life, and we've suffered in this one. There are about a million things that could go wrong if we go home. I don't know how I'd survive if I lost you again."

I sat silent and let his words wash over me.

"It's not that I don't want to stop Sumi and get you back inside your body," he continued. "Of course, I want her to pay for what she's done to us. But more than that, I want to keep you safe. It doesn't matter what body you're wearing, you're still my Senshi. And I will love you from this life into the next. If you're tired of fighting, just say the word and we'll disappear."

I chewed my lip. He was right—with Sumi and the Network expecting us, there was a pretty big chance we'd fail in our mission to get my and Q's bodies back. How easy would it be to just drive to Mexico? Or anyplace where Kim and I would never be found? We could spend the rest of our lives alone and together.

But as tempting as that sounded, could I really stand to wake up every day, look in the mirror, and stare at a face that wasn't my own? And what would happen to Quentin? If he'd been apprehended by the Network, he'd be stuck in a cell forever as Whitely. I couldn't let that happen.

And what about my mom? Sumi had no problems killing her own parents. Why would she hesitate to do the same to my mom or the other samurai?

I wouldn't risk anyone's life for a chance at escape.

I shook my head. "We have to go back. I know the odds are stacked against us and the risk is huge. But we have to at least *try* to fix the mess Sumi made. Q's counting on us. We can't desert our friends."

Kim stared at me a long moment. Finally, he sighed. "I know. Your desire to always do the honorable thing is one of the many reasons I love you." He reached forward and tucked a loose strand of hair behind my ear, letting his fingers linger on the back of my neck. "We'll get through this."

Not wanting him to sense my doubt, I forced a smile onto my face. Meanwhile, I couldn't help but worry about what would happen if we failed. If I was captured or...worse, then this might be the last few hours I had with Kim—ever. An invisible weight pressed against my chest and I strained to keep my smile locked in place.

As if reading my thoughts, Kim dropped his hand and frowned. "Do not worry. We *will* defeat Sumi and get your body back. And afterwards...I don't really know." A slow grin appeared on his face. "Huh. What do you want to do afterwards? After this whole mishap, I'm not really too keen to work for the Network because—"

"They're idiots?" I offered.

"I was going to say because they tried to kill us. But your answer is just as good. So if we don't work for the Network, what do we do?"

I let his question swirl around my mind a minute before I finally shrugged. "I have no idea." I chuckled. "It's crazy because a few days ago I thought I had it all figured out. I was going to attend a local college and get a criminal justice degree. I assumed I'd work for the Network for the rest of my life."

"And now?"

"I don't know." I shrugged. "I couldn't join an organization that tried to hunt me down. But at the same time, it's not like there are a lot of job openings for reincarnated samurai these days."

"I was thinking the same thing."

I tapped my thumbs against the steering wheel. "Which is

unfortunate, because we could really use a few more samurai right now."

"I agree." He rested his elbow against the window. "I hope our friends are faring better than we are."

"Me too." With Sumi and Whitley as the wolves in sheep's clothing, the other samurai were in considerable danger. And to make it worse, they had no idea. "If Sumi or Whitley hurts any of them . . . " I bit off the rest of my words, and my hands tightened around the steering wheel until my knuckles turned white.

"I know." I watched his jaw flex out of the corner of my eye. He didn't say anymore, and he didn't have to. His intent blazed like fire in his eyes.

I glanced nervously at him. "You know we can't kill them, right? I'm Whitley's soul mate and you're Sumi's. If they die, so do we."

He nodded, his jaw flexing. "I'm not worried about Whitley—he's an idiot. But Sumi is dangerous. If I have the chance to make sure she never hurts anyone ever again, I'm going to take it."

Cold fingers clamped around my throat. "What are you saying? If you get the chance, you'd sacrifice yourself just to kill her?"

He said nothing, his eyes trained on the road ahead.

"Kim!" I turned, accidentally swerving the car onto the shoulder in the process. After quickly righting it, I glared at him. "I won't let you do it. We've been through too much in this life to lose each other again."

He shook his head. "I'm a samurai, Rileigh. I don't know how to be anything else. And as a samurai, I will sacrifice everything to make sure the people I care about are kept safe."

"No." I shook my head. "No. No. No. No. I won't let you do it. There has to be another way, Kim."

He looked at me. "Is there? Because so far, nothing else has worked. The longer Sumi is left alive, the more dangerous she becomes. How many people does she have to kill before we put an end to her?"

I pressed my teeth together so hard my jaw ached. "None. Because I will figure out another way. So don't do anything stupid."

When he didn't answer me, I glanced at him. He sat, looking straight ahead, with his lips pressed into a thin line. I knew that look—it was the same look he wore before he charged into battle. I knew then he'd made up his mind and there was no talking him out of it.

So I didn't bother.

We were past the point of words, anyway. Lucky for me, I had an advantage in that I knew his plan. If he had the opportunity, he would kill Sumi. So now it was my job to stop Sumi on my own before he had the chance.

The clock was ticking. I needed a plan, and I needed it fast.

26

An hour before we reached St. Louis, Kim told me he was feeling better and offered to drive. And as tired as I was, I let him.

As we drew closer to the city, his eyes flicked from the road ahead to the rearview mirror. I, on the other hand, kept my eyes locked on him. I watched for any signs he'd begun to suspect I was plotting against him. There was no way I would let him sacrifice himself for a chance to kill Sumi. But the problem was, I still hadn't come up with a plan and with us drawing closer to St. Louis by the second, I was nearly out of time.

Oblivious to my worries, Rosie stuck her head out the back window and happily panted in the wind.

A pang of jealously twisted through me. How awesome it would be to be a dog—to have no worries other than finding a soft place to sleep and learning what time dinner would be served.

We passed a sign announcing that St. Louis was only thirty miles away. "We're getting close," Kim said. "We need a plan."

"I agree," I answered, even though I knew mine would have to go against his.

He tapped his thumbs along the steering wheel. "We can't go to any place the Network might suspect we'd show up at. So your condo is off-limits."

I nodded. "The same goes for your dojo and apartment. I'm sure they're watching those places as well."

"Yes." His fingers continued to drum a taiko war rhythm on the steering wheel. "We need a place where we can assess the situation. A place we can regroup and wait for an opportunity to strike. So the question is, where is the last place they would expect us to go?"

I thought about that. With Whitley posing as Q, Quentin's house would be out, and so would Drew's apartment. Michelle's house was probably being watched. So that left...

I smiled at Kim the same moment his eyes locked with mine. A knowing grin pulled at his lips.

"Braden," we said in unison.

Kim turned his attention back to the road. He continued to drum the war beat as he drove.

I settled back into my seat, happy with our plan. It wasn't that Braden wasn't as capable a warrior as the rest of our friends, but his goofy demeanor and distracted tendencies made him appear less of a threat, even though I knew he was every bit as deadly as the rest of us. But because of his outward appearance, the Network would assume he'd be the last of the samurai we'd contact.

That didn't mean we wouldn't have to be careful. I was sure

Sumi and Whitley were working hard to convince the rest of the samurai that I'd brainwashed Kim and we were coming to kill them. It wasn't going to be easy to convince Braden I was really Rileigh, and it would be even more difficult to convince him if he decided to attack.

Hopefully, it wouldn't come to that. We needed all the allies we could get. And let's face it—Rosie wasn't exactly intimidating.

Darkness streaked across the horizon like thick brush-strokes from a calligraphy brush. If Gene's assumption was correct, with night approaching I had less than twelve hours to switch bodies with Sumi before the change became permanent.

I stared at Sumi's reflection in the side mirror, her eyes boring into mine until I had no choice but to look away. As much as it would suck to stay trapped inside the body of my enemy forever, maybe I could learn to live with it—especially if it was a question of Kim's life.

I chewed on my lip as I tried to come up with a plan to ensure Kim wouldn't kill Sumi. But a half hour later, as Kim parked the car along a narrow St. Louis street, I hadn't come up with an answer.

I rubbed my burning eyes and sucked in a deep breath. All my hours without sleep were definitely catching up to me. And now, more than ever, I needed to be on full alert.

Worried lines pinched Kim's forehead. "How are you doing?"

"I'm exhausted," I admitted. "But I know I have to keep going. It's not like I can afford the luxury of a nap."

He reached for my wrist and squeezed lightly. "Soon. This will all be over soon."

His words caused a flutter of fear to stir inside my heart, because I wasn't exactly sure whose end he was talking about.

"But first," he continued, "we need a plan."

I turned my head to the row of brick houses outside my window. Each house was an exact replica of the one beside it, distinguishable only by their landscaping and whether or not a chain-link fence crossed the narrow strip of grass separating the lots.

I recognized Braden's house only because I'd been there before. It had only been a year since Q and I had gone to Braden's house after we'd found out Michelle had disappeared. So the good news was, I knew the layout. "Did you see any suspicious vehicles when we pulled up?"

Kim shook his head. "No. But that doesn't mean they're not out there."

"Right." I surveyed the parked cars, looking for anything out of the ordinary. Unfortunately, with only a single dim streetlight and my lack of danger premonitions, there was no telling who could be lurking in the shadows. "We can't just ring the doorbell. We should take a quick assessment—find out what kind of situation we might be walking into."

"Agreed." He gripped the door handle. "Do you want high ground or low?"

As tired as I was, the least amount of ground to cover, the better. "High. What about Rosie?"

We both glanced behind us at the dog grinning and thumping her tail.

Kim frowned. "It's a cool night. She should be fine in the car with the windows rolled down. Hopefully this won't take long."

Hopefully was right.

"Let's go." He opened the car door and stepped out onto the street. I did the same, making sure to close the door as softly as possible. I hunkered down against the car until Kim crept along the vehicle and joined me. He looked down both ends of the sidewalk before motioning to the corner of the house, indicating which direction he would take.

I nodded.

He set off in a sprint, and I stayed close at his heels. He paused at the edge of the house, leaned over, and laced his fingers together. I only had to put my foot in his hands before he launched me into the air. Landing on the roof in a crouch, I glanced over the side and gave Kim a thumbs-up.

He nodded before darting into the backyard.

From my new vantage point, I surveyed the entire street. Except for a yellow lab who eyed me curiously several yards over, the street remained empty of life. Still, my heart hammered inside my chest, warning me that things were seldom as easy as they appeared.

Keeping low to the shingles so as not to call attention to myself, I crept along the roof to the back of the house.

Once I reached the apex of the roof, I had a clear view of Braden's empty backyard. The only movement came from a rusted swing that swayed lazily in the wind. Wherever Kim was, he was doing an excellent job at staying hidden.

I cleared the apex and climbed down the other side until I reached the roof's edge. I swung my head over the ledge and peered into Braden's window to find it dark and empty. I pulled myself back up on the roof and frowned. If Braden wasn't home—where was he? With Sumi? I sank back on my heels. With time running out, we needed to find him. Kim and I didn't stand a chance without allies.

A car door slammed shut from somewhere nearby.

With a gasp, I flattened myself along the shingles, muttering a silent prayer that we hadn't been followed.

Another car door slammed, followed by the sound of voices in conversation. I heard the metal gate squeal open, and the voices moved into the yard below.

With my pulse racing, I debated what to do. Any movement might draw attention to my location. I had no choice but to remain as still as I could.

"I still can't believe Sumi kidnapped Kim." I recognized Michelle's voice. A second later, she appeared below me. She walked to the wooden deck and sat on the steps.

"We don't know for sure that's what happened," Braden answered. He, too, appeared below me and sat beside Michelle.

She shook her head, her auburn curls bouncing like springs around her head. "Of course that's what happened. Dr. Wendell said Kim was chasing after her when she escaped, and he never reported back to the truck." She shrugged. "What else *could* have happened?"

"I don't know." Braden leaned forward, propping his elbows against his knees. "This whole situation ... Doesn't something feel *off*?"

Michelle chewed on her lip before answering. "Yeah ... I didn't want to say anything around Rileigh and Dr. Wendell because I didn't want them to think Sumi was messing with our heads again. Do you think that could be it?"

"Maybe?" He sighed. "I know it sounds crazy, but I've had this really bad feeling ever since Sumi and Whitley were captured. I can't explain it. The only thing that makes sense is if Sumi *did* mess with our minds. Do you think we should tell the others?"

"I don't know." Michelle tipped her head back to the night sky and I held my breath, praying she wouldn't glance in my direction. "Rileigh's been so..." She was quiet a moment, as if searching for the right word. "Stressed," she said finally.

Braden nodded. "She definitely hasn't been herself, that's for sure. Maybe she's just worried about Kim?"

"Maybe..."

A small wisp of hope fluttered through me. If they had doubts about the situation, maybe there was a chance I really could convince them I was Rileigh.

Michelle turned to Braden. "Thanks for letting me stay with you tonight."

Braden wrapped an arm around her shoulder and drew her against him. "Of course. If what Doctor Wendell says is true, and Sumi really is headed back to St. Louis to kill us, I'm not going to let you out of my sight."

She smiled and nestled her head against his shoulder. "You don't think I can handle myself?"

"What?" Braden looked down at her. "You think I want you here so I can watch over you?" He snorted. "Did you consider maybe I want you here to protect *me*?"

Michelle laughed.

"But as powerful as Sumi is," Braden continued, "I'm even more afraid of your dad. He's not going to kill me, is he?"

"Relax." Michelle shook her head. "He'll never know I was here. I told him I was spending the night at Rileigh's."

Braden nodded and leaned back on his hands. "That's

good." He was quiet a moment. "I just wonder how long we have to worry about Sumi. With all the Network guys here plus us, she'd have to be pretty stupid to come back."

Not stupid, I thought. *Just desperate.*

"Maybe she's desperate." Michelle echoed my thoughts, sending a chill spiraling down my back.

"Desperate for what?" Braden answered. "If it's Kim she's after, isn't he with her?"

"That is the question, isn't it?" She shook her head. "Kim is all she ever wanted. If she has him, what on earth would she come back here for?"

"Dunno," Braden answered. "It doesn't make sense, does it? I just wish Kim would contact us. I'd feel a lot better knowing he's okay—even if he is under mind control."

Just then the bushes in the back of the yard made a soft rustling noise. A second later, Kim pushed through and stepped into the middle of the yard.

Michelle gasped and Braden scrambled to his feet.

I clasped my hand over my mouth and swallowed my own startled cry. Was this really the right time to reveal himself? Then again, it wasn't like we had the luxury of waiting for the perfect moment. I just hoped he knew what he was doing.

Before they could say anything, Kim raised his hands. "I'm fine. And, no, I haven't been brainwashed."

"Kim! Oh my God, I'm so glad you're okay!" Michelle ran to him and threw her arms around his waist.

"Um, babe?" Braden grabbed Michelle's arm and pulled her away from Kim, putting several feet between them. "We don't know for sure that's really *our* Kim." He gave Kim an apologetic look. "No offense."

Kim frowned. "Of course it's me."

"Well, *yeah*." Braden rolled his eyes. "But how do we know Sumi hasn't brainwashed you again? If you were brainwashed, of course you would say you weren't brainwashed. That's kind of the point of being brainwashed, isn't it?"

I fought the urge to smack my palm against my forehead. Leave it to Braden to complicate things.

Kim blinked in confusion. "I really don't—"

"Besides," Braden continued, "if you are brainwashed, how do we know you aren't here to kill us?"

Michelle's eyes widened as if she were considering the possibility. "Are you here to kill us?" She straightened her posture, shifting her weight to her back foot—a stance that would let him know she was prepared to fight.

Kim smiled. "You are wise to be on guard. It lets me know I've trained you well." He held his arms wide and turned a slow circle. "As you can see, I am unarmed."

Braden made a face. "Dude, that doesn't mean anything. Your entire body is a weapon."

Kim's smile grew wider. "Yes, it is. So you should also know that I've been here, watching you since you arrived. If I had any murderous intent, I could have executed it a dozen times now."

Braden and Michelle exchanged uneasy glances.

Kim shook his head. "I hate how Sumi's powers have created mistrust between us. I am in trouble, and need you two on my side now more than ever."

"What kind of trouble?" Michelle asked. "Is Sumi nearby?"

Kim glanced up, meeting my eyes in a silent plea to remain

quiet awhile longer. I motioned him to hurry. He nodded once and turned back to Michelle.

I said a silent prayer he would get them on our side. With their help, we were sure to convince Drew, and possibly even Dr. Wendell. Then Sumi would be the one in trouble.

The thought made me grin.

But no sooner had my lips curled into a smile than a stabbing pain erupted in my shoulder. I flinched and glanced down, only to find a tranquilizer dart lodged below my collarbone.

Oh, crap.

I whirled around and looked for the shooter, but already my vision was hazy. Everything more than a couple feet away became a blur of color. I knew I should signal Kim, but a wave of tingling warmth flooded through my body and my arms became too heavy to move.

The only part of me that remained alert was my heart, which skittered wildly inside my chest. Despite my best efforts to fight the drug, I slumped against the roof. The heavily sanded shingles scraped against my skin as I slowly slid to the edge. I wanted to brace my legs against the gutter and claw my fingers into the shingles, but my body refused to listen.

"Rileigh isn't who you think she is," Kim continued, his voice sounding far away. "Sumi performed a ritual that allowed her to switch bodies with Rileigh. Now Rileigh is trapped inside Sumi's body while Sumi is inside Rileigh's body. I need your help to switch them back."

"What?" I could hear Michelle's surprise through the velvet fog of unconsciousness pressed against me. "C'mon, Kim. That sounds impossible, even for Sumi."

"Yeah," Braden agreed. "We know Sumi's powerful and all—but switching bodies? That's crazy."

"Kim." Michelle's voice was low and soft, the way one might speak to a frightened animal. "Don't you think the more logical explanation is that Sumi's manipulating your mind again? Making you *think* she switched bodies with Rileigh? We need to find her, Kim. We know you were with her. Where is she?"

I'm right here! I wanted to scream, but I only managed a low gurgle no one heard. Invisible weights pulled at my eyelids, and it took every ounce of strength I had to keep them open. The alternating whirl of rooftop and sky flickered before my eyes as I lazily tumbled down the roof. I said a silent prayer Kim would look up before I fell to the ground. Somewhere around here, a Network agent lurked, and I couldn't afford to get caught. Not after all we'd done to make our way back home.

My eyelids drifted shut.

"Kim!"

The shock of hearing my own voice from outside my body fluttered my eyes back open. I watched helpless as I—or, at least, Sumi in my body—ran into the backyard. Even through the haze clouding my vision, I could see the katana strapped to her back—*my* katana.

The burn of anger boiled beneath the numbness inside me. Still, I couldn't move. My leg hung over the gutter, and it was only a miracle no one had looked in my direction. But I couldn't go unnoticed for long. As badly as I wanted to hold on, my fingers were beginning to slip.

Things were definitely not going according to plan.

Kim swiveled on his feet and jerked back. "You!" His hands curled into fists. "You've made a deadly mistake coming here."

Sumi looked at Michelle and Braden. "I told you his mind's been manipulated."

Michelle and Braden exchanged worried glances and retreated to the deck.

"What? No!" He turned to them, his eyes pleading. "The only minds being poisoned here are yours. This is Sumi!" He gestured to my body. "You can't trust her. You must believe me."

"No, Kim." Sumi shook her head. "I'm the same Rileigh I've always been. It's you who's been brainwashed. We know you're working with Sumi, and you've come back here to kill us all."

He took a step toward her, and her hand fluttered to the handle of my katana. "You're a liar. I would never hurt my friends. But you?" He flexed his fingers. "You, I can't wait to kill."

I had to stop this! But how? Unconsciousness beckoned me with silk fingertips. One of my hands slipped from the edge of the roof and dangled beside my leg.

"Easy, Kim." The voice belonged to Dr. Wendell.

I squinted. A blurry Dr. Wendell shape moved into the yard, followed by a blurry Quentin shape. I couldn't be sure, but it looked as if Q—or rather, Whitley—held a dart gun in his hand.

So Whitley had shot me. I should have known. If I made it out of this alive, he and I were going to have a little chat.

"Nobody is going to kill anyone," Dr. Wendell continued. "I just need you to calm down until we can get Quentin here to clear your mind. Everything is going to be okay."

Even through my hazy vision, it looked like Whitley shot Sumi a fearful look. He knew as well as I did that he didn't have Q's healing abilities. Maybe once the others realized—

"Everything is not okay!" Kim yelled, interrupting my

thoughts. "That"—he pointed at my body below—"is Sumi! Why won't any of you believe me?"

This couldn't be happening. We needed our friends to believe us, not turn against us. And now, thanks to the tranquilizer dart, I couldn't even make a run for it. I was royally screwed.

"Kim, we know you've come here to kill us," Dr. Wendell answered. "Because that's what Sumi wants."

"That's not true," Kim said.

"Okay, fine." Dr. Wendell folded his arms across his chest. "If you're not working with Sumi, and you're not here to kill us, then please explain to us why you brought her here?" He lifted his arm and pointed at me.

No sooner had he done so than I lost my battle with unconsciousness. Darkness shrouded my vision and pulled me inside myself. From a faraway place, I thought I heard Michelle gasp as I lost my grip and tumbled to the ground below, right at the feet of my now enemies.

27

The first thing I noticed when I blinked my eyes open was the crushing pain throbbing inside my skull. I tried to lift my head, but it only rolled lazily on my neck as I took in my surroundings. A card table had been pushed against the far wall beside a row of lockers. Beside me was a countertop, complete with sink and cabinets overhead. Gradually, the pieces fell into place inside my hazy mind.

I was in the dojo's break room.

I tried to stand, but something held me in place. Craning my neck over my shoulder, I found that my hands were bound with duct tape to the sides of the folding chair I sat in.

A chill coursed through me, and I snapped awake. I struggled against the tape, but it was bound too tightly. "Son of hibachi," I muttered.

"Good morning."

I jerked my head up and found me—or, at least, Sumi

inside my body—standing in the doorway with her arms crossed over her chest. My katana hung at her hips. Even more important was the beaded leather bracelet wrapped around her wrist—a bracelet I would have to cut loose if I hoped to get my body back.

Sumi walked into the room and the door swung shut behind her.

Morning? This was even worse than I thought. If daylight was here, that meant Quentin and I were nearly sealed inside these bodies forever. How much longer did we have before the transformation was permanent? An hour? Minutes?

Anger burned through me as Sumi walked toward me, a smug smile on her face. Clearly, she thought she'd won—and hadn't she? Because of her I'd lost my body, my best friend, my life, and now—*oh my God.* "What have you done with Kim?" I snarled.

She waved the question away with a look of annoyance. "Nothing… yet. After you fell off the roof, that idiot Dr. Wendell tried to shoot him with the tranquilizer gun, but Kim dashed off and we haven't been able to find him."

I wasn't sure if that was a good thing or a bad thing. Sure, I was glad Sumi hadn't been able to capture Kim. But that meant his plan to kill her was still on. And in my current condition, I wasn't in the best position to stop him.

The break room door pulled open, and Dr. Wendell stepped through. His eyes narrowed when he caught sight of us. "Rileigh, what on earth are you doing in here? You know Sumi is extremely dangerous and shouldn't be addressed alone."

She batted her eyes innocently. "I know. I'm sorry. I was hoping I could get her to tell us where Kim is hiding."

218

I'd never wanted to punch myself in the face so badly. Instead, I rolled my eyes and looked at Dr. Wendell. "Please tell me you're not falling for that load of crap."

He frowned. "Excuse me?"

I tried to shrug, but the duct tape prevented me from doing more than a head bob. "You can't really believe that I—or *Rileigh*—would ever tell you she's sorry."

His eyes narrowed. "If you're trying to make me believe that you're Rileigh trapped inside Sumi's body, forget it. You're wasting your time."

"Why's that?"

"Because I know Rileigh very well. I live with her, and I would think I would notice if she weren't herself."

I arched an eyebrow. "*Right.* Just like you noticed when our building elevator was sabotaged by ninjas. And you were certainly on top of things when Whitley snuck into my bedroom."

"Uh." He scratched at his temple as he looked between me and Sumi.

Sumi shot me a murderous look before waving a hand in the air. "Nice try, *Sumi.* But I already told him how you used your powers on me to get me to reveal personal information."

I snorted. "Dr. Wendell, seriously. You don't believe this load of crap, do you?"

His eyebrows squished together and he opened his mouth, but no words came out.

"Don't worry, Dr. Wendell." Sumi glared at me as she walked to the counter and snatched a roll of duct tape from the top of the microwave. "I can tell she's confusing you with her lies. I'll take care of that." She ripped a small piece of duct

219

tape from the roll, walked over to me, and placed it over my mouth. "There." Sumi smirked. "No more lies."

If looks could kill, I would have vaporized her into a puddle of ooze.

Dr. Wendell frowned. "Right." I couldn't be sure, but I thought I detected the faintest hint of uncertainty in his voice.

Sumi must have noticed as well. Her smirk melted into a scowl. "So when is the Network truck getting here?"

Dr. Wendell blinked several times before glancing at his watch. "Uh, I'm not sure exactly. But I would imagine within the hour."

Panic seized my chest in an icy grip. An hour? How on earth was I supposed to get out of this mess within an hour? And if I didn't, I'd be back on a truck bound for New York— and this time I wouldn't have my ki powers to help me get out.

"You don't know for sure?" Sumi huffed.

He gave her a silent look before answering. "I don't know the exact time, no. But they'll be here soon enough."

Sumi turned to me, an indecipherable expression on her face. "You should probably call them to confirm."

His brow furrowed. "And you shouldn't be alone with the fugitive."

Sumi's eyes never left mine—which was really trippy considering they were *my* eyes. "Then send Quentin in here. Maybe he can get some information out of her with his mind powers?"

I pulled against my restraints but only succeeded in rubbing my wrists raw. I knew as well as Sumi that Whitley didn't have mind powers. But I also knew my chances of survival plummeted the second Dr. Wendell walked out the door.

He turned for the door, hesitating long enough to fill me

with desperate hope. A second later, he shook his head and pushed through.

Sumi ripped the tape from my mouth. White hot pain burned across my face and I was certain that as long as I remained in Sumi's body, I would never have to wax again. She leaned down so only inches separated our faces. "We're going to have a conversation." She pulled a dagger out of her boot.

My throat went dry as she brought the blade to my face. I didn't know what kind of conversation she had planned, but I thought it was safe to assume we weren't going to discuss the Cardinals' chance at the Series.

She jabbed the dagger into the bottom of my chin. Pain exploded where the tip tore into my skin. I clenched my teeth together to keep from crying out. I wouldn't give her the satisfaction.

"You're going to tell me where Kim is," she hissed in my ear. "Or else things are going to get messy."

I fought the urge to groan. Why did things always have to get messy? Why couldn't enemies ever offer to settle their scores with a game of *rock-paper-scissors*? Instead, I curled my lips and spoke through clenched teeth. "I have no idea."

"You're lying!" She dug the knife blade deeper into my skin.

I flinched and balled my fingers into fists. Something warm and sticky began to trail down my throat. "Careful. Are you sure you really want to damage your own body like this?" I asked.

She laughed. "As if I care. I'm never going back into that body. So save yourself some trouble and tell me where Kim is."

My eyes darted to the bracelet at her wrist. It was close enough to touch, if I weren't bound to the chair. There had to be a way I could break free...

"I'm warning you, *Rileigh*." She spoke my name as if it burned her tongue. "If you don't tell me where Kim is, I will kill you. I'll tell the others you broke free, attacked me, and I had no choice." Hate blazed in her eyes like a torch, so hot I could almost feel the heat emanating from them.

I glared back, my jaw throbbing from having my teeth clenched together. *Think, Rileigh!* I needed a plan, which meant I had to stall Sumi until I came up with one.

"Why do you care so much about finding Kim?" I asked. "He hates you. You know that, right?"

She flinched at the word hate and jabbed the knife deeper into my skin. Pain flashed across my vision in white streaks. "No. Kim's confused, that's all. And it's because you're always ruining things. He said he was disgusted by my powers—but now I don't have them anymore. And once you're gone, he'll remember that he loved me first. He'll see that I've given up everything to be with him, and he'll love me again."

And she honestly believed that—I could see it in her eyes. For the briefest second, I almost felt sorry for her. How awful to spend a lifetime loving a man who would never love you back.

She pressed her lips together. "If you really don't know where Kim is, then I have no further use for you." She pulled the point of the knife from my chin and laid the long edge of the blade against my neck.

Son of hibachi.

I went rigid, afraid any movement would drive the blade into my skin. I considered screaming, but knew Sumi would slit my throat before I even opened my mouth.

I struggled to calm my heaving chest. I couldn't believe that after everything I'd done, Sumi was going to win. And worse still, once she killed me, there'd be nothing I could do to help Quentin.

Sumi grinned. "I've been waiting a long time for this."

I refused to close my eyes. If she was going to kill me, I wouldn't give her the pleasure of seeing me flinch. I tilted my chin so I could meet her stare head-on. How ironic—the last thing I would see before I died would be my own eyes staring back at me.

"Got any last words?" she asked. "Not that I care."

"Yeah." I licked my dry lips. I knew if I wasn't around to stop Kim, Sumi was as good as dead herself. "See you on the other side."

28

What the hell do you think you're doing?"

Sumi kept the knife at my neck as we both turned in the direction of the voice.

Any other time, having my best friend interrupt my impending murder would be a good thing. But considering it was really Whitley inside Q's body, I was hardly relieved. Rock, allow me to introduce you to Hard Place.

Sumi pulled the knife from my neck and I exhaled loudly. "What I'm *doing* doesn't concern you, Whitley," she said.

"Is that so?" He folded his arms across his chest. "That happens to be my soul mate you're poking with a knife. So, yeah, that concerns me. If she dies, so do I—a fact I'm sure you're well aware of."

"I'm fine. Thanks for asking," I mumbled.

Sumi shot me a dirty look before sliding the blade back

inside her boot. "I wasn't going to kill her—I was simply trying to get her to tell me where Kim is hiding."

Whitley made a face that clearly showed he did not believe her. "You know, I agreed to help you in this insane scheme because you promised you would stop hunting me down. I've done everything you asked. I tricked Rileigh and her healer friend into going to the gym. I agreed to swap my life with his so he couldn't use his power against you—which, by the way, made me the proud owner of the most ridiculous car in existence. All this, and yet here you are, with a blade to her neck, which is really a blade to *my* neck. Call me crazy, but I'm starting to get the feeling you don't want to keep your end of the bargain."

I shook my head. "You're just now realizing that? How many times does she have to kill you?"

Sumi huffed. "Stop being so dramatic. I already told you I was only questioning her. Don't you think if I wanted to kill you I could have done it a hundred times already?" She extended her hand, and Whitley shrank back. Having no power of his own—unless you counted his ability to be a super ass-hat—was it possible he didn't realize Sumi no longer had hers?

She pointed to the door. "Now I want you to go back out there and tell that annoying doctor you did everything you could to try to get information out of her." She pointed at me. "But her mind was too strong for you to break."

I strained against the duct tape until my skin burned. Still, it held fast. "Don't do it," I told him. "She's lying. She's going to kill me the second you walk out that door."

Whitley's frown deepened.

"Shut up!" Sumi snarled. She turned to Whitley and pointed at the door. "What are you waiting for? Get out of here!"

He took a step backward.

"No!" I knew my life depended on whether or not he stayed. "If you leave me alone with her, we're both as good as dead."

Sumi whirled on me. "I thought I told you to shut up!" Her open hand connected with my cheek hard enough to topple me over, chair and all. My head smacked against the concrete and white fireworks exploded in my vision.

The duct tape, however, remained intact. So not only was I still taped to the stupid chair, but now I was sideways and taped to the stupid chair. *Not* an improvement.

Sumi brushed her hands together. "Now Whitely, I believe I asked you to wait outside. And please make sure we're not interrupted."

"You don't have to listen to her," I said. "She doesn't have her powers anymore."

Sumi's eye's flew wide and her mouth snapped shut.

Whitley's lips curled into a grin. He cocked his head. "I'm sorry. Say that again?" *Oh, crap.* I pressed my lips together, realizing too late I'd made a horrible mistake. I needed Whitley to stay so Sumi wouldn't kill me. But now that he knew Sumi was powerless, would he try to kill her and in the process kill Kim?

"You're dead," Sumi whispered, her eyes blazing. Slowly, she withdrew my katana from the sheath at her hip. "I'm going to kill you in this life and every life thereafter." She raised the sword over her head. "I'm going to take from you any chance of happiness—just like you've taken mine."

Fear squeezed my throat as I tried in vain to shimmy the chair backward. I'd barely made it an inch when she swung.

"Not so fast!" Millimeters before the blade met my neck, Whitley caught her arm and spun her around to face him.

The sword wavered in her hands. "Let go of me!"

Whitley brought his face next to hers. "Make me." Before she could respond, he made a fist, reared back, and punched her in the jaw.

I couldn't help but flinch. That *had* to hurt.

Sumi spun a lazy circle before she collapsed to the floor. She let go of the sword, and it clattered to the ground just out of reach of my fingers.

Sumi jerked her head and blinked. An angry red welt bloomed across her chin—*my* chin, really. "How dare you! I should kill you right now!"

Whitley smirked. "Go ahead then, princess. Give it your best shot."

Son of hibachi. This was exactly what I didn't need right now. With Kim and the Network on their way here, I needed to be back in my body before they arrived—*not* breaking up a fight between my two worst enemies—a fight that would leave either Kim or myself dead.

I craned my neck over my shoulder. My katana was only an inch away—if only I could work my way over to it without being noticed. I glanced back at Sumi as she slowly climbed to her feet, her murderous gaze locked on Whitley. Yeah, I think I had a few minutes on my own.

Whitley raised his hands, his fingers curled into fists. "You're not so tough without your powers, are you?"

She bared her teeth. "Who says I need powers to kill you?" She raised a hand over her head. Balancing on one leg, she lifted the opposite knee.

Awesome. It was about to get all kung-fu up in here. Which meant I had to stop this before someone got killed. Using all of my strength, I heaved my weight backward and managed to scoot a hair closer to my katana. I tried not to groan. If I kept it up, I'd reach the blade by tomorrow.

Sumi cried out and launched herself at Whitley, and the two became a blur of flying fists and feet.

I had to hurry.

I sucked in a deep breath and prepared myself to try again. But before I could move, a weird drifting sensation came over me. I shook my head, trying to dislodge the woozy feeling, but it remained. Had Sumi hit me harder than I thought? Or maybe it was the surreal experience of watching my own body locked in mortal combat with the body of my best friend.

Whitley jerked back and placed a hand against his head as if to steady himself. Did he feel it too?

Sumi looked at me and smirked. "You're almost out of time."

That's what that was? The feeling of my spirit severing ties with my old body? A lump pushed up my throat, and I struggled to swallow it down. I couldn't let that happen. Again I threw my weight backward, and again I was rewarded with another fraction of an inch. Only this time, I extended my index finger and was able to touch the edge of the katana's hilt. Success! Now I had to hurry.

Sumi narrowed her eyes at me. "What are you—"

Whitley charged her before she could finish. He swung a foot for her head, which she quickly ducked before it made contact.

Carefully, I coaxed the handle into my hand and flipped the sword around so I could saw into the tape. The drifting sensation grew stronger as I worked. It was the same feeling I got when I plummeted down the incline of a rollercoaster—a feeling that my insides were no longer connected to my outsides.

I didn't have to be a metaphysical expert to know that was probably a bad thing.

From the looks of Whitley and Sumi's sudden sloppy fighting, I knew they were experiencing the same thing as well. Whitley's punch went wide, wobbling over Sumi's head. Her clumsy attempt to duck sent her staggering backward.

Yep. I had to hurry.

I continued sawing feverishly until the tape gave a pop as the blade cut through. I pulled my arm free and set about sawing the tape on my other hand. Second by agonizing second, the blade ate into the tape until it finally broke open. Once free, I climbed to my feet, my legs wobbling as the floor seemed to move beneath my feet.

Sumi snapped her head up as I approached, her eyes growing wide.

Whitley only laughed. "Well, this just got interesting." He folded his arms over his chest as his body wavered. He nodded to Sumi. "How do you like these odds? Now it's two against one." He winked at me. "Help me take her down and I'll make sure you get back inside your body."

I spun my sword in a slow arc in front of me. "And then what?"

He hesitated. "We'll hand her over to the Network, of course."

Right. As if I couldn't read the lie on his face. He wasn't going to stop until she was dead. And as much as I would love to have Sumi gone from my life once and for all, I couldn't risk

Kim. "You screwed me over last time I trusted you. Why should I believe you now?"

He shrugged a shoulder. "Because we both want the same thing. Common interests unite."

"Normally, yes. But this time, we don't want the same thing." Before he could react, I grabbed his wrist and slipped the tip of my sword beneath the leather-wrapped bracelet.

"Hey! What are you—?" But before he could finish, I jerked the blade forward, slicing through the bracelet. It fell to the floor in tattered pieces.

Warmth radiated through me. If nothing else, I'd saved Q.

Whitley looked at me, his eyes wide with horror. "No. I won't go back. I won't let them lock me away." He spun on his heels and ran for the door. He pulled it open and staggered into the dojo where he collapsed to the ground before the door had a chance to swing closed behind him.

Sumi placed a hand on her hip. "Thanks for taking care of *that* for me. If I didn't hate you so much, I might say we make a good team."

I turned to her, my sword held out in front of me. "Yeah, well. Let's see how well you like me once I have you back in your own body and you're locked inside a jail cell."

She laughed and adjusted the wrapped bracelet on her wrist. "As if that's going to happen. Powers or no powers, I'm not going back inside a body wanted for murder. Especially not with the Network on the hunt." She snorted. "I'm not going anywhere."

"You're wrong."

Sumi and I whirled around to find Kim standing in the

doorway. He held a katana in each hand. Behind him, Q's body remained motionless on the dojo floor.

Sumi made a choking sound before she spoke. "Kim, thank God! I'm so glad you're here! Sumi's trying to kill me."

His eyes narrowed. "You know as well as I do she isn't Sumi. *You* are."

"No." She held her hands out. "That's not true, Kim. She's poisoned your mind again—making you believe her lies."

"Is that so?" He took a step toward her. "If you're really Rileigh, tell me how you like your nachos."

Sumi paled. "What? That's a ridiculous question. What does that matter?"

"How do you like your nachos?" he repeated.

"I—I—" She took a step back and shook her head.

I smirked. "Extra jalapenos." Triumph buzzed through me like an electric current.

"No!" She raised a trembling finger at me. "I won't let her steal you from me again. We can finally be together now, Yoshido—just as we were meant to be in the past. I've given up everything for you—even my powers—just like you wanted. All of this"—she threw her arms wide—"I did for you. So I could be exactly who you want me to be."

Dr. Wendell pushed the door open. "What on earth is going on in here?" His eyes swept over the three of us, lingering on Kim's extended blades. "Kim?"

Kim ignored him. "Don't you get it, Sumi? It's not your powers that kept us apart—it's *you*. You're twisted on the inside, and switching bodies isn't going to change that. You hurt the people around you when you can't get what you want. I could never be with someone like that."

Her shoulders slumped, giving her the appearance of a broken doll. "No," she whispered.

He took another step closer. "I'm going to make sure you'll never hurt anyone else ever again."

"Wait a second." Dr. Wendell pressed his hand to his temple. "You mean Rileigh really *is* Sumi? And you really are … " His eyes met mine.

"We're going to have a talk later about that tranquilizer dart," I answered.

Tears sprang from Sumi's eyes and she let out a wail. "You don't mean that, Kim. You loved me once. You can love me again."

"No." He shook his head. "Our marriage was arranged to unify our families. I never loved you. And I never will."

She hugged her arms around her waist and sobbed. If she hadn't tried to kill me several times over, I might have felt sorry for her. *Might.*

The sinking feeling inside me grew, and I stumbled backward.

Kim shot a worried glance in my direction. "Are you okay?"

I pressed my palm against my forehead to keep the room from spinning. "We don't have much longer until the change is permanent."

He turned to Sumi. "Take the bracelet off and prepare to die."

Sumi clutched her wrist to her chest. "You would kill me? Even if it means you die too?"

"If it means you never hurt another person I love, absolutely."

"Kim, no!" I rushed to his side and placed a hand on his

shoulder. "The Network is on their way here. Once I get my body back, they can lock her up, and we'll never have to worry about her again."

He frowned and shook his head. "Isn't that what we thought last time? And then look what happened. She found a way to switch bodies with you. As long as she's alive, she's a threat—she'll always be searching for a way to hurt you. I'd rather die than give her another chance." He glared at her.

I stepped in front of him, blocking his path. "I won't let you. We lost each other in the last life—I won't lose you in this one."

His eyes softened. "Rileigh, I—" But before he could finish, Sumi kicked my hand holding the katana. The sword sailed from my grasp and tumbled to the floor. With a gasp, I dove for it—but Sumi was faster.

With my sword clutched in her hands, she scrambled backward toward the door.

I took one of Kim's katanas from him and pointed it at Sumi's chest. "Do you honestly think you're going to defeat the two of us?"

She licked her lips. "I don't need to defeat you." She lifted the sword and dug the sharpened edge against her own neck. "I just need to escape. And if you don't let me go, I'll slice your pretty little throat. Not only will Kim die, but you'll lose your precious body—forever."

29

Japan, 1492

Chiyo ran her hand along the edge of a trunk her men had deposited inside her tent earlier in the evening. She undid the latch and pulled open the lid. Several daggers waited inside. She smiled and withdrew a blade with a delicate gold handle. Tonight's robbery had gone well. A few more like it, and she'd be set for life. Not too bad for a girl on her own.

She put the blade back when the candlelit silhouette of a man holding a sword passed outside her tent. With a gasp, she whirled around with her hand extended. Her men knew better than to sneak up on her unannounced and not expect death. But before she could release the electricity pulsing from her fingers, the man pushed open her tent flap and revealed himself.

Impossible. Chiyo's stomach clenched and her hand dropped to her side. "Yoshido?" What on earth was he doing, not only in her camp, but inside her tent? Unless... she snapped her mouth shut and grinned. "You have finally come for me! I knew you would not give up!" She ran to him with her arms extended. *Finally* she'd have the embrace she'd always dreamed of.

Before she could fall against his chest, he jerked out of reach. "Chiyo?"

She stopped and frowned. "Of course it is me. Who else did you expect to find?"

The look of surprise on his face gave her the answer—anyone *but* her. He shook his head, his eyes wide. "What are you doing here?"

"Obviously not being rescued," she replied bitterly. She silently cursed herself for thinking he might actually be here for her. Would she never learn? She pressed her lips together and balled her fingers into fists. She thought she'd long ago squashed the part of her that wistfully longed for married life. She was a powerful kunoichi now. She needed no man.

But if that were true, why did her heart ache in the presence of this one?

"I do not understand," Yoshido said. His gaze swept across her tent, lingering on the overflowing trunks of silks and weapons. "I was told you were dead."

She lifted her chin. "You were lied to."

His eyes returned to hers and he readjusted his grip on his sword. "Then show me the leader. I will kill him for you."

She almost laughed. "Where were you two years ago?"

His brow furrowed in lines of confusion. "What do you mean?"

She turned to the nearest chest and sat on it. "You never came. You were my betrothed and you left me to suffer."

He jerked back like he'd been struck.

"And not only that," she continued, "but when I finally managed to escape on my own, I went looking for you. And I found that you had ... already moved on." She turned away so he wouldn't see the hurt on her face.

"Oh, Chiyo." He moved toward her, but she halted him with a glance.

"No, Yoshido." Anger burned through her. "I have only ever wanted your love," she spit, "*not* your pity." She gestured at the crates and chests stacked around her tent. "Does it *look* like I suffer? I bet I have more wealth now than you could ever have offered me. Perhaps I am better off." Even as she said the words, she knew it was a lie. She did suffer, especially now with him in front of her, reminding her of everything she couldn't have.

His eyes widened. "*You* are the kunoichi?"

She smirked. "Do not look so surprised. I did what I had to do to survive. Did you think I was going to wait for you forever?"

Just then, a woman pushed aside Chiyo's silk-covered doorway and stepped inside her tent. She wore the armor of a samurai and her withdrawn sword dripped with blood. A quiver of fear rolled down Chiyo's spine. This woman reminded Chiyo of a tiger, in that she was beauty and death intertwined.

"Senshi," Yoshido said, his voice thick with sorrow.

Of course. Chiyo pressed her jaw together so hard it ached. As if it wasn't enough for him to come here and open old wounds, he had to bring his harlot with him as well. Did he think she was stupid? That she didn't know he hadn't been true to his word? She glared at him. She wanted to hear him say the words out loud, to admit his wrongdoing. He owed her that. "Who is that?"

His eyes narrowed in warning. "She is none of your concern."

This time Chiyo did laugh. She should have known he was not man enough to admit it. "Some samurai you are—making promises you never intended to keep."

"That is a lie!" His eyes blazed in anger. "Look at you! Look at what you have become. I only had one betrothed, and she was killed by bandits. You *are* a bandit." He turned and looked at the woman beside him. "We are going." He reached for her and the woman slipped her hand within his.

The second their fingers laced, Chiyo felt a rip through her heart. As much as she'd tried to convince herself she was better on her own, having Yoshido hold hands with another woman reminded her how much she'd been in love with him—and how much she still was.

He turned to leave and pain surged through her. Yoshido was a samurai—which meant he was bound by honor. Surely he would not forget his promise to her.

"Yoshido, no! You cannot leave me!" She tried so hard not to fall apart, but despite her best effort, tears streaked down her cheeks and she fell at his feet. She twisted her hands into his obi and tried to pull him away from the woman he held so tightly to. He had intended to marry her once. So how could he now dismiss her so casually? "You promised. You *owe* me."

"My debt to you has been repaid tonight." He tried to pull his obi out of her hands, but she only tightened her grip. His eyes narrowed. "Release me."

Never. As long as she had breath in her body, Chiyo would

never let him go. He was her samurai. *Hers!* And he would be again. "How can you say that? You have repaid nothing!"

"You are wrong. On this night, I am walking away from you and allowing you to live. If you want to keep breathing, you will leave this area and never return." He looked at the woman with him and gave a slight nod.

Before Chiyo could move, the woman sliced through Yoshio's obi, barely missing Chiyo's fingers. The two of them turned and walked from her tent, leaving her with only a fistful of silk.

No. She couldn't lose him. Not again! "This is not over!" Chiyo shrieked after them. "Yoshido, you will be mine!" Sobs ripped through her words. "You will be mine," she moaned before collapsing onto the ground. She remained there, shaking and crying until the sound of someone clearing their throat made her jerk her head up.

The same samurai that Chiyo had shocked unconscious in Yoshido's village stood before her. He smiled and extended his hand. "I believe I can help you with that."

"What?" His words didn't make sense. Why on earth would he want to help her? Cautiously, she took his hand and allowed him to pull her to her feet.

"What if I told you I can solve both of your problems?" he asked. "I can get rid of the girl and deliver Yoshido to your door. All for a small payment, of course."

Chiyo pulled her hand out of his grip and narrowed her eyes. She knew better than to trust someone so easily. "Who are you?"

The samurai laughed. "How rude of me!" He gave an exaggerated bow. "Allow me to introduce myself. My name is Zeami."

30

My breath caught inside my throat and I tightened my grip on the katana. "Sumi, if you don't take that damned bracelet off, we're going to be stuck like this." My insides felt like they were being stretched like rubber bands. I knew we had minutes at most.

"Yeah?" She winced and dug the katana deeper into her neck with trembling hands. The trickle of blood widened to a stream. "Then you have to make a decision. What's worse? Spending your life in my body with Kim or spending your life in my body without Kim?"

I licked my lips and tried to steady the blade in my trembling hands. Without any other options, what choice did I have?

Kim stepped forward.

Sumi raised her hand, halting him. "I wouldn't." Blood coated her fingers, shiny and slick. "I've got nothing to lose. So what do I care if your little girlfriend gets stuck in my body, huh? Kind of fitting." She laughed. "You say you don't want me. And yet, as long as you're with her, you'll be forced to look at my face for the rest of your life."

Her words hit me like a shuriken to the chest. I knew Kim loathed Sumi as much as I did—if not more. Would he still be able to love me if every time he looked at me, he saw her face?

I looked to Kim for a plan, but the panic in his eyes showed me he didn't have one. Dr. Wendell hadn't moved in the last couple of minutes. And considering his eyeballs appeared to be on the verge of popping out, I sincerely doubted he was going to be any help.

"Do we have an understanding?" Sumi took another step back. "I'm going to leave, and I don't want to be followed. If I am, I will end this body."

A bitter taste burned my throat. If I was going to be stuck inside this body forever, I'd want Kim alive—even if he couldn't stand to look at me.

Kim pressed his lips together. A hundred emotions passed through his eyes. Still, he said nothing.

The decision was mine.

I lowered the katana to my side. "Leave," I growled.

"Rileigh—" Dr. Wendell began.

"No," Kim interrupted. "She's right. We have no choice."

Sumi smiled. "We have an agreement then."

I stared at her a moment, trying to commit my own face to memory, knowing it might be the last time I ever saw it. How do you say goodbye to yourself? Finally, I gave a curt nod. "Whatever. Just get the hell out of here. Nobody wants to see you again, anyway."

Her eyes flicked to Kim's, and when he made no move

to argue, her lips twitched. "You won't." She spun around and pulled open the break room door.

Quentin waited on the other side.

"What the—" Sumi stumbled backward.

He caught the swinging door with his hand and stepped after her.

For one horrible second, I was sure Whitley still inhabited my best friend's body. But then he smiled—a look that was all Q. "Hello again." He rolled up his sleeves. "I've been looking forward to seeing you."

"No." Sumi shook her head as she continued her backward retreat. "How did you regain consciousness so quickly?"

He shrugged, his grin widening. "I guess you can say it takes a lot to keep me down."

She raised the katana in front of her, pointing the tip at Q. "I'm warning you. Stay away from me."

"Oh, I will—right after I do this." Before she could react, he spun around the extended blade and caught her wrist. A flash of light erupted beneath his fingers.

Sumi groaned, and her eyes rolled into the back of her head. She fell forward and Q caught her in his arms.

My own sword fell from my fingers as I struggled for breath. "Q! You're really okay?"

"Yeah." He grinned and lowered Sumi to the floor. "This is sure an improvement from the cell I'd been stuck in." He laughed. "I guess Whitley's in for a bad surprise, huh? Anyway, I'd hug you, but we don't have time." He lifted Sumi's arm. "Who gets the honors?"

"Allow me." Kim stepped forward and slid his sword

beneath the bracelet. He jerked up and the bracelet fell to the ground in pieces.

The stretching feeling inside me ceased.

Kim, Q, and Dr. Wendell all turned to me at once.

"How do you feel?" Kim asked.

I shrugged. I sure didn't feel any different. "Fine, I guess." I looked at Quentin. "Am I supposed to feel fine?"

He frowned. "I don't know. I don't think we can compare our experiences. I'm a healer, after all. My transformation probably went a little easier because of it."

"Right." I fought off the wave of panic that rolled through me by concentrating on my fallen body. Q's healing touch had done more than knock out Sumi. The cut on my body's neck had already scabbed over, and the angry welt on my chin was nothing more than a blush of color. "So when is this going to happen? Shouldn't I pass out or something? That's what Whitley did after I cut his bracelet."

Quentin nodded and chewed on his lip—a telltale sign he was hiding something from me.

Kim and Dr. Wendell exchanged uneasy glances.

"What's wrong?" I asked.

"Rileigh, I—" Q pressed a hand to his mouth as if unable to speak the words. But he didn't have to. The expression on his face told me everything.

A ball of ice settled inside the pit of my stomach. "No," I whispered. I reached for Kim, and he was instantly at my side. I wound my arm around his, hoping this touch would keep me from falling to pieces as the world crumbled around me.

"It's not working, is it?" Dr. Wendell asked the question I knew was on all of our minds.

Quentin only shook his head.

A gasp ripped through my chest.

"Why isn't it working?" Kim shouted, making me flinch. "Why isn't she changing back?"

Q looked at me and sucked in a breath. "It's not working," he answered, "because we're too late."

31

No." Kim gently pulled free from my grip and took a step backward. "You're wrong. You haven't given it enough time to work."

"Let's all take a deep breath." Dr. Wendell raised his hand. "If we calm down, I'm sure we'll figure this out."

I sank to my knees and stared at my unconscious body—the body that was no longer mine. Blond hair I would never brush again splashed across lips that would never again kiss Kim. Hands with green fingernails, which I'd painted only days ago, rested on the floor.

A sob bubbled up in my throat. I quickly swallowed it before it could escape. Turning away, I pressed my fingers against my lips for extra insurance.

"Rileigh?" Quentin held out a hand. I accepted and he pulled me to my feet. "What do you need? What can I do?"

"Nothing." My voice came out flat. "If you can't put me back inside my body, there's absolutely nothing you can do."

"Is that true?" Kim asked. "Is there really *nothing* you can do?"

Quentin shrugged helplessly. "I'm a healer. My powers affect the body only. To affect a soul, you would need..."

"Ki powers," I offered.

Kim's eyes widened. "But you no longer have—"

"My ki powers. I know." I shook my head sadly. "So it's true. There's nothing to be done."

"Don't say that," Dr. Wendell said. "This isn't the end of the world. Yes, losing your body is horrendous—but you're alive. Isn't that enough?"

"Enough?" I looked at him as the first hot, angry tear trailed down my cheek. "I just turned eighteen. I didn't *just* lose my body. I lost my life!"

Dr. Wendell opened his mouth, but I cut him off. "Don't you get it? I had plans to go to school. And with Kim back, maybe we could have traveled... or do whatever college-aged kids do. But now I'm trapped inside the body of a girl wanted for *murder*. No matter what, I'm going to spend the rest of my life in a cell."

"No." He shook his head. "I'll make sure of that. After I explain the situation to the Network, they'll make sure the charges disappear. After all, what good is a secret government agency if they can't rig a murder trial?" He gave a lame attempt at a smile.

"All right." I folded my arms across my chest. "Let's say your stupid Network—which has made my life a living hell these last forty-eight hours, by the way—gets me off the hook.

Then what? What life can I go back to? What about my—"
I choked back a sob and exhaled before I could finally form
the word. "Mom? Am I just supposed to show up looking like
this?" I thrust my arms outward. "And expect her to believe
I fell asleep one day and woke up in another body? What are
you going to tell her about her daughter?"

Dr. Wendell's mouth opened and closed several times as he
appeared to search for an answer—an answer I knew he didn't
have because there *was* no answer.

Q squeezed my shoulder. "We'll figure it out one thing at a
time."

"Will we?" An edge of hysteria crept into my voice. "Let's
make a list. Right now I'm trapped inside a murderer's body,
I no longer have my ki powers, and *this*"—I pulled at the tank
top I wore—"is the only outfit I own. And let's not forget I no
longer have a place to live."

"That's not true." Kim grabbed my arm and turned me
around.

I tilted my chin so I could meet his eyes.

"As long as you breathe air, you have a home—with me."

"What?" I wiped my tears with the back of my hand. "You
can't be serious. I'm wearing the face of our worst enemy."

He pulled me toward him, shaking his head. "When are
you going to realize I don't care about things like that? I don't
care what face you're wearing. I love *you*, Senshi. Not for what
you look like, but for the way you make me feel when I'm
with you. You've taught me that every death, every life has a
purpose. And no matter how many times I'm brought back to
this planet, no matter how many bodies or lives pass between

us, the familiarity that is you—that is *us*—will always be the wind that guides me to where you are."

He lifted a hand to my face and trailed his thumb down my cheek. "We can leave if you want. If this is too much, we can go. Forget this life. Let's pack our bags—tonight—and make a new one."

I brought my hand to his, as if to make sure this wasn't a dream. Could I really do it? Could I leave everything I'd always known and run away with him? I chewed the inside of my cheek as I considered his offer. After all, with my life stolen, what did I have to stay for?

"Kim, let's not do anything hasty." Dr. Wendell approached us with a frown. "We need you here. The Network—"

Kim turned away from me with a scowl. "Screw the Network!"

Dr. Wendell's eyes fluttered wide as he took a step back.

"Lord Toyotomi was right," Kim continued, turning back to me. "We sacrificed everything as warriors. And what has it brought us? Only death and suffering." He shook his head. "I'm beaten, and I'm so tired. I can no longer remember what I've been fighting for—but I'm pretty sure it's not what I *should* be fighting for."

I swallowed, my throat suddenly dry. "What's that?"

"Us. I've forgotten to fight for us."

My chest tightened, making breathing nearly impossible. I opened my mouth to speak but found I couldn't get the words out.

"So what do you think?" He placed his other hand on my face and drew me closer so I could feel the heat of him radiating through my clothes. "Will you leave with me? Will you fight for us?"

I placed my hands over his and, for the first time in nearly two days, I felt at peace. Kim was right. We'd wasted too much time fighting. We'd lost so much. Didn't we deserve this, finally? "Yes," I answered.

He grinned. "Say it again."

I laughed. "Yes. Let's leave this all behind us."

He drew me closer until his face eclipsed the room and all that remained was him, me, and the kiss that had survived five hundred years.

32

Kim?" Dr. Wendell's voice brought me back to the dojo. "Are you sure this is wise? What about your work at the dojo?"

Kim slid an arm around my waist. "Drew can take over. Or Michelle. Or Braden." He shrugged. "Or close the damn thing. I don't really care."

I couldn't help but laugh. I'd never heard him speak so flippantly about his work.

"But don't you think the others will be upset?" Dr. Wendell crossed his arms over his chest. "They depend on you. How can you leave them behind?"

A muscle in Kim's jaw tightened as he raised his chin. "We're not in Japan anymore," he answered. "They do not need a leader. Maybe our absence will be a good thing for them." He shook his head. "I can't help but wonder if we've

kept on as samurai because it's all we've known. But now..."
He shrugged. "They are free to follow their own paths."

"But they're your friends."

"We'll visit."

Dr. Wendell sighed and rubbed his face. "Look, it's not that I don't think you're capable of making your own decisions, but I do think you might be entering into this a little rashly."

Quentin's mouth quirked into a sad smile, and I felt the first stab of sorrow through my joy. "You have to do what you have to do," he told me. "I only want you to be happy. But if you leave—I'll miss you like crazy."

"I know." I gently slid free from Kim's arms and fell against Quentin. He quickly enveloped me in his arms.

"You're my best friend," he whispered against the top of my head. "And you'll always be—no matter where you are or what you look like."

I pulled back, half-laughing as fresh, hot tears trailed down my cheeks. "Ditto. I promise I'll call or email as soon as we get..." I looked up at Kim, who only shrugged. I laughed. "Wherever it is we're going."

"You better." Q gave me another squeeze before slowly backing away.

"Of course."

Kim pointed to what used to be my body, still unmoving on the floor. "When the Network arrives, make sure they lock her up—and keep her locked up this time."

Dr. Wendell nodded. "You know we will." He was quiet a moment. "The other samurai are supposed to be here soon. Are you sure you wouldn't rather wait to see them—to say a proper goodbye?"

"No." Kim shook his head. "It's time to finally start our lives. I know the others will understand when you explain it to them. Tell them I'll get in contact as soon as we get settled. If they decide to follow, they're welcome to join us." He nodded at Quentin. "That goes for you, too, but it also means you can't tell anyone where you're going. If she somehow gets free again"— he motioned to Sumi—"I don't want to risk the chance of being found."

Quentin nodded. "I appreciate that. I'll let you know."

Kim looked at me, an eagerness in his eyes I hadn't seen in a long time. "Are you ready?"

Was I? Was I ready to walk away from everything I'd ever known—my life? My friends? My family? Just to finally be with the man I'd loved for almost five hundred years?

Oh, hell yeah.

But there was one thing still left unsettled. A bugging sensation wiggling inside my stomach. "My mom…"

Kim frowned. "I know you want to say goodbye. I understand—but she won't recognize you."

"I know." I nodded. "It's not that." I turned away from him and gave a pointed look to Dr. Wendell. "You have to take care of her. You owe me that."

He was quiet a moment before clearing his throat. "Rileigh, listen. I'm your handler—well, at least I was. And that meant part of my job was to keep a close eye on you." He shoved his hands in his pockets. "At first, my interest in your mother was strictly business-minded. I saw her as an opportunity to get closer to you."

A small flame of anger flickered inside me. Reflexively, my fingers curled into fists. "Go on."

He sighed. "I just want you to know that after I got to know your mother, I'll admit I did fall for her. She's a remarkable woman, Rileigh—amazing, really. Just like her daughter."

The flame inside of me extinguished and my fingers uncurled.

"You should know," he continued, "that I care for your mother a great deal. And I will look after her as long as she'll have me around."

The knot of anxiety inside me loosened. After my grandmother died, I was the only real family my mother had. I had no idea what Dr. Wendell would tell her about me—but I hated to think she'd have to suffer alone. At least I could leave now with the comfort that she'd be looked after by someone who genuinely cared for her. "Thank you," I said.

He nodded. "You should also know that, even though the two of us haven't always seen eye-to-eye, I've also grown to care about you a great deal." He sucked in a shaking breath. "I'm going to miss you." He lifted a finger and pointed it at Kim. "And I want to know when you've arrived safely . . . well, wherever you go. Don't disappear forever."

Disappear forever. The words echoing inside my mind made my gut clench—not because Kim and I were finally going to be together, but because we were going to walk away from our current lives and never look back.

Kim's fingers slipped into mine. "Are you ready?"

I bit my lip. Was anyone ever ready to leave their life behind? I sucked in a breath and shrugged. "I guess I am. It's not like I have a bag to pack. I don't own anything."

He shook his head. "You're wrong. There are two things that belong to you—this." He bent over and picked up my discarded katana from the ground. After handing it to me, he took my free hand and placed a hand over his heart. "And this."

His heart beat under my open palm, as if it wanting to leap into my hand. I swallowed, my throat suddenly tight. "That's all I need."

And it was.

33

Kim loaded the last duffle bag into his car and slammed the trunk while Rosie danced around his feet. The other samurai had arrived sooner than we'd expected and now stood half-circled around us like mourners at a wake.

"Rileigh, I'm so sorry we didn't realize Sumi was impersonating you sooner." Michelle's lip trembled, her eyes sparkling with unshed tears.

"Is that why you're leaving?" Braden asked. "Because we failed you?"

Kim whirled around. "Of course not! No one here failed anyone. We're leaving because it's going to be too hard for Rileigh to remain here and be reminded of the life she no longer has. We're off to claim a new one."

Drew folded his arms across his chest, his lips tight.

Kim placed a hand on his arm. "Brother, this isn't forever.

Once we're settled, we'll let you know where we are and you can join us."

Drew's face softened. "Really?"

Kim smiled. "Of course. We're family. A lifetime doesn't change that."

Drew looked away, and for a moment I feared that would be the end of their goodbye.

Kim must have thought so, too, because his smile dissolved. He started to turn, but Drew caught him by his arm and pulled him in for a hug, thumping his fist against his back as he did. "Brothers," he whispered.

"Forever," Kim agreed. He slowly pulled away. "That goes for you as well." He cast pointed looks at Michelle and Braden.

"What about the Network?" Michelle asked. "What about our jobs as samurai?"

"We will always be samurai," Kim answered. "The Network doesn't determine that. Besides, I think it's time we stop fulfilling the missions of others, and instead focus on our own mission."

"But what's that?" Braden asked.

Kim arched a single eyebrow. "*That* is your mission—to figure it out."

Braden frowned. "Now you're starting to sound like Lord Toyotomi."

My breath caught at the mention of his name. Kim and I exchanged quick glances before both of us looked away. We hadn't mentioned to the others that we'd seen him, and I could tell by Kim's reaction he wasn't eager to bring up the subject. How would they feel knowing we'd found him only to lose him again? Our first stop on our journey was to find out if he was okay. If he wasn't . . . it was probably for the best the others didn't know.

I glanced over my shoulder at the dojo. Q stood in the doorway and waved. With my throat tight, I waved back. I knew he couldn't come out because he and Dr. Wendell were standing guard over Sumi until the Network arrived—and for that, I was glad. I could hold my emotions inside as long as there was distance between us. But if he were to come out here and put his arms around me, I was sure to fall apart.

"Rileigh?" Worry laced Michelle's voice. "Are you okay?"

I was quiet a moment, unsure how to answer. I glanced at my reflection in the car window, still surprised to see Sumi's face staring back at me. Would there ever be a time when I could look into a mirror and own the reflection staring back? "I hope so," I answered. "Maybe with time."

She nodded and opened her mouth to say something when Rosie scratched my leg and began to whimper.

Kim looked down at her and frowned. "What's the matter, Rosie? I just took you for a walk."

Rosie yipped and spun circles around us.

"I wonder what's gotten into her," Kim muttered.

No sooner had he asked the question than a yellow taxi pulled into the parking lot and stopped in front of the dojo doors.

Kim and I exchanged uneasy glances. It wasn't like we were expecting anyone—especially not in a taxi.

The car door opened on the side farthest from us, and someone climbed out. A moment later, the door closed and the taxi pulled away, leaving its passenger behind.

My heart dropped into my knees. *No. It couldn't be.*

Yipping, Rosie bolted to Gene and spun in circles around

his legs. I pressed my hand over my mouth, still not believing the sight before me.

Braden was the first to speak. "Um, do any of you know this guy?"

"Gene," I whispered, through my fingers.

"Who?" Michelle asked.

After petting Rosie long enough to get her to stop hopping, Gene looked in our direction and smiled. "You made it! I never doubted it for a second." With his cane poised in front of him, he made his way over to us.

"How?" Kim asked, his eyes wide. "You were horribly out-numbered."

Gene chuckled. "A skilled warrior goes into a fight knowing his only fight is with death. An unskilled warrior goes into a fight only to win."

"Look, I'm sorry to interrupt." Drew narrowed his eyes. "But exactly *who* are you?"

"Ah, Seiko." Gene reached out and clasped Drew's arm. "Still looking out for your brother, I see."

Drew made a choked noise and the color drained from his face.

Braden crossed his arms. "How do you know that?"

"Yeah," Michelle added. "What's going on?"

Gene let go of Drew and clapped his hands together. "Yorimichi and Kiyomori! How wonderful! You're all here."

Michelle swallowed before answering. "We are. And since you know so much about us, would you care to explain who you are?"

Gene grinned. "My dear samurai, could it be you do not remember your old master?"

Michelle gasped and Braden staggered back as if he'd been punched. Drew, on the other hand, remained motionless.

Gene rested a hand on Rosie's head and her tongue rolled out of the side of her mouth. She sat and her tail swished the ground at his feet.

"My dear samurai," Gene began, "while I've waited a lifetime for this moment, I'm afraid a proper reunion will have to wait. I'm here to help our Senshi."

Even though I couldn't see his eyes through the dark glasses he wore, I could feel his gaze settle on me.

"Things have not been set right," Gene said. "I can feel it."

I swallowed several times before my throat loosened enough to allow me to speak. "I'm so thankful you're all right, Gene. But I'm afraid your trip here was wasted. I ran out of time. I'm . . . " Emotion cracked my voice. "I'm stuck this way."

"Hmm." Gene frowned. He reached out and grabbed my arm and gave it a squeeze. "Maybe you are stuck this way—but maybe not."

"No." I gently pried my arm free from his grip. "I'm afraid it's true. My friend Q is a healer, and he confirmed it. This is who I am now."

Gene tilted his head down. "We're manipulators of ki, you and I, correct?"

"I used to be," I answered.

Gene waved my words away. "So you know better than most the true state of the spirit. It is not an immovable object but something fluid. Spirit is always moving, always flowing."

My hands began to tremble. "What are you saying?"

He shrugged. "I'm saying this would have been no problem

258

if I'd reached you before your spirit rooted inside this body. Now? Things are a bit tricky. But that's not to say it's impossible."

"What do you mean *tricky*?" Kim asked.

"Whatever ritual was performed, Rileigh's spirit was severed from her body, allowing it to be moved into another. Typically when a spirit is drained from a body, the end result can be quite dangerous."

"More than dangerous," I added. I thought about all the times I'd used my ability to manipulate ki in battle, knowing what would happen to me if I used all of it. "It could be fatal."

"Exactly." Gene nodded, his lips set in a grim line. "Death is a very real possibility. But that's where I come into play. I can use my own spirit to sustain your bodies while we attempt the switch—something that wouldn't be possible without another ki manipulator."

"You're saying it's possible?" Hope swelled inside me like helium, making me feel on the verge of floating.

"Yes," he answered. "But I won't lie to you. There are risks. I've never attempted anything like this before."

Kim grasped my hand tightly and spun me to face him. Lines of worry creased his brow. "You don't have to do this," he said. "I meant it when I said I don't care what you look like. My feelings for you will never change."

"I know." I squeezed his hands. "But it matters to me." I glanced at my reflection—Sumi's reflection—in the car window. "Any other body, and I could handle it. But to see *her*? Every day for the rest of my life?" I shook my head. "If there's even a small chance I could get my body back—my *life* back—I have to try."

For several heartbeats, Kim said nothing. Finally, he nodded. "If you're sure this is what you want."

"I'm sure."

Kim sucked in a breath. "All right. We better hurry. The Network will be here soon, and we don't need them interrupting us."

Gene grinned. "And I don't think they're going to be too excited to see me again."

Braden shook his head. "I still can't believe this is happening."

Kim met my eyes, and I silently nodded. This was the right decision. I knew there were risks, but any chance I had to get out of my enemy's body was a chance I had to take.

34

With my back against the dojo's rubber mats, I stared at the ceiling and tried to pretend this was just another training session with Kim and the samurai. Still, I couldn't help but glance to my right at my unmoving body beside me. "You have no idea how weird this is," I said.

"I think *I* have a pretty good idea." Quentin kneeled beside my body's head. "Don't worry," he said when he caught me glance at it for the umpteenth time. "If she wakes up, I'll zap her."

I swallowed and watched Gene light the ring of candles he'd placed around our bodies. When he finished, he turned to me with a smile. "Are you ready?"

I clenched my jaw and swallowed. "Let's do this."

The door separating the dojo from the lobby squeaked open. I tilted my chin to see Dr. Wendell, Kim, and the other samurai step inside.

"Well?" Gene asked.

"We should have more time than I expected," Dr. Wendell answered. "I just got off the phone with the Network, and they told me they were delayed in Ohio. Something about having all the tires on their vehicles slashed?"

Gene grinned. "I guess fortune smiles upon us this day."

I gave him a knowing look. "Fortune? Is that what we're calling reincarnated daimyos these days?"

"Never you mind that." He rubbed his hands together. "Let's get started." He kneeled between me and Sumi and glanced over his shoulder at the samurai hovering by the door. "I'm sorry. This is a delicate procedure, and I'm going to need complete concentration. If you would all be so kind as to wait outside."

Alarm rang through me like a bell. I didn't want Kim to leave. If anything went wrong, I needed him close by.

Dr. Wendell opened the door and ushered Michelle, Braden, and Drew back into the lobby.

Kim didn't budge.

"Kim?" Dr. Wendell called.

"Can't he stay?" I asked Gene. "I'd be calmer if he were here. And I know he won't distract you."

Gene was quiet so long I was sure he was going to say no. Finally, he shook his head and chuckled. "Like he'd leave even if I said no?" He waved Kim over.

Seconds later, Kim hovered over me. Lines of worry pinched his brow.

"Sit, sit." Gene patted the mat beside my head. "The only rule—and it's extremely important—is that you mustn't touch her. No matter what. Understand?"

Kim opened his mouth to argue, but Gene cut him off with the wave of his hand. "Do not doubt for a minute that I can remove you from this dojo in an instant. This is a delicate ceremony involving the transference of spirit. There's no telling what outside contact could do. We don't want Rileigh to accidentally end up inside your body with you, do we?"

My heart quivered against my ribs. "That's a possibility?"

Gene shrugged. "There's no telling what could happen. So let's just plan on being safe over sorry."

Kim kneeled beside me, his eyes wide.

Gene looked at me. "Rileigh, are you ready to begin?"

My pulse thrummed like an electric current inside my veins. Was I ready? What if it didn't work? Or worse, what if something went wrong and my spirit bled out for good?

My throat went dry as I considered the possibilities. But then I thought of my mom, and Q, and everyone and everything I'd have to leave behind if I couldn't get my body back. I had to try, for them and for me. I couldn't surrender my life to Sumi without a fight.

I bit my lip and nodded.

"Very well." Gene held his arms out. "Hands?"

Quentin plucked Sumi's hand from the ground and placed it into Gene's.

After a moment of hesitation, I closed my eyes and reached out my hand.

A second later, Gene's fingers gripped mine and an electric current jolted through me where our hands met.

I gasped and arched my back.

"Hang on, Rileigh." Gene's voice wavered with strain. "Your spirit may be rooted inside Sumi's body, but it's eager to break free. The first thing we need to do is sever the root."

I wasn't sure if he was right about my spirit wanting to break free—but I could certainly feel something breaking inside of me. What felt like an invisible rope wrapped around my insides, pulling tighter and tighter until I thought I might burst.

A gasp of pain pushed through my clenched teeth.

"Rileigh?" Worry laced Kim's words.

"Breathe, Rileigh!" Gene squeezed my hand. "Just try to relax. You might feel a tugging sensation."

Before I could ask him what he meant, a stabbing pain pierced my chest. Unable to open my eyes, I was sure my insides were being ripped apart by daggers. A scream tore from my throat.

"What's wrong?" Kim shouted. "This can't be right."

"I'm—I'm not sure." Gene answered between labored gasps. "I think her spirit's been too deeply embedded inside the body. I-I think it might be ripping her apart."

A fire erupted inside of me, burning white-hot beneath my skin as it blazed a trail across my body. With an agonized cry, I opened my eyes to find the world around me shifting and out of focus, like I was looking through the glass of a fish bowl. Kim was nothing more than a dark shadow above me.

"Gene!" Quentin cried. "Look! We need to stop this."

I didn't have to see to know he was pointing out the trail of blood dribbling from my mouth. I could taste its coppery sweetness as it bubbled up from my throat and spilled over my tongue. No matter how much I gagged, coughed, and spit, I couldn't rid my throat of blood. I was literally choking in it.

Gene released me. From a faraway place, I felt my hand hit the floor.

"Oh, my God." Kim's voice drifted inside my head, sounding

miles away instead of above me. "Don't do this to me. Don't leave me."

I tried to say his name, tried to choke out an apology, but all I managed to do was cough up more blood.

"No," Kim whispered. "No!"

"Kim, don't!" Gene shouted.

I could no longer see him, but the moment his fingers touched mine, the fire inside me extinguished. Inside my head, I could hear nothing but the sounds of my own struggled gasps for air. Everything spun, from the ground beneath me to the space inside my head. I squeezed Kim's hand tighter, hoping his touch would somehow root me in place, but I only seemed to drift further away.

"Rileigh?" Kim's voice broke through the whirlwind. "Are you okay? Please, say something." His fingers pushed back the sweat-soaked hair covering my forehead.

No matter how many times I blinked, I was unable to bring the swirling colors into focus. I opened my mouth to answer him, but I couldn't force the words through my chattering teeth.

"I don't understand," Kim said. "Why is she shaking? Is she cold?"

"No," Gene answered, his voice full of fear. "I think—I think it may be a seizure."

A seizure? I knew I should be afraid, but I was too busy trying to fight for control of the body I was trapped inside. My muscles spasmed, my arms thrashed, and my head rattled against the floor.

"Rileigh, listen to me," Kim whispered against my ear. "You're going to be okay. When this is over, we're going to get into the car and we're going to leave. I meant it when I said I don't care what body you're in. To me, you'll always be Senshi—*my* Senshi. Do you remember our pact? What you promised me? You promised you'd never go where I couldn't follow. *You promised.*"

Through the tremors shaking my body, a memory came to me, so vivid I could almost smell the smoke from the fire pit in the corner of the room.

Japan, 1493

"You have to promise me." Yoshido stared into Senshi's eyes, drawing her in until she felt sure she would fall and drown inside their black depths.

She laughed. "Yoshido, what on earth could I promise you that you do not already claim? You have my heart. What else is there?"

"It is not enough." He shook his head, his expression a curious combination of desperation and fear. "With you—it is never enough."

She stopped polishing her katana and set it aside. "What would you have from me then?"

"Promise me that . . ." He paused long enough to clench his jaw. "If something should happen to either of us, promise me that you will not go anywhere I cannot follow."

Senshi frowned and reached for him. "Yoshido—"

He shook his head and sidestepped her grasp. "*Promise me.*"

She snapped her jaw shut. A hundred questions raced through her mind. Why was he asking *now*? And what kind of place could she go where he couldn't find her? Still, she would promise. She would always give him whatever he wanted. *He* was and always would be her greatest weakness. "Of course."

"You have to mean it." He took her hands within his, his skin rough and calloused from a lifetime of wielding a sword. "Because *this, w*hat we have together—they will build statues of us and write songs about our love."

She couldn't help it; a smile tugged at her lips. "Statues *and* songs?"

He nodded. "But the statues will crumble and in time, people will forget the words to the songs. But you and I? We will continue on as long as neither of us goes where the other cannot follow."

35

"Yoshido?"

"I'm here," he whispered.

But that wasn't right. The voice was wrong...and yet it wasn't.

Everything was wrong...and yet not.

I blinked open my eyes, but couldn't see past the black hair matted against my face.

Slowly, the pieces fell into place. Gene...the ceremony... the shaking.

I rolled onto my knees. "It didn't work?"

"Easy, Rileigh." The voice was Q's. "You suffered a major seizure. Maybe you should stay down a little longer."

I shook my head but it did nothing to dislodge the hair stuck to my sweat-soaked face. "No...can't..." The Network would be here any minute. But when I tried to move, I found I couldn't. Disappointment wrapped around me like ropes, keeping me anchored to the floor. I'd had one chance at getting my body back—getting my *life* back—and it didn't work. It looked like I was going to be stuck as Sumi forever.

Kim's sandalwood cologne enveloped me, rustling the memories of a lifetime ago and making my head swim. "Rileigh." There was no mistaking the relief in his voice. "It's going to be okay."

A lump rose inside my throat and no amount of swallowing could dislodge it. "But it didn't work." Slowly, I lifted my head up.

His hand slid under my hair and rested against my chin. "The only thing that matters to me is that you're all right." With his free hand, he smoothed the hair away from my face and that's when he froze, his eyes wide and locked on mine. A strangled sound emerged from his throat.

"What's wrong?" Gene asked.

"I don't believe it," Kim answered, his voice barely a whisper.

"What's going on?" Quentin rose from his spot beside my old body. He walked toward me only to stop after a couple of steps. "Oh, my God."

"What is it?" I brought my hands to my face, expecting to feel some sort of disfigurement, scar, or anything else that might be the reason for their reactions.

Gene stretched his hand out. "Give me your hand."

With a thick pulse in the back of my throat, I placed my hand within his.

Gene jerked upright. But just as quickly, a smile spread across his face. "Now *that* was unexpected."

"What?" I snatched my hand back. "What's going on?"

Gene shook his head. "Your soul was too deeply rooted in

that body to be removed. But my ki energy must have awakened your ki energy. And when Kim touched you, he reestablished your connection with your past life."

"It's amazing. I never would have thought it possible." Quentin shook his head, his eyes wide. "You're … you're … "

"Not Rileigh anymore," Kim finished.

I glanced over my shoulder at my old body, lifeless on the ground. "I know. I'm stuck as Sumi."

Smiling, Kim shook his head. He reached out like he was going to touch my face, but stopped as if suddenly afraid. "You're exactly how I remembered."

"What does that even mean?" I backed away from him. "Somebody better tell me what's going on, like *now*."

Quentin plucked my sword off the ground and handed it to me. "See for yourself."

I hesitated. I knew that when I looked at my reflection, it would only confirm my failure. But with Kim and Q watching me with eager expressions, it wasn't like I could hold off the inevitable. I grabbed the sword and lifted it to my face. I expected to see Sumi's eyes staring back at me.

I never expected to see my own.

The sword fell from my hands. *Impossible.* Maybe the seizure had messed with my brain and now I couldn't see correctly. "Something's wrong with my eyes," I told Q. "You-you have to heal me."

"Nothing's wrong with you," Kim said. "You're perfect." A second later I let out a yelp as he lifted me off my feet. Too surprised to stop him, I allowed myself to be carried swiftly across the dojo before he deposited me in front of the mirrors on the far wall. "You're … you again."

Shock froze me in place as I took in my reflection. I couldn't move—couldn't breathe. Finally, I raised my hand to the mirror. My throat was tight and my chest rigid as I stared into the eyes of what could only be a ghost.

Not a ghost, whispered a voice inside my head.

"It's impossible." But the moment my palm touched the reflection, a cold spark ignited beneath my fingers. It traveled through my arms like ribbons of silk until my entire body tingled.

My ki was back.

As if to prove the point, a burst of energy escaped my open palm, swirling around me and fanning the dark hair around my face.

In the mirror, I watched Quentin approach cautiously from behind. I spun around to face him, examining my hand as I did.

Quentin's brow furrowed. "Are you... who I think you are?"

I glanced over my shoulder at the mirror. My reflection smiled back. "Yes."

"Quentin." Gene shuffled toward us, his hand extended. "Allow me to introduce you to Senshi."

"Whoa," he answered.

I nodded and pressed my hands against the mirror, as if I could somehow reach through and grab my reflection to ensure she was real. Whoa was an understatement.

Kim appeared over my shoulder. "You've been through so much. How are you feeling?"

I turned to him and ran my fingers along his arm, curious if he would feel the same to my new skin. "Better than okay." I looked up at him and smiled. "I feel…" I searched for the perfect way to describe it. Being Senshi again felt like slipping on a favorite pair of jeans. She was the embrace from a friend after a too-long absence. "I feel like I'm home."

He placed his hands against my cheek and dipped his head so our foreheads touched. He opened his mouth to say something, but a moan from the back of the dojo jerked us apart.

"I think Sumi's waking up," Quentin said. "Do you want me to knock her out again?"

"Please." Gene nodded. "I wouldn't want the Network to have any more *difficulties.*"

"You got it." Quentin jogged to the back of the room and crouched beside Sumi.

Gene sighed as he watched Quentin work. "Such a shame—a young life wasted. I know she's done terrible things, but I believe she only ever wanted to be loved." He shook his head and held his hand out to me. "Are you ready to say goodbye?"

No. But I knew with the Network on their way, I wouldn't get another chance. With a lump in my throat, I followed Gene as he walked over to my old body. Together, we stared at what remained of Rileigh Martin. An invisible cord ensnared my chest and pulled tight. I knew I wasn't so much saying goodbye to my body, but rather goodbye to an entire life.

Quentin moved beside me and slid his arm around my waist. "It's a lot to take in," he said.

I nodded. "If I can't be Rileigh—at least I can still be me."

He nodded and gave me a squeeze. "I can sense a *but.*"

"You're right." I nodded. "It's almost perfect. I'm not Sumi—*but* I still can't go home. I still lost my old life."

Quentin was quiet a moment. "Maybe not."

36

Japan, 1493

Chiyo pulled back on the reigns and halted her horse beside Zeami. Together, they sat mounted before Yoshido's village. Her bandits stood behind them, their dark clothing making them almost invisible beneath the night sky. It had taken months of planning and waiting for the perfect opportunity for attack. And tonight was finally the night.

Chiyo's pulse thrummed with excitement. For two years she'd waited for this moment. And now, at long last, it was finally here. She wouldn't allow any mistakes. "You understand our deal?"

"Of course," Zeami answered. "Kill the girl and bring you Yoshido. In turn, I get to take over the village." He lifted his hand and smiled as blue sparks danced from his fingers. "How does this work again?"

Chiyo frowned. Zeami had been all too eager in his

demand that she loan him some of her power. She hoped it wouldn't impact the job he had to do. "I am a healer," she answered. "That means I have complete control of the body. Those blue sparks?" She nodded at his hand. "Your brain is full of them. I merely enable the body to manipulate them."

His grinned widened as he watched the sparks fly.

"Please keep in mind"—she laced her words with warning—"that your power is only temporary. It will fade."

His smile dissolved and he dropped his hand.

"I am only allowing you to have it long enough to kill the girl and anyone else who would stop you from bringing me Yoshido. Understood?"

He waved her concern away. "There will be no problems."

"There better not be." She narrowed her eyes. "Because I continue to learn more about my abilities by the day. Today I discovered something interesting about my talents."

He arched an eyebrow. "Do tell."

Chiyo turned to one of the bandits behind her and lifted a finger. "You there. You are a dog."

The man dropped on all fours. He sniffed the ground before lifting his head and bellowing at the moon.

Chiyo faced Zeami and was pleased to find his mouth slightly ajar. It would serve her well for him to remember the importance of his mission—and what she would do to him if he failed. "Unless you want to spend your days scratching at fleas—or *worse*—Yoshido is to be brought to me alive. Is that understood?"

He snapped his mouth closed and swallowed. "Perfectly."

"Good." She pointed to the village below. "Now go and bring him to me."

Zeami nodded and waved the men behind him forward. "Time to move!"

Chiyo's stomach fluttered with excitement as she watched her small army descend down the hill. After nearly two years, Yoshido would finally be hers. Her newfound ability had been like a gift from the Gods, urging her forward in her plan. Once she had Yoshido, she could make him forget about Senshi and they could finally be married, like they'd intended all those years ago.

She tightened her grip on the reins. Soon. She'd have everything she ever wanted.

She'd finally be happy.

———

Senshi jolted upright from her sleeping mat, her startled gasp rousing the man next to her.

Yoshido, accustomed to her premonitions, awoke in an instant and grasped beside him for his sword. "How long do we have?"

"The enemy is almost here."

37

My cell phone buzzed on my desk.

I crammed the last T-shirt into my bag, zipped it up, and grabbed my phone. I had a text from Kim.

We're outside waiting.

I grinned, slipped the phone in my back pocket, and double checked my duffle bag one last time to make sure I had my passport and ticket—both provided by the Network in an attempt to make up for trying to kill me.

"Rileigh?"

I spun around to find Debbie standing in the doorway with a sad smile on her lips. "If you don't hurry, you're going to miss your flight."

"I know." I nearly choked on the words. Only two days had passed since I'd lost my former body and assumed I'd lost my mom as well. But thankfully Quentin was able to alter her mind so when she looked at me, she only saw the old me. We weren't sure it would hold forever. But for now, it was enough.

"Are you certain you don't need me to drive you to the airport?" She absently twisted a ring on her middle finger. "I don't mind."

"That's okay." I slipped the duffle bag over my shoulder. "My friends are already waiting outside."

"Right. I forgot." She sucked in a deep breath. "I know this was my idea. I wanted you to travel. It's just hitting me all at once. My baby is an adult now—leaving the house to explore the world." Her eyes glistened with unshed tears. "You're going to call me, right?"

I swallowed to keep the tremor out of my voice. "Every day. I promise."

She nodded and motioned me forward for a hug. I let the bag fall from my shoulder and threw my arms around my mom's waist. I shuddered when I thought how close I'd come to losing her—my only remaining family.

Reluctantly, I pulled back. "I'm going to be late, Mom."

"I know." She dabbed at her eyes with the back of her hand. "Have fun and be safe."

I picked my bag off the floor. "I will."

"You have your passport?"

I nodded.

"Money? Your cell phone?"

I laughed. "Yes, Mom! If you don't let me go, I'm going to miss my flight."

"C'mon, Debbie." Dr. Wendell appeared behind her and gently pushed her out of the way. "She has to go."

"Okay, okay!" She threw her hands in the air and stepped aside. "Can't a mother be concerned about her only daughter?"

She dipped her chin and gave me a pointed look. "You make sure you call me if you need *anything*. Got that?"

"I will, I promise. But I really have to go." I stepped around her into the hallway.

"I love you, baby."

I stopped, a lump thick in my throat. For those words, everything I'd gone through to get my body back, including almost dying, had been worth it. Without turning around, I answered, "I love you, too, Mom."

I marched down the hall before I succumbed to the tears burning in my eyes. I'd nearly reached the front door when a hand grabbed my arm. "Rileigh?"

I turned around and came face-to-face with Dr. Wendell.

He blinked before shaking his head. "It's so crazy seeing you in a different body. Even crazier that your mom can't see it."

"Thank God for that." I adjusted the strap on my shoulder.

"Right." He nodded. "Listen, I know you guys say you're done with the Network—but we could sure use you. What exactly are you going to do while you're gone?"

I shrugged. "Not sure."

"Where are you going?"

"Everywhere."

"When will you be back?"

"Dunno."

He sighed and pinched the bridge of his nose. "And *this* is exactly how I know you're really Rileigh. It doesn't matter what you look like—you still have the ability to drive me crazy."

I grinned. "It's a gift."

He laughed. "Well, I just want you and the others to know there will always be a spot for you in the Network."

"Thanks, but don't hold your breath."

He frowned. "But you're samurai. What else are you going to do with your lives?"

"I'm not really sure..." I shrugged. "I think it will be fun to figure out." Before he could argue, I threw my arms around him and squeezed. "Take care of my mom."

He made a startled noise, but when I made no move to let go, he wrapped his arms around my shoulders and squeezed back.

He said nothing when I pulled away, only stared at me with his mouth slack.

"Take care." I turned away from him, threw the door to the condo open, and rushed into the stairwell. I practically leapt down the stairs until I reached the ground floor. When I emerged in the lobby, I immediately spotted Kim outside standing in front of a taxi van.

I ran through the doors, laughing as Kim picked me up and spun me around.

"I've missed you so much," he whispered against my ear.

I leaned back so I could stare into his dark eyes. "It's been what? Not even twenty-four hours?"

"Too long." He pressed me against his chest, burying his face into my neck.

"Guys!"

I turned and spotted Quentin leaning over the driver in the front seat. "Save the huggy-kissy for later. We're late."

The side door of the minivan slid open and Drew, Michelle, and Braden waved to me from the backseat.

Kim gave me a devious look. "It's not too late for us to make a run for it. We could disappear, just the two of us."

I swatted him. "You know as well as I do we're all stuck together for life."

He gave a dramatic sigh. "That I do." He carried me to the van, depositing me on the sidewalk so I could climb inside. I settled into the middle seat and Kim climbed in beside me.

Braden leaned forward, resting his arms on the back of our seats. "So what are we going to do first when we get there?"

Kim smiled and stretched an arm around my shoulder. "Whatever we want. That's the point."

"I'm so excited!" Michelle drummed her fingers against her knees. "I can't believe we're finally going back to Japan. I wonder how different it will be—if there will be anything left to remind us of home."

Drew said nothing. He only bobbed his head along to whatever he was listening to on his iPod.

"It doesn't matter." Kim shook his head. "Japan's not home for us anymore—and neither is St. Louis."

I looked at him. "So where exactly is home then?"

The van lurched into traffic, jostling our bodies together.

He smiled. "Anywhere we're all together."

Smiling, I settled my head in the curve of his neck and watched the passing buildings as we made our way to the airport. He was right.

We were finally home.

Photo by Kyle Weber

About the Author

When Cole Gibsen isn't writing she can be found shaking her booty in a zumba class, picking off her nail polish, or drinking straight from the jug (when no one is looking). Cole currently resides in the Greater St. Louis area with her husband, daughter, and one very cranky border collie.